101 Things To Do
With A Dead CEO

Bonnie Aona

Books may be purchased at www.amazon.com or by contacting the author at:

www.bonnieaona.com/contact

Cover and Book Jacket Design: Kalah Allen
Interior Design: CreateSpace/BonnieAona
Publisher: Bonnie Aona
Editor: Max Regan
Cartoon Editor: Jack Pollock
Creative Consultant: Ron Bueker

Library of Congress Catalog Number: 2016903651
Bonnie Aona

ISBN-13: 9780997231700 (Paperback)
ISBN-13: 9780997231717 (Kindle)
ISBN-10: 099723170X

1) General Fiction 2) Mystery/Cozy 3) Humorous

First Edition Printed in the United States of America

Dedication

To Deirdre Garvey, Meg Grant, and Kate Cox, friends in comedy and survivors of idiocy and every crazy situation, I gleefully and gratefully dedicate this romp to you, knowing I will be laughing with you about all this and more for the rest of our lives. I'm counting on it.

101 Things To Do With A Dead CEO

Table of Contents

Cast of Characters

Jo (Josephina) Galvan, Lead Software Engineer: Workaholic, high-anxiety, refuses to drive anything but a manual transmission, loves her grandmother and her friends, hates idiots.

Luce (Luciana) Savodsky, Lead Software Engineer: Balanced, cool, most of the time, anyway. Jo and Luce are colleagues who became best friends.

Manny (Manfred, a.k.a. Shit-For-Brains) Wimple, CEO of McWare: Highest priority is practicing his golf swing.

Red Nails (Cinda) Janx, HR rep, wanna-be Project Manager: Ambitious, well-dressed, well-manicured.

Steve Scott, Engineering Manager: Ace problem solver, technically savvy. Engineers are his favorite people.

Wayne Oakley, Software Engineer: Dependable, affable, with a Wyoming twang.

Jim McGraw, Software Engineer: Team player, terrific collaborator.

Sherm (Sherman) Chrisman, Software Engineer: Expert, excellent memory for technical details.

Vijay Patel, Miracle Intern: Smart, diligent, quietly phenomenal.

Lonnie Schuster, Software Engineer: Manny's best friend, still in search of his forte.

Liz (Elizabita) Czernak, Administrative Assistant: A survivor, she hears everything, knows what to hide, and keeps McWare running with no thanks from senior management.

Illyena (Grandma) Galvan, Jo's Grandmother: A fearless protector of her beloved granddaughter, she is the sweetest person and everyone loves her.

Mystery Geek: The name says it all.

1

You Say That Like It's a Good Thing

"A CAR. I'LL BET we each get a car." Jo Galvan reached a petite hand toward the extra-large latte to grab it from the long white counter at Ozo's Coffee. A silver earring in the shape of an Abyssinian cat caught the glinting ray of early morning sun through the curly black hair escaping from a thick ponytail. "No, after all that work, management would be so appreciative that it's gotta be better than a car." Jo dropped her change in the tip jar as the young red-headed barista flashed a quick smile, pulling two more shots of espresso that sent the rich dark aroma of coffee into the air.

The barista poured the two shots simultaneously into a tall cup, steamed the milk, added it to the espresso, and spooned the foam on top before setting it on the counter, smiling up at the next customer. Luce's long slender hand curled around her own latte. "A trip. It has to be an all-expense paid week in Hawaii for our entire team. Do they still sell bikinis in Boulder in September?" Nearly six feet tall with ash blonde hair that fell in a fluid line to her shoulders, she was as much the visual opposite of her best friend Jo as they were alike in spirit and opinion.

"Let's just wait and buy them in Hawaii." Out of habit, Jo glanced at the wall clock, calculating the remaining minutes of freedom.

Absently brushing an escaping dark curl behind her ear, she inhaled the rich fragrance as she took a healthy swig of her latte. Jo turned around, looking up at Luce as she pointed to her friend's tee-shirt. "Nice outfit!" Saluting her latte in the direction of the six-and-a-half-foot, sandy-haired man coming through the door, Jo called, "Steve, you can be our fashion judge."

Jo posed side by side with Luce, showing off their oversized tee-shirts emblazoned with matching large black block letters on the front and back. Steve's long, angular face broke into a wide grin, his green eyes laughing as he hooted, "'Actual Size.' Good one." He ordered a herbal tea, and soon his big hand enveloped his own large to-go cup.

Jo nudged, "I conned Luce into starting a new fashion trend for the corporate awards ceremony."

Luce shuddered. "It's my chance for a day without cashmere. Jo dared me, so I had no choice."

Jo smirked. "You know that we wore these just for our Shit-For-Brains CEO."

Steve sipped his tea. "I'm sure Manny will be impressed. So, Ms. Galvan and Ms. Savodsky, are we ready for the Geek Oscars?"

Boulder's early September sunshine exploded through the wall of windows, lighting up Luce's natural blonde hair. "We've got exactly ten minutes to come up with a way to get out of this thing," Jo said.

"Aren't you looking forward to the fabulous award we're getting for all our stupendous efforts?" Luce asked, leading the three outside to the nearly cloudless blue sky of the parking lot.

Jo sighed, "Sadly, no, never, zip, zilch, nada."

Luce stared down at Jo in mock horror as she whined, "But we're getting something great, like a big pile of money. Right?"

Jo reached up to pat Luce's shoulder. "Not this time, but almost as good. It's a pony."

Luce clicked her Prius open, raising the electronic key high in a victory salute. "A pony! Wow, I always wanted my very own pony. I'm so happy."

Steve mimicked parental chiding as he said, "Jo, you shouldn't lie to your best friend." Jo hung her head in pretend shame. "Manny's going to pay off your college loans. You have to promise to act surprised."

Jo sauntered to her restored candy apple red 67 Mustang hardtop, grumbling, "I really don't think that will be a problem." She stopped and turned to Luce and Steve. "Why doesn't Shit-For-Brains Manny give the whole team an award? We finished the Rhombus software together, night after nightmare."

Luce grumbled back, "Because he only notices stars, mostly his own."

Steve dug through his pockets for his Audi keys. "Luce is right. Manny is really rewarding himself for the great job you two and the team did on Rhombus. You can take the team out for lunch afterwards and expense it to me."

Jo nodded. "It's a deal, but on one condition. You're coming too."

Steve's large hands, so at home with a basketball, gave a thumbs-up. "Deal, I can use a free lunch even if I'm paying for it. I'll race you to the Boulderado, unless you really want Manny's undivided attention by walking in late."

The warm fall morning air whispered across Jo's face, and her attention was caught for a moment by the resolute beauty of Colorado's Flatirons mountain faces under the high blue dome of the Boulder sky. "Shit-For-Brains Manny gets so twitchy happy when he hands out awards, as if coming from him makes it all worth it. He's so oblivious he thinks reality is on television."

Luce got into the Prius. "I have a sick feeling they won't start without us."

Jo unlocked her car and got in. "It's 8:50 AM and this day already feels like a lost cause."

Jo carefully set the latte in the cup holder and ran her hand over the custom leather seats of the Mustang as the engine hummed to life. It was her chariot, her pride and joy. She mused that all corporate awards should be in money, chocolate, or time off so they could be shared. Giving awards just to her and Luce felt weird.

2

Start-ups 101

To: rookie-pup
From: Lord&Master

An old geek proverb goes like this, "Before the world was formed, there was chaos, written in Fortran." That's one of the first computer languages, from the Era Before the Internet, Smart Phones, and Facebook (E.B.I.S.P.F.). You're probably asking, "How did people ever live like that?" They ate carbs without guilt, true story.

Today's high-tech world is a different one, and not just the thing about the carbs. Software is written in newer languages, and the buzz goes something like, "Any technology will sell if we spin it right." Denial is a beautiful thing.

Every day some MBA or engineer wakes up with the bright, shining thought, "I know I can do better on my own with a couple of engineer friends. God, if it worked, it would be beautiful." But for the proper number of syllables, those words might as well be the Start-up Entrepreneurs' Haiku.

But you know what happens. Schedules are missed and revenue projections fall down the slippery slope of PowerPoint slides, from bright green heights to red puddles. The military has a term for this situation, SNAFU, i.e., situation normal, all fucked up. Military intelligence is not always an oxymoron

Entrepreneurs spawn start-up companies to build something shiny, spin the idea as a ticket to an early fortune, pull engineering talent together and let the geeks figure it out or take the blame. Start-ups are privately funded, allowing them to operate in secret, where ethics and job security don't exist.

You think you know enough about the world of high-tech start-up companies. Self-delusion is the evolutionary vehicle of denial, but no less a house of cards. You must be crystal clear about our mission, willing to learn, and willing to do whatever it takes.

A con intentionally separates people from their money, but a start-up company is only a con if it fails to deliver on the investors' expectations. Long after the investors have forgotten the Big Idea, they remember the date the profit piper is coming.

Learn to use the unparalleled commitment of brilliant engineers to full advantage, and be ready to replace them with the next batch. Truth be told, "*Caveat* burnout" is the hidden agenda of corporate sharks, and not a bad hobby either.

Beware, indeed, for paying the piper requires the ritual sacrifice of engineers.

~Sent from my iPad

3

The Geek Oscars

STATELY COLUMNS FLANKED the huge glass and brass double doors that welcomed visitors to the historic Boulderado Hotel. Jo and Luce walked through the original part of the hotel's beautifully restored stained-glass canopy ceiling. Ascending the cantilevered cherry wood staircase from the ground floor to the mezzanine brought a rush of elegance that made it worth attending McWare's company meeting in the hotel's conference center.

They hurried past the lovely restored period chairs arranged in pleasant little groupings near quietly beautiful paintings. Walking felt like floating as they crossed the thick carpet toward the new wing. Luce gazed at the details in the ceiling. "I wonder what it would be like to live here?"

Jo noticed the intricate details of the restored antique elevator. "You would miss the puppies, not to mention the family heirloom furniture."

Luce pushed the elevator call button. "The furniture I could do without, but I do love Hekili and Kula, the world's best Labs, and I would miss my condo in Gunbarrel. I was just daydreaming about hiding from my parents when they visit me from Portland."

Jo watched the elevator's floor location lights change. "You can't get far enough away from your parents, and every day I wish I had mine back. I'm so lucky to have Grandma."

When Jo was six years old, her parents died in a car accident. Grandma was the one who broke the news to her. Jo moved into her grandparents' home. She brought all her father's big flannel shirts because that's what he wore when she snuggled against his chest for a bedtime story. She also brought her mother's hairbrush, hand mirror, and two soft shawls with little beads on the fringe, one black and the other creamy white.

Luce stepped into the elevator and held the door. "Your Grandma is such an amazing lady. She makes me miss my grandfather."

Jo followed and pushed the button for the first floor. "She's not exactly your typical grandmother. She thinks a hand-held device is a screwdriver, and no one on Earth loves a socket wrench set like Grandma."

As they exited the elevator, Luce adjusted her long-legged stride to match Jo's shorter one. "She can fix anything."

Jo hurried to keep up with Luce's longer strides. "As long as it was invented before the Internet and she has a printed manual for it."

Luce swigged her latte. "It's so cool that she fixes all the old lawn mowers and VCRs your neighbors have."

Jo checked her messages. "She loves it. It's an excuse for her to hang out with her friends and gossip. She isn't interested in the Internet except email but she only does that in the morning when she first wakes up. She thinks Google is Gmail."

Luce checked her iPhone. "She might be the only person on the planet who isn't addicted to surfing the Net. The Internet will probably be our downfall, or the people who control it will."

Jo scanned her cell phone for unread email. "I thought the Internet was designed by frustrated engineers who couldn't get a date. Was that redundant?"

Luce took a gulp of her latte. "UCLA engineers worked with Stanford engineers. A couple of them had actually dated. See, there's hope for your OkCupid ad. You're a twenty-seven-year-old, physically fit female in Boulder who isn't actively dating, so it's time."

Jo's walk slowed as they rounded the corner to the meeting room hallway. "And who else in this conversation is twenty-seven and dateless? In the spirit of the Divine Ms. M, my standards are lower than they used to be for dating, but I have them, nonetheless."

Luce smirked. "And you managed to use nonetheless in a real sentence." The lithe, blonde young woman nudged her barely five-foot-tall, raven-haired friend as they ambled down the hall on a more or less parallel path. They stopped outside the double doors of their doom, and Luce took a deep breath. "Today we have to accept an award from the world's biggest sleazebag. This meeting will be like the flu but will only last a couple of hours."

Jo stared at the open door. "So the choice is unemployment or spending the next few hours in hell for money?"

"Hi, Jo. Hi, Luce." Liz, Manny's administrative assistant, hurried past them, carrying an armload of plaques and papers. Her short dark hair framed a porcelain complexion, and her grin came with a knowing wink. "Congratulations in advance."

Luce called to the woman's retreating back, "Hi, Liz. Do you need a hand with that?"

Liz looked back with a wink. "I'm good. I'm two hours away from a cigarette."

Jo intoned, "Deep breaths, Liz, deep healthy breaths."

Liz tossed her retort as she disappeared through the open door to the meeting room. "Not in my job description."

A booming male voice exploded behind the two women, startling them. "It's runt and beanstalk. Are you advertising your IQs?" Lonnie Schuster's thick-muscled frame barreled toward them. He was wearing his usual loud striped rugby shirt, tattoos covering his left arm. As they quickly jumped back to get out of his way, he grabbed a sleeve of each of their matching tee-shirts, pulling them along as he continued with his trajectory.

Jo reacted with visceral disgust. "Get your hands off us!"

Luce yanked both her and Jo's sleeves free of his meat-hooks. "Quit being a jerk, Lonnie."

Lonnie smirked. "Careful, you wouldn't want our CEO to get a bad impression about you two from his best friend." He disappeared into the meeting room as Jo steadied herself against the hallway wall, her heart racing as her face reddened with anger.

Luce touched Jo's arm. "Are you OK?"

Jo took a deep breath against the beginning flush of an anxiety attack. "I hate that creep. I hate this whole thing."

"Breathe, Jo. I'm right here with you. All we have to do is walk up together and accept our consolation prize, not do espionage."

Jo managed a feeble grin despite the pounding in her chest. "OK, let's get it over with." Jo looked at the placard by the door with the meeting information, making a mental note of the WiFi password.

They stepped into the spacious meeting room, its beautiful Victorian décor as inviting as the three large windows looking out to the sun and blue sky of a gorgeous fall day in Boulder. Jo and Luce crossed the plush, red patterned carpet, waving to the line of young men in tee-shirts and jeans sitting in the very back row. Each member of their engineering team clutched a large cup of caffeine for dear life

Luce raised her cup in salute to them. "I love how they decided where to sit by mathematically calculating the seats that are the farthest point from the podium. Can you imagine cramming all of McWare's employees into the executive conference room at our little building?"

Jo slouched into a chair in the eighth row, her annual pair of jeans contorted, one foot under the opposite knee, shooting for points in the Most Unladylike category. "Our engineers' meeting room is big enough, but Shit-For-Brains Manny wouldn't feel comfortable there. I hate these meetings. Please, can I leave now?"

Luce crossed her long, denim-clad legs. "I don't see a shift in the universe happening in the next thirty seconds."

"Manny is such a cretin, and a plaque is nothing, less than nothing for all the work and overtime we did on the Rhombus project. It feels like we're getting a gold star for killing ourselves."

Luce muttered, "He couldn't find a clue if it was gift-wrapped. We built a team that saved the Rhombus project, so he owes us at least repayment of our school loans, if not an organ."

Jo leaned back in her chair, memorizing the pattern in the room's high ceiling. "He has no heart, no balls, and his brain is MIA. Loan repayment it is."

Luce said, "At least we're not assigned to save the GuardShark project. That would have been the all-time death march."

Jo covered her ears with both hands. "Don't say that name. Let's hold out for a project that will get us home by 5:00 PM, with time off for our vacation in Hawaii."

Luce closed her eyes. "In my mind, I'm packing. Three bikinis, three pairs of earrings, flip flops, all in a carry-on bag."

Jo gazed absently around the room, noticing that Liz sat by herself in the row in front of Jo and Luce. A pair of accounting assistants sitting a couple of rows in front of them half-turned to glance pointedly in their direction, one with pursed lips and another rearranging herself in discomfort.

Luce whispered, "Oh look, we have an audience." Jo rolled her eyes.

Steve waved as he walked past them to sit next to Liz, pushing his chair back a bit to give him almost enough leg room, and turned around with a quick grin as he hoisted his herbal tea in their direction. A loud popping from the front of the room turned everyone's attention to the small stage.

Cinda Janx, the HR manager, tap-tap-tapped her talons on the live microphone, the staccato sound echoing as the walls closed in, sealing their fate. "Silence your cell phones before Manny begins the meeting."

Jo studied Cinda over the rim of her to-go cup. The nails were not just red, they were a Chinese red, perfectly manicured, rendering her hands an icon of fashion-perfect glamour, complemented by the matching mouth. And then there was the hair, a Not Found In Nature Red in a short little cement-and-forget style that would stay put even in a Category 5 hurricane. She wore a grey tweed blazer paired with a von Furstenberg black wrap dress and black stilettos, accented with small gold earrings and an effortless little saffron scarf. But the long red nails fixed the stares of nearly everyone in the room as she stood at the lectern. Cinda belonged in an upscale mall, not in a software engineering company.

Jo checked the time on her iPhone, closing her eyes tight against the hours stretching toward lunchtime. *I wish I had learned to meditate.*

Manny Wimple, the CEO, ascended the podium with the walk of a wanna-be golf pro and sat down, crossing his legs and bouncing one ankle up and down like a coked-up model in a GQ ad. From his precisely blonde-tipped brush cut, perfect white teeth and navy Hugo business casual blazer to the tailored Arnold Palmer golf pants and Gucci tasseled loafers, he was as well-packaged as his smile, painted on like an afterthought.

Manny's power was like everything else in his life, assumed and pointless. So far he had perfected only the anti-Midas touch. Fortunately, he touched little and left often for the golf course, freeing his employees to do the real work.

Jo popped open her Mac and used the hotel's WiFi to read and answer her email as the droning monotony of Manny's voice lulled her into a semi-consciousness state, catching up on Dilbert strips, playing online solitaire, and Googling any keywords that came to mind. She felt a nudge from Luce's arm that startled her. Suddenly remembering what was about to happen, she looked pleadingly at Luce, who shrugged in response. Jo braced herself for the announcement.

Manny brandished his laser red beam at the PowerPoint slide on the digital screen and clicked to the next slide. 'Leadership Award—Josephina Galvan and Luciana Savodsky—Rhombus Product Technical Leads' screamed in bold letters under the McWare corporate logo.

His voice sounded like a chipmunk on crack. "C'mon up, girls!"

Jo and Luce rose and walked to the podium. Jo felt the room spinning out of her comfort zone as they faced the audience. Luce pointed to both tee-shirts and turned to wink at her shorter friend. Jo felt an involuntary grin, breathed, feeling lighter, and put her hands on her hips to match Luce's pose for full effect. Raucous laughter and applause erupted from the back row of engineers as titters rippled across the rest of the room.

Manny stood motionless, holding a plaque in each hand, his face etched with a tight smile as he waited for attention to refocus on him. When the room quieted, he silently held out the simple pieces of wood to Jo and Luce, glaring at their tee-shirts.

Luce reached for an award with her left hand and graciously extended her right hand to meet Manny's handshake, but Jo froze. She felt paralyzed as Manny's hand hung in the air holding an award she didn't want, her own hands uselessly glued to her sides. She felt the room tilt as the sea of eyes bored into her. Luce's hand closed on Jo's award and handed it quickly to Jo, who barely moved to grasp it.

Luce stepped past Manny to the microphone. "Jo and I would like to thank our team for all your hard work on the Rhombus product. You are hands down the best engineers we've ever worked with. We will be celebrating at Spruce Restaurant downstairs in the Boulderado after the meeting. Thanks everyone!"

Jo and Luce stood together at the podium, smiling at their team as cheers exploded from the back of the room. Amid the applause, Jo noticed Shit-For-Brains Manny locking eyes with Red Nails Cinda, their mutual expressions dripping with disdain folded into tight little smiles.

Manny ended the meeting as Jo and Luce returned to their seats. They grabbed their backpacks and empty cups, motioning to the team to follow them. With every step away from the meeting room and Shit-For-Brains Manny, Jo relaxed, surrounded by the geeks' banter. They clambered down the elegant stairs and crossed the lobby to Spruce Restaurant. The band of engineers waited at the hostess stand next to the long gleaming oak bar until the lithe young brunette hostess returned to seat them at a large table in the porch section of the restaurant.

"Here's to the greatest team ever. *Salud*!" Jo raised her club soda as a variety of beverages were lofted in victory, a beam of light from the porch windows bouncing off her glass. She sank back in her chair at one end of the oak table.

Steve offered the next toast, towering above everyone else even when seated. "Here's to the brainiest software engineers!" Cheers went up amid another round of clinking glassware, interrupted only by the fugue of ordering lunch as their server moved around the table. The restaurant filled as the tide of Boulder's Friday afternoon lunch crowd rolled in.

Jim McGraw, the software architect, took a healthy pull of his Fat Tire beer. "So how are we going to kill some time while we're waiting for lunch?" His Dartmouth Computer Science hoodie stretched across his broad shoulders, proudly announcing his alma mater. His ginger hair and deep resonant voice reflected his Scots heritage.

Sherm Chrisman, a software engineer, put down his Dogfish Head beer. "We always do CEO or manager jokes. How about non-work jokes?" Sherm's lean frame was sculpted with the taut musculature from climbing rock faces, crags, and sheer drops that felt like home. He approached engineering problems similarly, never hurrying the process when a crucial misstep could mar the outcome. His faded jeans were paired with a 2012 Bolder Boulder tee-shirt from the local 10K race. The team was used to seeing him in a race shirt from every year he had run in the annual event.

Wayne Oakley, a systems engineer, drawled, "That might be a stretch for these folks, but I'm up for it." Wayne's lanky body was topped by an untamed ponytail that was a comfortable fit with his seasoned cowboy boots and the Cheyenne Frontier Days silver buckle decorating his hand-tooled leather belt. He wrote software and kept all the computer servers, equipment, and automated tests running amid the tenor of his irreplaceable humor.

Vijay Patel, the part-time intern, put down his glass. "Finally, a non-geek joke-a-thon. I might actually be able to keep up." His black hair formed the backdrop to dark lively eyes, and he proudly wore his Team India cricket jersey that prompted the running joke from his engineering teammates to explain the sport. As soon as he had caught on to their humor, he'd emailed the link to a website for 'Cricket For Dummies,' threatening to quiz them.

Jim raised his beer with a large muscular hand. "Dream on, rookie." Good-natured laughter sparkled around the table. "Hey, Jo, great cartoons. You've got Manny's idiot look down, except for the hair."

Sherm leaned forward, his elbows nudging the gleaming flat-ware, and looked directly at Jo and Luce. "Did you really draw those by yourself or did Luce help?"

"She did it!" Jo and Luce pointed at each other, until Jo admitted, "*Mea culpa*, it's all me. Luce has a little too much class for graffiti."

Sherm pointed his beer bottle in Jo's direction. "Too bad you can't turn Manny into a cardboard cut-out and just put him different places, like those garden gnomes."

Jim chuckled. "Maybe you could draw him as something useful, like a crash test dummy."

Wayne grinned. "Or a paperweight."

Luce waved her hand. "You could turn him into a Manny-kin and dress him up. Do him as a scarecrow for Halloween."

Steve laughed from his spot at the end of the table, where he had more space for his long arms and legs. "Do we need to order dry erase markers? At the rate these ideas are coming, we'll be up to one hundred in no time."

Jo ducked her head as if she were dodging a fly ball. "I don't know if I could handle drawing him that many times knowing I'm going to have to deal with him every day. I doubt medical science would even be interested in him after he's dead."

Vijay piped up, "That's what you could draw, things to do with a dead Manny."

Sherm pounded his beer bottle on the table in his excitement. "Why stop with Manny, why not all idiot power-tripping CEOs?"

Jo brightened. "How about 101 Things To Do With A Dead CEO? That sounds like a good start. But I don't have time to draw 101 different cartoons. Of course, if I had help …"

Jim's voice boomed from his thick chest. "How about a contest? We could all come up with ideas and vote on the funniest one."

Luce yelled down the table, "That's it, let's do a cartoon contest. 101 Things To Do With A Dead CEO."

Jo raised a fist straight over her head. "Done. Best entry wins by consensus of the whole team."

Wayne cocked his head at her. "Wins what?"

Jo didn't skip a beat. "A plaque, of course. Everyone's in?"

Vijay nearly choked mid-sip. "No, not me. I don't know how to draw cartoons."

Sherm eyeballed Vijay. "Too busy playing cricket?" He reached for his beer. "Jo, don't you worry about drawing Manny so realistically? What if he sees your cartoons, or ours? At least you changed the hair, a blonde Afro instead of blonde spikes."

Wayne pointed his beer bottle at Sherm. "I wouldn't worry. Manny wouldn't be able to find our conference room with a GPS and a trail of bread crumbs."

Luce smirked. "Maybe with a trail of caviar and Veuve Cliquot."

Jim turned to Jo and Luce. "OK, we'll bookmark that topic. Do you two know what we're working on next? Will it be something with normal hours, or the GuardShark project from hell?"

Vijay sipped his water. "What's GuardShark?"

Steve leaned forward, propping his chin on his big hands. "GuardShark was a software product that protected computer accounts, electronic files, and personal data from hacking, catfishing, and viruses. It had market clamor written all over it. Manny killed it when the old team told him customers wouldn't buy it without cyber security certification, and then he fired the team that built it."

Jo's voice had an edge when she said, "My friend Cate was the lead engineer on GuardShark. Manny forced her to fire everyone on the team before he fired her." She frowned. "Manny is so stupid he wouldn't listen to her when she told him that certification just required passing a set of standard tests."

Jo saw the face of her former mentor, Cate, who had first interviewed her for the job at McWare. Cate's cluster migraines began during the stress of leading the first GuardShark project. Jo felt a stab at her heart remembering Cate's face the day they hugged good-bye, with Cate's warning for Jo to watch her back and stay healthy. After she was fired, Cate couldn't afford to COBRA her medical insurance benefits and had to move back with her family in rural Kansas to rest and heal before she could look for another job.

Steve shrugged his shoulders. "He said testing would cost too much. Ironically, GuardShark could make McWare an instant leader in computer security software."

Jo felt her heart turning over. "What Manny did to Cate and that team … He used them and then threw them away, all because they were honest with him."

Jim looked at Wayne. "Didn't anyone tell that team the first thing engineers at McWare learn to do is lie to management so we can get our jobs done?" The team erupted in laughter as the server set a big tray of food on a stand next to their table.

Jo grinned at the waitress. "Sorry we're a little rowdy. We will leave someone to apologize for the rest of us, or leave you a great big tip, or both."

The server smiled as she began distributing the plates of luscious-looking food, each artfully composed with subtleties of color and texture. "The tip will do. Let me know if you need anything else, or hear any good chef jokes."

Luce set down her iced tea. "So there's no chance GuardShark will be resurrected?"

Steve shrugged as he unfolded his napkin from the utensils. "Sooner or later Marketing or someone on the Board or one of the investors will push for it."

Jo beheld the happy group with a satisfied grin before her gaze suddenly froze. One by one, each engineer around the table went silent as they turned to follow her eyes to the approaching couple. A ray of sunlight glinted off Manny's blonde-tipped brush cut, only to explode in the unreal red of Cinda's helmet hair. Manny sauntered through the doorway of the restaurant's porch, following Cinda's half-step-ahead lead. Wearing identically fixed smiles with lines of eerily glowing teeth, they descended on the engineering team's table, making eye contact with no one.

Jo's brain went into panic mode. *What are Shit-For-Brains Manny and Red Nails Cinda from HR doing here? They couldn't possibly be stupid enough to believe they were invited. Oh, right, they could.*

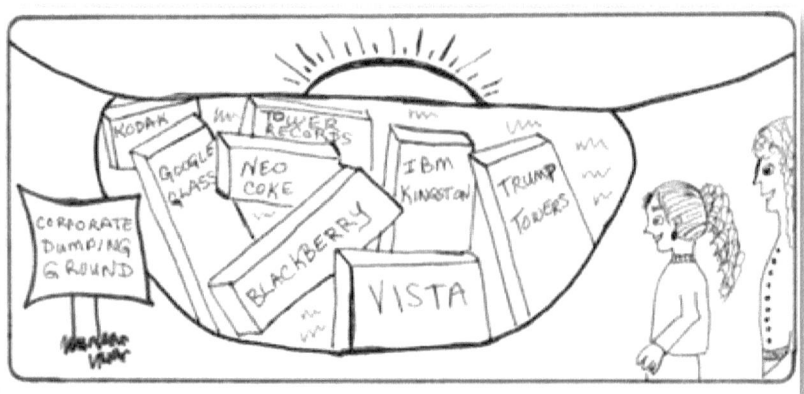

YEAH, BUT THIS TIME IT'S GONNA WORK,
AND IT'S GONNA BE BEAUTIFUL.

4

MAWM Lands

Red Nails spoke through a plastic Cheshire cat grin. "Hey, party animals! Looks like a great lunch. You deserve to celebrate. Congratulations on the Rhombus product."

Manny oozed schmooze. "You really got lucky with that one, but let's see you pull it off again. We picked your team to save the GuardShark project. You can't just be winners on this one, you've got to be champions. Josephina and Luciana will share technical leadership. This project is critical to the company's success, so you'll have to get it together and be perfect this time."

Jo's head was throbbing, threatening to become the size of a beach ball. Her glass was in jeopardy of losing contact with her hand as she sat suspended in disbelief.

Red Nails sparkled as more of her blazing white teeth came into view. "I'm so excited that Manny made me the project manager for GuardShark. It's a win-win!"

Jo's face was a mask of shock. "We have to take over the GuardShark product, and you're in charge? Wasn't that product cancelled?"

Manny shrugged as he turned to leave. "That's water under the bridge, Luciana."

Jo stared at his retreating back. *He only knows names from the PowerPoint slide.* "She's Luce. I'm Jo."

Manny tossed his exit line as he walked away. "We'll meet with you girls on Monday morning to hammer out the details so your team can finish GuardShark ASAP."

Steve turned to Red Nails. "Jo and Luce need time to review the work that has already been done on GuardShark before the planning discussion."

Red Nails waved as she turned to follow Manny. "We'll just wing it. Next Monday I'll attend a class on project management, but I know I'm leaving everything in great hands. Let's sync up when I return to the office, after I get caught up on email, so like, Wednesday?"

Jo's gaze fixated on the impossibly red hair. *She has nothing in her brain under that hair. She stopped learning after the color red.*

Red Nails wriggled giddily. "Hard to believe the day could get any better, huh?! We'll let you get back to your party. Just see what you can get done before Wednesday."

Did she just say that? Jo's jaw was as tight as her clenched fists hidden under the table. She shot Luce the same look that stared back at her from Luce's ready-to-kill face. *Breathe. I'd breathe better while wringing their necks, one right after the other.*

The brainless duo exited through the wood-paneled doorway. The engineering team sat in stunned silence.

"Fuck," Jo finally gasped in a hollow voice.

"Amen to that fuck," Luce observed.

A cascade of voices arose, chanting in chorus.

"Double fuck."

"Fee-uck."

"Fuck me swinging from a treetop."

"Fuckery doo, baby."

"How the fuck did this happen?"

"Jo and Luce, did you know anything about this fucking crap?"

In unison, Jo and Luce responded emphatically, "No way!" They looked around the table at their team, reeling in the wake of rapidly vanishing hope.

Jo grasped for logic but was left empty-handed. "So this is our reward for completing a successful product delivery? We're assigned a worse project on which, wait for it, Red Nails is the project manager?"

Luce held her head in her hands. "We should have fucked up a little."

Jo clenched her fist. "We should have fucked up a *lot*."

A shadow of doom settled over the table until Sherm rallied, raising a sinewy arm in a circle to include the group. "So what does this mean for us?"

Jo felt rage leaking through her voice as she said, "Luce and I will see what we're up against at the meeting on Monday. Let's forget it for now and celebrate Rhombus."

Luce looked up from her hands. "That's right. We'll figure out how to get everything done. I say the hell with them."

Jim punctured the air with his fork. "We need a code name. GuardShark has marketing spin written all over it."

Sherm signaled their server. "I don't usually have another beer until after my run, but right now we definitely need more drinks. I'll throw 'Doom' into the codename hat."

Jim raised his bottle to the server. "We haven't had beer in the house for eight months and three weeks since Jenna can't drink while she's pregnant. I have daydreams about Old Chicago's World Beer Tour. How about 'Kegger' for the code name?"

Wayne watched the server approach. "How about 'Phoenix,' as in rising from the ashes?" He ordered a Fat Tire Amber Ale.

Luce shook her head No at the server before turning to Wayne. "Didn't the firebird go down in flames?"

Vijay waved away the server. "No, its magical feather just caused problems for whoever stole it. Icarus flew too close to the sun and fell into the sea."

Steve laughed. "Vijay, that's both appropriate and impressive." He ordered Guinness Stout, handing his empty bottle to the server.

Vijay grinned sheepishly. "Doom sounds almost happy in comparison to the rest of the ideas. GuardShark must be a killer project."

Jo ordered a club soda. "It's the Make-A-Wish product. As in, just once before Manny dies, he wishes he could see that product happen."

Luce reached for her iced tea. "It would take a miracle to get him to let us run all the certification tests."

Jim pounded the table. "Hey, let's call it the Make-A-Wish Miracle and just use the acronym MAWM. Nobody but us would have a clue what we were talking about."

Sherm shot Jim a look. "It sounds like we're saying 'Mom.'"

Jo snickered, "In my head, I will always think of it as Make-a-Wish, Motherfucker, but that's me."

Luce raised her glass. "MAWM it is!"

As soon as the round of drinks came, toasts were raised. Gourmet entrees were consumed with less than the deserved level of gastronomic enjoyment and, without discussing it, another round of drinks was ordered, followed by a final round of softer beverages and coffees.

Steve looked around the table at the engineers. "This might feel like your last meal before another death-march project, but I promise that Jo, Luce, and I will fight for a sane product schedule."

Jim set his BrewDog/Oscar Blues bottle on the table. "I could look at the GuardShark software over the weekend, find the tests the old team wrote and try to run them. That might give Jo and Luce a better shot for that planning meeting with Manny on Monday."

Sherm brushed bread crumbs from his tee-shirt as he turned to Jim. "I can help you. They had great engineers on that team. I'll bet if we add more tests from the start, and remember to lie about doing that, we might have a shot at getting GuardShark done without killing ourselves."

Steve looked at Sherm and Jim. "That's generous of you two, but I hate to see you work on the weekend when you deserve a break."

Jim crossed his arms, hunching his brawny shoulders. "I need to do this. Just knowing the truth about what shape GuardShark is in right now will improve my ability to sleep. Besides, when my wife goes into labor, I'll be in new-father mode."

Jo threw her napkin on her nearly empty plate. "Good point. Let me know when you decide to run the tests and I'll help."

Sherm shook his head. "You and Luce put in enough overtime. We've got this covered. We can email our results to everyone on Sunday."

Jo nodded. "OK, I guess that's one of those offers I'd better not refuse."

After the party crumbled to a support group, Jo and Luce said goodbye to the team and thanked Steve, who stayed behind to pay the bill. The two women made their way to the parking lot and leaned on the metallic red hood of Jo's Mustang, sunning themselves as they watched the panorama of clouds crawl across the bright blue sky.

Jo rubbed her forehead. "Shit-For-Brains and Red Nails have lousy timing."

Luce's voice punctuated the air. "Could there be a more asinine choice for a project manager?"

Jo felt the low throb of an on-coming migraine. "Her first assignment should be buying malpractice insurance for both of them. I just know we're always going to be thrown to the wolves as long as Shit-For-Brains runs the company."

Luce anxiously twisted a lock of blonde hair as she grumbled, "Red Nails will be out next Monday, doing email Tuesday, so we won't need funeral arrangements or new jobs until Wednesday. God, my parents would be overjoyed if they thought there was a chance I would have to move back to Portland to work for them."

Jo shook her head as she unlocked the car door. "I won't let that happen. Friends don't let friends work for contractors who are screwing the environment, especially not wealthy controlling ones."

Luce sighed as she clicked the Prius door open. "You're a good friend, but this is bad, worse than the Rhombus project." She walked to her car, which was parked next to Jo's.

Jo called to Luce, "All we need to do is finish GuardShark, work around Red Nails' idiocy, and keep the team from dying. No pulse, no paycheck."

Luce turned back to Jo and each woman took a breath before chanting in unison, "We're faith healers, miracle workers, we never sleep. We will survive."

Luce caught Jo's eye. "I assume you have some inspiration to channel."

Jo clenched and unclenched her hands, wiggled her fingers, and shook her hands loosely. "Yes, I'm off to my art studio."

Luce waved as she climbed into her car. "I'm so proud. Hasta."

Jo drove off in the Mustang, waving half-heartedly to her best friend. *Luce is as worried as I am.*

5

Power 101

To: rookie-pup
From: Lord&Master

You are a shark. Own it, work it, be the killer. A shark is all about power, so get comfortable. Better yet, get hungry for power. Having it, using it, abusing it, and knowing the difference. You are the power player, the one who always wins.

We answer to no one except the few who are more powerful than us. The losers can exhaust themselves on commitment and that anathema, teamwork. We aren't defined by a job description. We focus entirely on our next feeding frenzy. Sometimes we feast on our enemies and sometimes we eat the underlings as hors d'oeuvres, whatever the situation requires.

This is your big break, and a troubled project is your perfect storm. Throw the underlings to the wolves to take all the risks. Use them, burn them out, blame them, they are a dime a dozen, and there are more lined up behind them, eager for the job.

Someone always has to lose. Get comfortable with winning, with doing whatever it takes. You are a shark. Get hungry for your next kill.

~Sent from my iPad

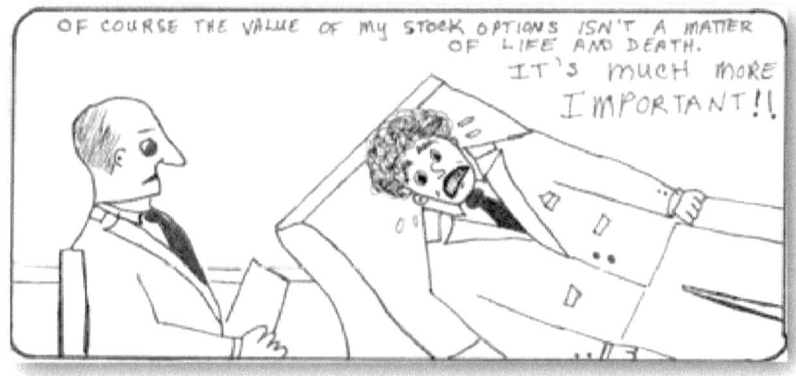

6

It Was a Dark and Stormy Night

THE SIGN ON the door was typed in a tiny font, almost hidden due to its placement under the door knob, 'Tomb of the Unknown Meeting.' The placement of the sign was intentional. Jo stood in the back hallway of McWare's otherwise empty office building, letting the evening's quiet hush her anxiety.

Jo opened the door to the engineers' lair, where all team meetings and technical discussions were held. The whiteboards dominated the large windowless square room, even in the dim light that flowed through the open door. Indeed, there was more whiteboard space around the perimeter of the room than wall space. Erasers and a dozen dry erase markers lay haphazardly on the trays along the lengths of whiteboard.

She grinned, remembering the free-for-all riffs that flew through the air that late night three years ago when the team problem-solved their way through technical difficulties to create McWare's first marketable software product, TrackRecord, a project management system. The CEO took all the credit, and the battle lines were drawn with the engineers.

The large space served two purposes. It was the engineers' scratch pad of diagrams, lists of buzz words and phrases, a few dates, and occasionally the name of a person or a code name. It was a room of secrets. Secret meetings. Secret knowledge. Secret jokes. Secret frustrations. Yet the room had a sense of safety, and the freedom of expression that blooms in secret.

A square table took up the middle of the room, surrounded by comfortably upholstered rolling chairs with armrests. Jo, Luce, and Steve had fought budget wars with management for this collaborative work environment, including wired access to McWare's data servers. Manny's reluctant agreement was one of the rare times he had done something to benefit the engineers, aside from frequently leaving the office and occasionally leaving town.

Jo clicked the light on as she closed the door to ensure privacy despite the empty building. She checked her iPhone, 5:32 PM. Moving to a blank area of board space, she grabbed a black marker and began to draw. Erasing and re-drawing, she got lost in the freedom of playing with dry erase markers on a sleek whiteboard.

After twenty minutes she stood back to survey her handiwork. The facial expression wasn't dumb enough and the hair wasn't as Hollywood, but she was only good for five minutes of picturing Shit-For-Brains in her head without risking projectile vomiting. Jo dabbed the final strokes to over-emphasize the blonde curls and the therapist's couch.

Crap, Sherm is right. I need to change more than the hair. Jo quickly replaced the golf outfit with a business suit. *He looks even more stupid. Score.*

A wave of giddy satisfaction from creative rebellion rocked her. She loved cartooning alone in the building long after the last engineer had fled for the weekend. The most frustrating days at work drew her like an addiction to the whiteboards in the Tomb, where her unsigned cartoons quickly materialized. She loved the team's game of coming up with the snarkiest captions. Like double chocolate frosting on triple chocolate brownies, their wisecracks made her revenge even more delicious.

One of the beautiful things about being alone was the freedom to abandon the urge to keep her attitude in check. *Art therapy, good.*

Jo threw the marker on the tray, pulled on her jacket against the rain smattering on the roof, but turned back for a moment to enjoy her work. Switching off the light, the Tomb was bathed in the dimness of the safety light, yet her newest caricature was visible on the white background. *Exit the artiste.*

Jo's hand was on the door knob when she heard Lonnie's loud grating voice in the hallway. "Don't bother, that's just the engineers' conference room." Jo quickly moved to the wall next to the door hinges just before the door swung open, hiding her behind it. Lights suddenly flooded the room. She pressed against the wall, holding her breath against her pounding heart as Lonnie growled, "See, it's nothing but whiteboards and scribbling."

A low warm voice quietly drifted from the other side of the door. "This is a scheme for multi-level security access, and that's a database design with pretty clever indexing for speed." Jo barely breathed, frozen in place.

Lonnie's impatience gave an edge to his growl. "What's clever?"

The warm voice moved two steps into the room, revealing a sweatshirt-covered arm to Jo's terrified eyes. "You wouldn't understand. Cool cartoons, must be some comedians on the team." Jo's heart kicked at her chest with a hollow thud.

Lonnie's growl sharpened. "Who cares? Come on, Seth. I'm meeting some friends. I'll give you a key so you can come back whenever you want." The room was suddenly engulfed in darkness, startling Jo as the door slammed shut.

Jo felt a rush of relief, gulping air, still gasping as the footsteps died in the hallway and the back door to McWare banged shut. The muffled growl of a high-rev four-stroke motorcycle engine purred from outside the building. *What was Lonnie doing at McWare on a Friday evening? When did he get into hot bikes? And where the hell did he find an intelligent friend?*

* * *

In the fall twilight, Jo turned off Vixen's engine and removed the key from the ignition. She was sitting, frozen in place, staring into the void, when the sudden wave of fear hit her. It felt darker than the heavily pregnant clouds scudding across the sky. Her heart beat like a fist, and her head felt like a basketball. Jo could not ignore the signals of a full-blown panic attack that she knew was about to arrive, with the added evil of a migraine chaser.

A sliver of moon rocked on its side, winking through the branches of the cottonwoods. A wisp of gauzy cloud fingered its way to the lower corner of the lunar comma that hung in the early September evening's sky. It all felt so quietly eternal, at peace in the constancy of nature. Jo closed her eyes, breathed in slowly, deeply, sighing as she let her breath go, go until the end, slowing her heartbeat. *Luce is right. I need to start doing yoga.*

She opened her eyes to gaze at the wide front porch of Grandma's house, the sturdy pillars, railings wide enough to sit on, and the generous roof that protected equally from rain, snow, and sun. The one-and-a-half story house on Bluff Street in West Boulder had been home most of her life, yet she saw it with new eyes in her need for its welcoming coziness and the safety of knowing she would always have a home, no matter what.

Her jaw clenched as she seethed, *How could Shit-For-Brains force the team back to eighteen hour days with no time to breathe and catch up with life? OK, breathe, just breathe. I don't know how I'll get through this. I can't let Grandma know anything is wrong.* Jo silently prayed to just be able to feel alive in her own body instead of that panicked horror of flying into a thousand pieces. So many things were out of her and Luce's control, including McWare's success and the security of their jobs.

Oh, God, Jo begged, *please don't let that happen to me. I don't want to worry Grandma.* She felt her heart cracking, the tears building behind her eyes. *I can't let Grandma see me cry. I won't cry until I'm in my room.* She took a few deep breaths, made her way to the porch and unlocked the front door. She sighed in gratitude for the moment of homecoming, never taking it for granted.

She passed the dark walnut end table in the living room, guided by a buttery pool of light from the amber glass lamp that cast long geometric shadows through the bentwood back of the old rocking chair. All the furniture except the couch had been in Grandma's family since the early 1900s, a testimony to careful, frequent maintenance. Jo and Luce helped pick out the ivory sofa when the springs of the old overstuffed couch finally bit the dust, keeping the old hand-embroidered pillows and the hand-knit throw, now draped over the arm of the couch.

Jo walked through the cozy living room, passing the old framed photographs of great- and great-great-relatives, to the workroom that long since had ceased to function in its original purpose as a dining room. The long table was perpetually buried under a thick canvas tarp to protect it from the tools and greasy parts of Grandma's project *du jour*, which ran the gamut from re-building a lawn mower to repairing a VCR or a garage door cable's spring assembly.

Jo smiled at the back of the small grey head, the slightly bent but strong body whose form was obscured by one of Grandpa's old work shirts. Her eyes went to Grandma's Croc Dual Sport Clogs in screaming yellow with orange grip soles in a size big enough for her corns. The small sturdy woman reached slender, capable fingers toward a tiny screwdriver from an organized layout of parts, her focus fixed on a worn repair manual. Jo stood next to her favorite person in the world. "Hi, Grandma. What are you fixing?"

As Grandma's face turned to her with a smile, Jo hugged her, kissing the soft cheek with its natural blush of sun from gardening her fresh vegetables. She loved looking into Grandma's sparkling blue eyes in her heart-shaped face, and the beautiful smile that greeted everyone she met with a joyful sense of delight. Grandma was in her happy zone. "Hi, honey. I just found the right size screw for this tiny little motor mount."

Jo's eyes roamed the table. "How old is that music box? Where did you find a manual for it?"

Grandma rotated the small screwdriver in a hand made strong from years of mechanical repair work and gardening. "It's probably twice as old as you are, honey. I'm fixing Molly's old jewelry box that's supposed to play a waltz while the ballerina spins. I found this manual for another type of music box, but it's the same idea." The older woman's hands nimbly made a tiny adjustment to one of the delicate gears on the antique. "I figured out how to restore the spinning mechanism and remount the ballerina so it doesn't wobble. I might have to get Gus at the clock shop to adjust the music mechanism."

Jo watched Grandma's deft moves. "I've seen old music boxes in his shop." Jo inhaled a delicious aroma. "Something smells good in here. Did you make soup?"

"Yes, chicken noodle with lots of vegetables. I made salad too, and you can make toast. There's a Tracy and Hepburn movie on TCM in a few minutes."

Jo knew Grandma loved her company, but lately Jo had been working such long hours that they hadn't eaten dinner together. "I think I can handle toast and tray duty. I don't see the TV trays. Did you move them?"

Grandma set the music box on the table and waved one lean arm at all the mess. "I put them in the kitchen. I needed more room."

Jo looked closely at the music box. "I wish I was that happy at my work."

Grandma's gaze held Jo's, her hand gently touching Jo's arm. "Is something bothering you about work, honey?"

Jo felt her throat tighten and she tried to swallow the knot, but it was too late. As her voice caught, a hot tear burned down her cheek, chased by a second one, and she felt her face give way.

Grandma quietly embraced Jo. "What's wrong, Jo? You had that big meeting for work today. Did something happen there?"

Jo's throat hurt when she tried to talk. "Luce and I got an award for all the work our team did, and we took our team to lunch."

Grandma gently held both of Jo's shoulders in her warm hands. "That sounds like fun. Luce is such a sweet girl, and you like your team."

Jo felt hot tears tracing chilly trails down her face. "We were having a great time when the CEO and his sidekick crashed our party to tell us we had to start work right away on a project that is a mess." Jo felt the tsunami of fear slamming her chest.

Grandma cupped her soft hand along Jo's cheek. "Honey, are you afraid of losing your job? I really don't think that will happen. Do they have anyone who works as hard as you do?"

Jo sucked in a hard breath, opened her eyes, and looked at the face of sweetness itself. "No, ma'am. Luce works as much as I do, but we're a team, and if they kick one of us out they will lose both of us."

Grandma looked into Jo's eyes and grinned. "Well, now, just exactly how stupid are the people you work for?"

Jo laughed, feeling the pain of her tight throat along with the comic relief. "Oh, I'd say they are way up there on the stupid scale."

"What is the most important thing to them?"

Jo laughed. "Money and power, and they are hungry for more all the time."

Grandma put her hands on her hips. "Well, how the heck are they going to stand a chance of making a dime off this bad project if they fire you and Luce? They might be stupid but I'll bet you can still count on their greed."

Jo's finger traced the edge of the collar of Grandma's faded blue work shirt. "That's them, all right, money-grubbing power brokers who can't wait to hit the links for their next golf game and martini. Luce and I will just have to figure it out."

Grandma patted Jo's shoulder. "You never know what you'll find until you start working on it. Maybe the problems will be easier to sort through than you thought. Grandpa and I used to figure things out together."

Jo put her arm around Grandma's shoulder, remembering the days she spent playing in her grandparents' repair shop. "I'd forgotten how long you and Grandpa had the shop. I didn't realize how different it must be for you to work alone. Maybe we can find you a mechanic buddy."

Grandma laughed. "I don't know who would put up with me! Anyway, I'm hungry, so let's eat. Can I still trust you to make toast?"

Jo put her hand to her forehead. "Remind me again, what do I do first?"

Grandma laughed as they made their way to the kitchen. When they were seated on the comfy couch with their tray tables laden with hot soup and thick slices of toast, Jo finally felt the knotted cable in her stomach unwind.

Jo's quiet moment was interrupted by an insistent paw poking her right ankle. She reached down to scratch behind Gizmo's creamy orange tabby ears, the kitty's eyes closing with predictable pleasure. A sudden pull on the laces of her left shoe revealed Gizmo's twin sister Jig, short for Thing-a-ma-jig, laying siege. "You two are fruitcakes," she laughed as she scratched matching kitty heads.

The lamplight caught the grey halo of little hairs that escaped the old-fashioned twist holding Grandma's long hair, anchored by cotter pins instead of bobby pins. *Grandma the Fixer.* Jo smiled, breathing a sigh of relief. Somehow, some way, she would figure out how to keep her job. *Be the Geek Warrior, the Fixer's Granddaughter.*

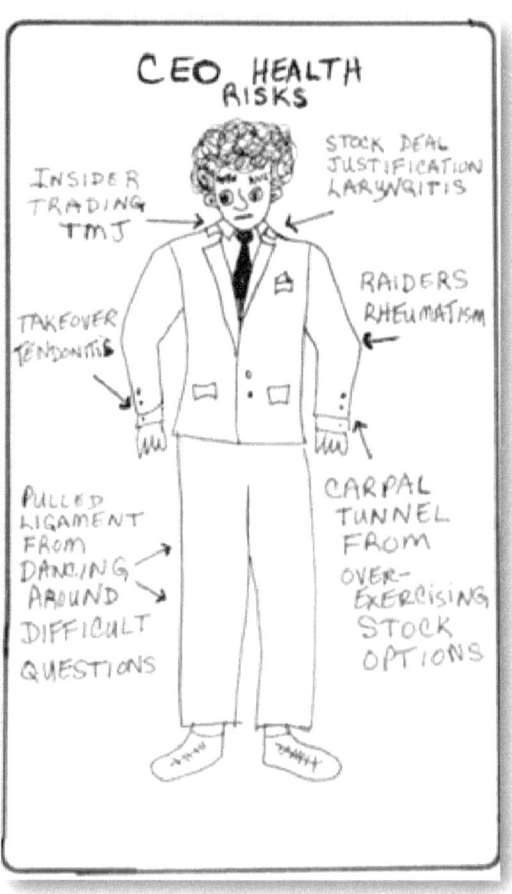

7

C[R]AP Day / CRAM Day

RRRRrrrrring! Jo grabbed for the alarm, stretched and snuggled under the covers. It was so nice to just lie there and let the morning air waft over her. *I could call in disgusted, but it would all land on Luce. Mondays should be outlawed. Mmm, bacon and coffee.*

After showering, Jo dressed in her engineering uniform of jeans and a tee-shirt, today's being a Kliban cat cartoon. Jo joined Grandma in the sunny yellow kitchen. She carried a bowl of Shredded Wheat to the old oak table, and sat down as Grandma handed her the plate of bacon. "Anything fun happening at work today?"

Jo crunched a bite of cereal. "Lunch."

Grandma sat down to her bowl of homemade granola. "You look worried, honey." She glanced at Jo before taking a healthy spoonful.

"Luce and I have to be in a meeting with the head of our company about the bad project. It will be a mountain of work." Jo gingerly freed the nearest bacon strip from the warm stack and pushed the plate closer to Grandma, who picked up a strip.

"You and Luce are the two smartest people I know. Your Grandpa and I worked long days in the shop, but we always enjoyed the work and seeing people."

Jo snapped a bite off her bacon strip. "The head of our company is a dimwit who doesn't think women are as valuable as men, no matter how hard we work." Jo crunched the rest of her bacon. "Should I pick you up over lunchtime to take the music box to Gus?"

"No, Don called this morning and needs his lawn mower adjusted, so I asked him to give me a ride instead of paying me. He's living on his Social Security checks, so that way it's just a trade, and he gets to visit with me and Gus."

Jo swallowed another bite of cereal. "You all watch out for each other. You're like a little village. I wish I had one."

"Oh, I think you do." Grandma smiled with a little wink, stirring her granola.

Jo crunched the last bite of cereal. "Yeah, I do have the Good Ship of Engineers to keep me afloat. I'd better get to work. Say hi to Gus and Don for me."

Grandma smiled. "I will. They always ask about you."

Jo washed her dishes in the sink, stacked them in the rack, and hugged Grandma before grabbing her backpack and heading for the front door. She drove Vixen through Boulder on streets still damp from last night's rain, the fall air pungent with dry leaves. Grabbing a latte at Ozo's, she stood for a moment enjoying the sun on her face before driving to McWare, where Luce sat waiting in the parking lot inside her Prius.

As Luce emerged from her car, juggling her latte and backpack, Jo read a message on her iPhone. "Did you see the GuardShark report Jim emailed? What a mind-blower."

Luce fished out her phone and scrolled her email. "All they had to finish was the password encryption, the hacker shielding, automated backups to the Cloud, and clean up the Help messages."

They went through McWare's back door. Jo gazed longingly at the Tomb as she and Luce walked quickly through the back hallway in the direction of the stairs.

"Most of the tests were written," Luce said as Jo pocketed her iPhone. "They only needed a few more weeks to finish GuardShark so they could run the certification tests. Can Shit-For-Brains actually be that stupid?" Luce's words echoed in the empty hallway.

"Evidently. We have to take Jim's advice and lie to management from the start."

"So we have a plan, lying by silence." Jo slowed her pace as they neared the stairs.

Luce sighed. "If Shit-For-Brains finds out how much of GuardShark is working, he will just add more features."

Jo's swiped her fingers across her lips. "Agreed. I am now affixing virtual duct tape across my mouth."

Luce sipped her latte. "CAP Day? Create A Plan Day should actually be CRAP Day. How about Create A Miracle Day? Then we would call it CRAM Day."

Jo tensed her shoulders, relaxed and did shoulder rolls as she walked, making her backpack dance. "I can't believe we're going to spend the next four hours listening to half-assed pontificating from Shit-For-Brains and the Ken dolls. Remember the first Rhombus meeting when they kept spelling words wrong and couldn't figure out their own notes?"

As the two women climbed the back stairs to the second floor, Luce said over her shoulder, "That's when we realized their ideas were basically ripped off from the competition. It's not too late to chew off our legs to get out of this meeting, is it?"

As they passed Liz's perfectly organized office, she looked up from arranging a plate of fresh fruit and called to them, "Manny and the marketing guys aren't here yet."

Jo snickered, "They probably stopped to buy us all flowers."

Liz laughed, "I already rinsed out my vase."

Luce wandered over to Liz's desk. "What are the boys getting for breakfast?"

Liz pointed to a pastry box from Longmont's Romana Cake House and the colorful fresh fruit. "I decided to go European today. Help yourselves to fruit. Manny said I shouldn't buy pastries for you girls because all women are watching their figures."

Jo winked. "Works for me, croissants conflict with my pizza diet." She grabbed a huge red strawberry. "You should just order food *you* like."

Liz grinned. "Robin Chocolates in Longmont?" Jo and Luce waved their fruit at Liz as they resumed walking to the executive conference room.

Jo followed Luce to the end of the second floor hall, but stopped in the doorway, hissing, "We forgot to buy winning lottery tickets on the way to the office."

Luce's tall frame crumpled against the wall. "Just think of this as our get-rich-slow scheme." She peeled herself off the wall and walked into the window-walled room. "We've got triple-shot lattes, laptops, and a complete abandonment of hope. CRAP and CRAM Day begins."

As Jo followed Luce into the executive conference room, the sheen of the long polished oak table caught her eye. It was in well-bred company with the rich carpet and stunning view of the mountains and sky. Jo and Luce sat down to set up their Macs in the otherwise empty room on the side of the table that afforded the best view. They immediately launched the Instant Messenger application to connect their computers.

[Jo: $5 bet? $1 a pt?]

[Luce: U R on]

Manny sauntered in twenty minutes late, dressed in a golf-ready navy polo shirt and khaki slacks. He was accompanied by two men in pinstripe shirts that had never seen a wrinkle or a stain, Countess Mara ties, and matching suspenders. They had names as predictable and forgettable as their contributions would be, so the engineers just called them the Ken dolls.

[Jo: the zoo]

[Luce: the circus, clowns running the show]

[Jo: 1 point]

Jo and Luce focused on their computer screens as Liz served espresso, croissants, and fresh fruit. As she moved around the table, a white reinforced elastic knee brace peeked occasionally from under the hem of her skirt.

Liz held the tray of espressos for Luce, who carefully took two of the small porcelain cups and smiled up at the dark-haired woman. "Thanks, Liz. This smells good." She handed one cup to Jo, who smiled and mouthed, "Thank you," to Liz.

Manny barked, "Liz, I need a yellow tie, one with stripes, thin ones. No dots like the last one you got." Liz nodded a discreet OK, but as she turned to go, she rolled her eyes when she caught Jo's look.

One of the Ken dolls muttered, "She probably doesn't read *GQ*." The other Ken doll set up his computer to display on the wall-mounted projector screen.

As Liz exited the room, Manny smirked at the Ken dolls. "Next time we hire a secretary, ask her if she knows Hugo Boss." On cue, the Ken dolls erupted in conspiratorial laughter.

Jo gritted her teeth in a hard stare at him that went unnoticed. She clenched her fist under the table in solidarity with the now-absent Liz.

Create-A-Plan Day should have been an opportunity to bring order out of chaos. Jo and Luce needed a complete picture of the work to finish the GuardShark software and a project schedule that assigned each engineer a realistic amount of work to complete by a delivery date. Simple math.

Manny sat at the end of the conference table, ignoring the engineers as he traded golf stories with the Ken dolls, occasionally interrupted by the buzz of a new text message on his iPhone. He tossed a strawberry to a Ken doll before starting the project planning with his traditional opening line. "Looks like the girls are ready to get to work."

[Jo: chauvinist comment. 1 point to me for calling it]

[Luce: 2 EZ]

One Ken doll threw a strawberry toward the trash can and missed. The other Ken doll projected the first PowerPoint slide, 'GuardShark Differentiators,' and handed Manny a laser pointer and a wireless mouse.

[Luce: goosebumps]

[Jo: pace yourself]

Manny clicked to the next slide, swirling his laser pointer at the top bullet item, 'Hocker detection.'

Jo typed notes into her Word document as she asked, in as neutral a tone as possible, "Is that supposed to say 'Hacker detection?'"

[Jo: 1 point]

[Luce: idiot's helping U]

Manny's focus jerked to his buzzing iPhone. "Looks like you girls are getting all this down. We can't afford to lose such epic stuff."

Jo and Luce automatically reached for their respective espressos as pointless discussion ensued among the trinity. The men devoured fruit and croissants, occasionally tossing pieces of food toward the trash can or each other.

[Jo: 2 hours to go, the litter mounts]

[Luce: pray for kidnapping]

Manny and the Ken dolls stopped playing when Red Nails slithered through the door. Manny whistled and winked at her. Jo's eyes fixed on the four-inch red stiletto heels, travelled to the postage stamp-sized black leather mini-skirt, coming to rest on the red-and-black sequined top.

[Jo: nails match shoes. Spanish judge awards 1 point]

[Luce: Rest of the skirt is where …?]

[Jo: MIA with her dignity]

Jo looked directly at Red Nails. "I thought you were going to a project management class today."

Red Nails sat facing Manny, crossing her legs as the red and black sequins of her blouse glinted. "I will be reviewing our training courses to add improvements. That's more important than learning about project management."

Luce stared at Red Nails. "Right, because project management is only your entire new job."

Cinda struck a saucy pose. "So, what is GuardShark? Pretend I don't know anything about it."

Jo coughed, not daring to look at Luce.

[Luce: pretend?]

[Jo: no problem]

Ken doll A offered Cinda the fruit tray, which she waved away. "GuardShark will make everyone's computers, smart phones, email, and web accounts completely secure," he explained.

Ken doll B handed an espresso to her. "It has state-of-the-art protection from hacking, catfishing, viruses, any type of electronic break-in. You will never again have to worry about having any of your online accounts hacked. Plus, automatic file backups to the Cloud."

Cinda stared at them, sipping her espresso. "So people need that?"

Jo stared at Cinda in shock before turning slowly to fix eye contact with Luce. *Where did Manny find her? God help us.*

Ken doll A grinned at her with a wink. "It has malware protection, so it's a license to print money."

Cinda stared at the list projected on the screen. "Does that help people shop at the mall?"

Jo resisted the urge to laugh. "No, Cinda, it's not m-a-l-l-w-e-a-r, it's m-a-l-w-a-r-e. It's shorthand for 'malicious software' that gets onto your computer from the Internet or a DVD or thumb drive. Viruses delete files and directory information. Spyware gathers data from your computer without you knowing it."

Cinda set down her espresso cup. "Wouldn't it be easier to just get a new computer and stay off the Internet?"

Jo and Luce sat stunned into silence while Manny and the Ken dolls erupted in laughter until they realized Red Nails was serious.

Manny teased, "Careful, Cinda, we don't want everyone following that plan. We have to make people believe they need all this security on their computers."

Cinda waved her red talons in dismissal. "Most of those people are just stupid or unlucky."

Jo stared at Red Nails. "You're kidding, right?"

Luce's jaw went rigid as the knuckles of her mouse-hand turned white. "*Those people* you're talking about *do* need all these security features." Her voice had a steel tone. "Ten million Americans had their identities stolen in the last year. It is the number one fear of American computer users. Thirty thousand websites are infected with some type of malware. You do the math."

Cinda scoffed, "You can't trust statistics. Stop worrying."

Luce's fists clenched as she spit her words. "My own Visa was hacked twice in one year. I had to work with my bank to get the hacker's charges removed. My second card number was sold to someone in the Ukraine who ran up charges to my $7,000 limit in a couple of hours."

Manny smirked. "I just love how cute long-legged blondes get when they're worked up. But we should plan meetings when they're not PMS-ing." Luce's face reddened as the Ken dolls grinned.

Jo couldn't make eye contact with anyone on the other side of the table, so she spoke to the list on the projector screen for Cinda's benefit. "Here is the list of features. Imagine someone stealing your purse with your keys, credit cards, checkbook, Social Security number, phone, address book, and the passwords to all your electronic accounts. GuardShark will protect your computer, phone, and all your files and contact information from Internet hackers—"

One of the Ken dolls cut her off. "Fingerprint ID. We decided to add that."

Manny tossed him a strawberry. "Right, the guys at the club are always forgetting their passwords."

Jo suddenly remembered a design discussion with a member of the previous GuardShark team. "Fingerprint ID requires software for optical scanning and accurate recognition of the fingerprint image, or capacitance scanning if the support for that capability is available in the computer, plus all the software to safeguard against hackers who try to trick the system. If someone steals your fingerprint ID, that can be worse than the usual ID theft."

Luce's voice had an edge. "That's a lot of extra work to add to the original design of GuardShark."

One of the Ken dolls shook croissant flakes off his designer tie in Jo and Luce's general direction. "You two always make it work. You could be looking at promotions out of this."

Over the longest hour in the history of high-tech, Cinda's attention drifted between adjusting her minimal attire, rearranging her legs to catch Manny's attention, and tapping her espresso cup with red talons while the slides were displayed and discussed. By 11:15 AM, GuardShark's feature list had been reviewed.

1. Malware protection against viruses, worms, trojans, and rootkits
2. Data protection for your critical files
3. Repair corrupted files
4. Full-system backup to the Cloud with super-encryption
5. Two-way firewall prevents unauthorized access
6. Parental controls protect your child from harmful Internet activity
7. Social networking protection ensures privacy on social media accounts (Facebook, Twitter, etc.)
8. Web search protection against potentially dangerous websites
9. Fingerprint ID

Ken doll A began packing his computer, oblivious to the mess on the table and in the vicinity of the trash can. Jo and Luce exchanged thank-god-for-early-lunch looks when Ken doll B clicked to the last slide. "Here are the numbers for our projected revenue, and the gotcha," he announced.

Manny beamed his laser pointer at the projector screen. "We anticipate high penetration of this product into the market, but only if we introduce it before the competition hears rumors. We need it in a month. Your team will have to pull out the stops on this one. It will be e-pic!"

Jo looked up from her computer, jolted, but was cut off before she could form a response.

Cinda beamed like a Barbie doll at Jo and Luce. "We know how much you like working at night. Just have your team work all day on GuardShark and test only after 5:00 PM. It's called 'divide and conquer.' We'll cover dinner."

Luce stared at Red Nails before saying to no one in particular, "'Divide and conquer' is a method for breaking down a mathematical algorithm into sub-problems that can be solved in parallel, combining the results of the sub-problems' solutions. You just described something that would be performed serially, not in parallel."

Red Nails winked at Manny. "I learned a lot of new things at the last conference Manny and I attended." Manny winked back.

Jo clenched her fists under the table, seething, as a rat-a-tat of anxiety knocked at her chest. She sensed Luce was as close to losing it as she was, and no wonder. *Why do idiots with power and money insist on making everything worse?*

Luce's hands gripped the arms of her chair as she spoke in a forced neutral tone. "We will have to obtain the international certification McWare needs to be competitive in the software security market. GuardShark has to pass a standardized test suite. We need at least a couple of weeks to run those tests and fix any problems so we can generate a passing report."

Cinda waved her talons. "Isn't that what we empower you girls to figure out?"

Jo watched Luce choke despite the fact that she wasn't drinking anything. *Did she really just say that? I want so badly to put her out of our misery.* Jo closed down her Mac. "Which tools are you considering for automated testing?"

Cinda's face froze in suspended animation. "What?"

Jo quickly simplified her question. "Do you want us to replace our current tests, or just add to the tests that are already working? What do you want to see on the test reports?"

Red Nails looked at her Fossil watch. "I have to run to a meeting, but we can catch up on all this at 3:00 PM for our first project status meeting."

Jo leaned close to Luce, muttering under her breath, "Look at all those questions flying over her head. We're supposed to have status by 3:00 PM today?" They nodded to each other to confirm a meeting later to draft the real plan for achieving such impossible deadlines.

Manny's gaze was glued to the sight and squeak of Red Nails' departing leather mini-skirt for several seconds, missing Luce's stunned expression and Jo's hand clenched for dear life. The clickety-click of stiletto heels in the hallway soon died, along with hope itself. His phone shrieked a shrill disembodied "Fore!", redirecting his attention.

Luce stood up and turned to Manny. "We need more engineers to build new tests."

Manny's iPhone beeped insistently. "Lonnie can help you until I need him."

Jo zipped her backpack. "Does Lonnie have experience testing software?"

Manny gave a thumbs up to the Ken dolls as he headed for the door. "Who cares? Anyone can test software." He gave Jo a sinister look. "Focus on getting the software to work instead of worrying about testing it."

Jo felt the rage rising in her. "Our team will make sure GuardShark lives up to every one of its promises."

Manny's phone beeped, his voice sharpened as he warned, "It won't be a problem if you engineers just don't screw it up like the last team. Worry about keeping your jobs. The customers can take care of themselves. GuardShark won't be any worse than any other security product that makes big promises." He began walking toward the door.

Jo fumed but quieted her voice. "We won't screw up …"

The Ken dolls exited the room behind Manny. Jo stared at the empty doorway, mimicking Manny, "Anyone can test software."

Luce growled, "I've got a fingerprint ID for him."

"Maybe we should go to a bar and drink our lunch."

Luce laughed as she snapped her Mac shut. "You don't drink alcohol." She turned to Jo. "What I really want is to get GuardShark done right. This feels like my chance to show my parents that writing software that benefits people is worth doing. I won't end up being a defense contractor like them."

Jo sighed. "Friends don't let friends become defense contractors. We'll find a way to get GuardShark done right, in spite of Shit-For-Brains Manny."

Luce shouldered her backpack, muttering for Jo's benefit, "Do you believe this?"

Jo seethed at full volume as she walked to the window overlooking the parking lot. "Shit-For-Brains is zooming off in his Porsche to the golf course, followed by his posse. You'd think they were hurrying back to the mothership."

Luce joined her at the window, staring at the exiting luxury vehicles. "They are. I wish aliens would land and take over. I would so much rather be enslaved by intelligent life."

Jo put her hands together in prayer. "Please God, let him hurt himself on the golf course."

Luce grumbled, "Like what? Pulling a ligament from dancing around intelligent questions?"

Jo turned to her best friend. "Have you started counting all the money we'll be making from our fat raises and promotions?"

Luce leveled a straight face at Jo. "Call me clairvoyant but I'll bet we came up with the same number."

Jo and Luce stood frozen in place. Jo leaned her forehead against the cool glass. "We're fucked."

Luce closed her eyes as if magic could and would fix the mess. "I imagine single syllable words will be best for writing my resignation letter. Otherwise the idiots might not understand I'm quitting."

Jo nudged Luce. "We're going out for lunch, just you and me, no work talk. We need to find your enthusiasm and my will to live. Are we doing Mexican, Chinese, Indian, or Thai?"

Luce raised her eyebrows. "For lunch or for our permanent escape destination?"

Jo playfully pushed Luce toward the door. "Let's play it by ear. I'll drive. Vixen makes a better getaway car. It's e-pic." Jo opened the door, stepping back to hold it open for Liz, who entered the room carrying a DustBuster.

Luce smiled at Liz. "I'm afraid the top dogs were as well-behaved as they've always been."

Liz sighed as she moved the trash can. "Money doesn't buy good manners." She flipped the switch and began vacuuming all the crumbs, the ends of her short dark hair dancing as she moved back and forth.

As Jo and Luce exited the room and ran down the back stairs to freedom, the high-pitched whine of the DustBuster blustered on.

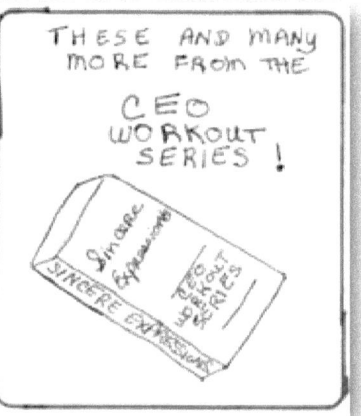

8

Method Acting

JO LEANED FORWARD in her chair at Illegal Pete's, a Mexican restaurant on Boulder's Pearl Street walking mall, inhaling the piquant aroma of her chicken burrito. "If only we could make Shit-For-Brains and Red Nails disappear."

Luce unwrapped her utensils, smiling down at her vegetarian tacos. "Got any ideas?"

Jo poured half a small bowl of extra-hot salsa on her burrito. "It cannot include touching them, too creepy. Does the criminal element ever have a two-for-one special?"

Luce put her iPhone on vibrate. "So, what I hear you saying is you want to find a hit person, but not just any hit person. You want a *cost-effective* hit person."

Jo threw up her hands. "Hey, I'm just being practical here. We have to cut corners."

Luce shook her head as she established a good hold on her first taco. "Seriously, what *are* we going to do?" She took a healthy bite of the little buffet of vegetables embraced in the joyful collaboration of crisp blue tortilla, barely melted Jack cheese, and tangy pico de gallo. She closed her eyes. "This is so good."

Jo's rhythmic forkfuls of the chicken burrito bathed in thick green pork chili were interspersed with satisfied sighs. "I cannot work with Red Nails for longer than sixty seconds a day. I hate her in deep and enduring ways that will undoubtedly lead to spewing of words and other substances."

Luce licked the delicious morsels off her fingers before grabbing the second taco. "As flakey as she is, sooner or later even she is bound to notice projectile vomiting."

Jo poured the rest of the first dish of salsa on the other half of her burrito. "We've got to think of some way to get everything done but stay under their radar."

"I've got it!" Luce finished off the taco. Jo's eyebrows wrinkled a frown, and Luce gestured theatrically. "We become actors who give glowing reports to the idiots while our team gets as much work done as possible."

Jo's fork punctured the air. "Me, act? Are you out of your mind? I don't even have a poker face. I'm all 'tell.'"

Luce dabbed taco shell crumbs off her face. "Maybe we could use that. You could overreact, or translate your deep frustration into a show of wild enthusiasm. Go ballistic with off-the-charts pro-nouncements. Use the angst, work it, own it." Luce hid behind her hands as Jo formed a cross against vampires with her fingers.

Luce threw the remaining half of the last taco on her plate. "C'mon, we can do this." She sighed, "If only I could be taco-level happy for the rest of my life."

Jo pushed her plate away, the little mountain of burrito bites overlaid with swirls of brick-red salsa. "I guess it can't hurt to try your Actors' Studio plan. But you have to coach me. This is going to feel weird, like wearing a dress and make-up to work."

Luce took a slow drink of water and set down her glass. "Acting is trying on another person. Think of it as a costume of the mind. I actually just came up with that."

Jo played with her water glass. "So now we're using The Method as a tactic to get our jobs done? Is it me or is this getting a little weird?"

Luce put the glass against her forehead. "We're way past weird. This is survival."

Jo took a last gulp of water and set down her glass, folding her hands on the table like a good student ready for class to begin. "OK, school me, Coach."

"The challenge is keeping a straight face while we manufacture positive energy every time we have to deal with them. They may be idiots, but they can smell fear."

Jo wiped her mouth with her napkin. "Predatory creatures are like that, although these yuppies wouldn't last two seconds in the wild. Imagine them being eaten by wolves. Now that's a happy picture."

"I suspect we have a more discerning class of wolves in Boulder County. But Jo, listen, I mean it. Do not show fear. It's that blood-in-the-water thing with those sharks."

Jo smirked. "Shit-For-Brains Manny could use some acting lessons to pull off sincere expressions and evasive responses."

Luce chuckled. "Coaching idiots like him would be a waste of time. OK, let's do a little role playing." Luce's voice dropped into a nasally whine. "Shit-For-Brains says, 'So girls, I would like you to finish the next set of product features before I leave for my golf game on Friday at 1:30 PM.' What do you say?"

"Bite me." Jo beamed a cheesy grin of triumph.

"Beep. Deduct 100 points. The correct answer is 'That's a great idea. Unfortunately, we could only get time on the special test systems for Wednesday through Friday next week, which will still allow us to make the scheduled delivery date.' So it's like 'Bite me' but sounds more professional and less like a personal pit bull attack. You see my point?"

Jo buried her face in her hands, muttering, "We're going to raise bullshit to new heights. I can practically smell the methane."

They paid the check, and let the Mustang fly them first class back to the office. Jo parked Vixen close to McWare's back door. "Now we get to deliver the bad news to the team." They walked slowly into the building and through the back hallway.

Luce sighed. "We should have brought treats to soften the blow."

The Tomb came alive when Jo opened the door and turned on the light. Her eyes cruised the cartoons on the whiteboard, and she noticed something out of place. The caption read, 'Of course the value of my stock options isn't a matter of life and death. It's much more important!'

"That's funny. Who did this?" Jo crossed and re-crossed her arms as she stood in front of her own cartoon, though it no longer felt like hers. "We're in and out of the Tomb all the time."

"One of the team must have come back late at night." Luce stood next to Jo, looking at the writing below the cartoon. "Does the handwriting look familiar?"

Jo shrugged, leaning closer to the caption. "Every engineer in the world writes in block letters. The team should be on their way, so I'd better put on my game face." Jo flipped open her laptop and attached the cable to the overhead projector.

Luce shook her head as she opened her Mac. "You won't win any acting prizes, but neither will they. I'll bet you real money one of them will be grinning at you."

As if on cue, voices from the hallway burst into the Tomb. Sherm nodded at the whiteboard, his hair still wet from his after-run shower. "Hey, Jo, you took my advice and changed Manny's outfit." He pulled a chair out.

Jim's thick rugby frame filled the chair next to wiry Sherm. "He looks almost life-like. I mean, in the cartoon." Sniggering spun around the room as the rest of the team took seats around the table.

Steve closed the door. "Did you have an interesting meeting this morning with Manny?"

Wayne crossed his arms, leaning comfortably back in his chair. "Interesting sounds bad." Vijay sat down next to him.

Luce displayed the PowerPoint slides. "The good news is the tests Jim and Sherm ran over the weekend show that most of the features are working. We didn't share that with Manny." Luce clicked to the slide that listed the features. "Since you've all been reviewing the GuardShark software while we were at the meeting, we thought you could tell us which features still need work. Here's the list."

Jo read the first bullet point. "Malware detection, blocking and destruction of suspicious files. That covers viruses, worms, trojans, rootkits, fraudulent websites, and suspicious email and file downloads."

Jim read through the test results from his computer screen. "Actually, all those things are done, but we need to add more testing for suspicious email and file downloads." Sherm popped open his Mac as Jo captured the work task for creating the new tests.

Luce moved the cursor to the next item. "Data privacy protection."

Sherm scrolled through the test results on his screen. "We need to add tests from computer accounts outside GuardShark's firewall to simulate hackers trying to get credit card, phone, address, and email information." Jo typed and clicked more notes.

Wayne turned to Jo. "Could we just use our personal email accounts to test from home? Or should we try to find someone who doesn't work on our team, or maybe someone who doesn't work at McWare?"

Steve looked up from his computer at Wayne. "That's a great idea. I wish we had access to a small army of teenage junior hackers. Let's start with testing from our personal email accounts from our home computers. I can test from my wife's account."

Jim shrugged thick shoulders. "My wife won't tell me her password, but that could be the pregnancy hormones talking."

Luce called out the next item. "Computer disk and file maintenance."

Wayne read off Sherm's screen. "Done, and the tests cover it well."

Jo looked up at the projector screen. "Backups to the cloud, with super-encryption."

Steve's big hand signaled to Jo. "The software needs more work, and I'd like to do that. The tests are good, but I may want to add more tests later." Jo captured Steve's tasks.

Luce called out, "Two-way firewall."

Sherm looked up. "The tests for that are doing a great job since they reported several problems. Sign me up to fix the failures."

Vijay raised a quick hand. "I looked through that software, checked the test results, and I've already figured out the fixes for most of the problems. That's another feature that we should test from our personal accounts on our personal computers." Jo typed like a fiend.

Sherm gave a thumbs-up to Vijay. "Hey, rookie, we're going to have to pay you real wages if you keep that up." Vijay's dark eyes glinted as he grinned.

Wayne nodded to Jo. "I can finish Parental Controls. Looks like the tests passed OK, but I want to set up tests from my personal computer." He winked at Jo. "I could use a small army of kids to help test."

Jo grinned. "Maybe we need to recruit at McDonald's." She shook her head and shivered. "No, I can't do McDonald's. You'll just have to learn how to think like a ten year old." Wayne winked and gave her a thumbs-up.

Jim pointed to the projector screen. "Sherm and I can take social networking protection. All the tests for that are passing, but we need to re-run the tests from our personal computers. That will also give us a chance to test the installation of GuardShark and the setting of personal preferences."

Sherm turned to Jim. "Couldn't we re-use some of the finger-print recognition we built for the Rhombus product that was axed to save time? I can look back in the design specs we did for it."

Jim nodded. "I'll find those files from the Rhombus software archives."

Luce looked around the table at the engineers safely tucked away in the Tomb. "Jo and I warned Manny and Cinda that GuardShark has to pass rigorous testing to receive the computer security certification. He graciously volunteered some of Lonnie's time to help us with that."

Jim exchanged a look with Sherm. "I don't think Lonnie will be happy about that. He told us testing was for interns. Sorry, Vijay." The dark-haired intern just shrugged.

Sherm sat back, crossing his ropey arms over his Moab rock-climbing shirt. "McWare can't risk getting sued if GuardShark has security holes. There are standard test suites available that cover the certification, so we can run those without Lonnie."

Jo got up and walked around behind Sherm to look at his computer screen. "I was reading about that over the weekend. Can you pull up the information on those certification tests?"

Luce moved next to Jo and read off Sherm's screen, "Common Criteria for Information Technology Security Evaluation is an international standard for computer security certification. It reports vulnerabilities in any software."

Wayne looked over Sherm's shoulder. "It's a gold-plated ticket for GuardShark if we can get it certified. Otherwise, GuardShark won't sell enough to buy Jo's lattes." A little wave of grins rippled around the table.

Steve looked around. "Would anyone be interested in working in pairs? Sometimes it helps to bounce ideas off each other and help each other run tests."

Vijay nodded. "We worked in pairs in my graduate projects classes. I'd be up for it."

Wayne turned to Vijay. "I'll work with you."

Jim looked at Sherm. "We've already buddied up, so we're good too."

Jo looked around the table. "Are you all OK with not mentioning to Manny or Cinda how much testing we're doing?" Heads nodded.

Luce turned off the projector. "Jo and I can create lots of status charts. We will even color them in since we all know how much management likes pictures." She was rewarded with several smirks.

Jo began closing down her computer. "The other piece of bad news is the daily status meeting Cinda will be holding at 8:30 AM in the executive conference room. She scheduled a meeting at 3:00 PM today to get a head start. I recommend you groan immediately so you can keep it all inside thirty minutes from now."

The team complied with a cacophony of zealous attempts to outdo each other's brand of guttural sounds. Jo and Luce exchanged knowing grins as they followed the team through the door.

9

Power 102

To: rookie-pup
From: Lord&Master

Being a shark is all about feeling your power. To feel your power, you have to do something only you can do, only you *would* do. Do you feel powerful? You will know it when you do.

Use the underlings as it suits your purpose, otherwise don't give them a second thought but learn to act as if you do. They are intelligent problem solvers, so you must keep them in the dark about your true game plan. They are desperate for approval, so mete it out in morsels and they will kill themselves trying to do what they believe will make you happy. It is a classic cat-and-mouse game, all part of the fun.

We only care about increasing our power and net worth. We have no use for a conscience. Utter selfishness simplifies our approach to life.

Remember, the control of money and power is your only goal. Money and power need each other, feed on each other. Money without power is just a dandy who is good for buying a round of drinks. Power without money is a back-street thug. You must use both in the right balance.

Today is a good day to be a shark.

~Sent from my iPad

EMPOWERMENT REQUEST FORM
(Complete in triplicate)
Please print

YOUR NAME: _____
YOUR IMMEDIATE MANAGER'S NAME: _____
YOUR AREA MANAGER'S NAME: _____
YOUR JOB: _____

AREA IN WHICH YOU REQUEST EMPOWERMENT: _____
WHAT DATE DO YOU NEED EMPOWERMENT? : _____
HOW LONG? : _____
  (If more than 24 hours, explain): _____
HAVE YOU EVER BEEN EMPOWERED BEFORE? :   ( )YES   ( ) NO
WITHIN THE PAST SIX MONTHS?:
  (If YES, explain): _____

IF YOU ARE EMPOWERED, DO YOU AGREE TO ABIDE BY THE RULES ESTABLISHED BY THE CORPORATE COMMITTEE ON EMPOWERMENT, AND BY YOUR LOCAL SITE EMPOWERMENT BOARD?:   ( )YES   ( ) NO
  (If NO, stop now)

JUSTIFICATION:
PLEASE JUSTIFY, IN DETAIL, YOUR REQUEST FOR EMPOWERMENT. INCLUDE SUCH INFORMATION AS:

- WHY YOU FEEL YOU DESERVE EMPOWERMENT (I.E., WHY *we* WOULD EMPOWER SOMEONE LIKE *you*)
- WHY YOU THINK YOU COULD DO YOUR CURRENT JOB BETTER IF YOU WERE EMPOWERED
- JUST WHAT IT IS THAT YOU WOULD LIKE US TO CONSIDER EMPOWERING YOU TO DO
- WHY CAN'T YOU JUST LEAVE IT TO US WHO ALREADY HAVE THE POWER INSTEAD OF GENERATING A LOT OF PAPERWORK SEEKING TO HAVE POWER DOLED OUT TO YOU?

YOUR REQUEST WILL BE REVIEWED BY THE SITE EMPOWERMENT COORDINATOR AND YOUR MANAGEMENT CHAIN (UP TO AND INCLUDING THE DIVISION VICE-PRESIDENT). YOU WILL BE INFORMED OF THEIR DECISION ON YOUR EMPOWERMENT WITHIN 90 WORKING DAYS. DO NOT CONTACT US FOR STATUS OF YOUR REQUEST.

10

Neo Vigilante

Jo stood in the corner of the executive conference room next to Luce, as far as possible from Red Nails' seat at the head of the table. She was staring at '3:05 PM' on her iPhone. The tee-shirted team sprawled in leather chairs, all sitting with a view through the wall of windows to the Rocky Mountains. The atmosphere was Us and Her.

Luce mumbled *sotto voce*, "Keep a straight face. Her kind can smell fear." She leaned her tall frame against the wall as she uncapped a water bottle.

Jo stood with her arms crossed. "If she hurts the team, I will take her out." Luce gulped and dropped her jaw, eyes wide in a mock Betty Boop face.

Red Nails switched on the overhead projector. Her rapid mouse clicks accompanied the bouncing cursor projected on the screen. "Give a brief status of your tasks on this list when I call your name. Wayne?" She looked around the table without seeing anyone.

Wayne waved his hand, smiling. "Right here, ma'am. I just do whatever needs doing."

Red Nails glared at Jo and Luce. "I see your project leads neglected to bring you up to speed. Every morning each engineer will report on their work assignments in alphabetical order. We're getting a head start this afternoon."

Wayne's kindly weathered face was all rural Wyoming politeness. "Ma'am, do you mean alphabetical by person, or alphabetical by the name of each task?"

"Alphabetical by engineer, of course." She rearranged herself inside her clothes, her back ramrod straight.

"Jim might be closer to the front of the alphabet." Wayne's smile disappeared as he caught Red Nails' icy glare.

Red Nails refocused on her screen. "Fine. Jim?" Jo clenched her fist, stiffening with disgust as her temples began to throb.

Wayne's broad grin lit his face. "He's at an appointment with his wife's doctor. Their baby is due soon."

Red Nails focused on her screen, clicking and typing. "He didn't update the vacation schedule."

"Well, ma'am, babies have a way of making everything else—" Wayne was abruptly cut off.

"Lonnie. Not here. I will talk with Lonnie later. Sherman?" Red Nails' laser focus bored into her computer screen.

"Everyone calls me Sherm. Social networking protections are done. What's next?"

Red Nails focused on her screen. "I will ask management. I will get back to you."

Engineers around the table exchanged what-the-fuck looks. Jo and Luce shrugged as if shaking off an evil spell. Sherm frowned at Red Nails. "We've always worked off the to-do list."

Red Nails' eyes appeared permanently fixed to her computer screen. "Who is available to take over Jim's work?"

Sherm waved his hand. "Jim and I are working together, so I'm covering for him. But he's coming back to work after the appointment with the doctor."

Red Nails glared at Sherm. "Only one engineer can be assigned to a task. Pick one."

Sherm flexed his hands as he looked from Red Nails to the screen and grumbled, "Twitter privacy protection."

Red Nails' tone cut like a knife. "Steve."

Steve answered, "I finished automated backups, so I can take another task."

Red Nails announced to her computer screen, "Steve gets the bug for password strength." She ignored the negative vibes swirling in the room. "Vijay?"

Vijay shifted in his chair. "I just started working on the two-way firewall."

Wayne turned to Cinda, smiling. "Now I understand what you're looking for. I'm working on Parental Controls and fixing a bug I found in the Help system."

"You're out of order. Next time wait until I call on you," Red Nails' eyes darted around the table like a caffeinated mosquito. Jo clenched her latte with a death grip. *Grandma could do a better job running this project.*

Jim's thick shoulders bumped the door with a noisy thud as he rushed into the room. "Sorry I'm late. My wife is home now." He pulled out a chair and sat down. "So, what did I miss?"

Red Nails' face was cast in stone. "This team has an appalling lack of understanding about proper status meetings. Tomorrow morning you will all attend the quality training class."

Jo exploded, "What? We're too busy to spend all of Wednesday morning in a training class. We have to keep GuardShark on schedule."

Steve cleared his throat. "Cinda, I teach that course, but not until January."

Red Nails' talons hit the keys with sharp pings as her voice took on a similar sharpness. "We have a new trainer teaching the course. Jim, update the calendar with your absence."

Jim grinned jovially. "Aye aye, Capt'n ma'am!" He winked at Jo, who shook her head as Luce gave him a thumbs-up.

Red Nails snapped her computer shut and stood up with a sharp push, her chair rolling back until it thudded against the credenza along the wall. She exited the room in the brisk walk of the self-important, the sound of her stilettos clattering away.

Jo massaged her skull, adopting a bad Russian accent, she said, "Dah-links, eez not training class, eez re-education camp."

Luce crumpled into a chair. "I can't believe we're going to lose a whole morning of work for a training class we don't need."

Jo looked around the room at each engineer. "Don't worry about Cinda. Just work off the to-do list and collaborate, share assignments, whatever works best for you."

Steve pushed back from the table and stood. "Let's meet in the Tomb to see where we're at."

Wayne's denim-jacketed shoulders shrugged a shiver. "Whew, the way Cinda talks to us is more like biting." He stood and followed Steve to the door.

Jim's deep laugh shook his chair. "I could bring her a teething ring from my wife's baby shower, or we could label the executive conference room 'Caveat Rabies.'"

Luce grinned at Jim as she passed him on the way to the door. "At least you felt empowered."

Sherm stood up, took a deep breath and stretched his arms and neck. "We should come up with an Empowerment Request Form, fill it out, and leave it in Cinda's office."

Jo grinned at him as the group made their way into the hall. "If we gave it an official-looking form number, she would probably process it. On a scale of one to two, her aptitude is nudging zero."

"Hey, Liz," the engineers greeted Manny's assistant as they passed her door.

She looked up from the documents on her desk. "Good meeting?"

Jim chuckled. "Empowering."

Liz deadpanned, "I feel that way every day."

Wayne pointed to the light as the team reached the back stairs. "How many project managers does it take to change a light bulb?"

Jim shook his head. "None, they like to keep employees in the dark."

Wayne opened his hands, spreading his fingers. "Ten. Two to find out if it needs changing, one to report the results to the administrative assistant, one to order the light bulb, two to get bids from contractors, one to notify the winning contractor, one to delegate an employee to tell the contractor which bulb to change, one to verify it was installed properly, and one to bill the contractor."

Jo and Luce were shaking, their laughter bouncing off the concrete walls as the team herded down the back stairs to the Tomb of the Unknown Meeting to sort out the details of their doom.

After the meeting in the Tomb, Jo grabbed her mug from her cube for a caffeine refill. Red Nails was getting coffee in the break room. Her back was turned, giving Jo a second to decide if she needed coffee bad enough to risk another brush with idiocy. Caffeine won.

"Hi, Jo. Is everything going OK?" Her shiny red talon tapped on her coffee cup.

Jo moved in close to the coffee and began filling her cup. *Just focus on the coffee pot, no eye contact.* "Just grabbing some coffee."

Red Nails felt far too close to Jo's personal space. "I haven't had a chance to get to know you. Say, you're not involved with anyone are you? I've got a brother who is looking for a date."

What ... the ... fuck??? Take a breath. Want to kill. No, wait, breathe. Don't turn around, no eye contact, you can do it. Focus on the coffee.

"Not interested." Jo fled as quickly as possible through the doorway.

Focus on the doorway, we're walking, we're walking, focus on the double doors, faster. Distance, lots of distance. Damned short legs. C'mon, faster. Damn, not fast enough.

The cheery-chirpy doll voice followed her. "Oh, that's too bad. So are you gay?"

What … the … mother … fuck??? Are you fucking kidding me? She really thinks lesbians are women who aren't interested in dating this pea brain's brother.

Jo hurried to her cubical and threw herself into her desk chair.

Work, just work, focus, don't look up if she comes over. Luce! I gotta talk to Luce!

Focus on the screen. Check the test reports, focus, damn it! God, I hate her. Breathe, stop, see the sunset over the Flatirons' mountain faces, breathe, fingers relaxed, hands unclenched, relax the jaw. I want to smack her. Breathe. See the pretty clouds. Relax the gut, belly breath. Out with the bad.

I'm an engineer, damn it, an intelligent, productive, accomplished engineer doing what I was hired to do, which does not fucking include dating that idiot's brother.

Maybe she really is that stupid. I have to breathe. God, I hate her!

Shit-For-Brains lets her do whatever her flea-sized brain wants to try, oh look, something shiny, I want to be a Project Manager, no, I want to be a cowgirl.

Wait, I feel a cartoon coming on. Luce will really love this one for Red Nails. I can use more colors, orange hair, blue bank teller shirt, and of course, screaming long red nails. Jo began to sketch. *Luce has to see this before I whiteboard it.*

Jo texted Luce: [Meet out back 20 mins]

11

Sisyphus Had A Last Straw Too

SITTING IN HER ready-to-spring pose on the bottom stair outside the back door of McWare's building, Jo fumed, "You gotta keep me from killing her."

Luce sat down beside Jo. "I'll do my best when the time comes." Luce handed the cartoon back to Jo. "This is funny."

Jo grumbled, "What, you think I'm not mad enough to kill her now?"

"It's know-how you lack. I think she has a good chance of living to see dinner." Luce grinned at the cartoon in Jo's hand. "You wouldn't want to lose your anti-muse."

Jo was livid. "Wouldn't I?"

Luce said quietly, "Red Nails is a walking example of a 'don't' list."

Jo rattled the piece of paper. "Can you even imagine being that shallow? What if you had to play her in a film?"

Luce pinched her nose to make her voice chirpy. "So, you're not involved with anyone? I've got a brother who is looking."

Jo made a cross with her index fingers. "Not interested. Be gone, evil one."

Luce squealed with delight, still pinching her nose. "OK, so you're gay. I have a sister and a mother who are looking."

Jo cocked her head. "You have a mother? Still not interested."

Luce poked her chin with an index finger, adding a Betty Boop quality to her high-pitched nasally voice. "Hmm, so not interested in men or women … so, you're …"

Jo threw up her hands. "Asexual!"

Luce, head and neck crooked in a human question mark, squeaked in an even higher pitch, "A what …?"

Jo put her hands on her hips. "Asexual! It means I don't fuck anyone, you complete idiot!"

Luce kept pinching her nose but she was having trouble keeping a straight face and staying in character. "But how can you live like that?"

Jo flexed both hands at Luce's impersonation of Red Nails. "Sex is like bridge. If you've got a good hand, you don't always need a partner."

Luce involuntarily grinned, trying to maintain her nasally voice. "Can I ask you a personal question?"

Jo posed with her hands on her hips. "Do you want to know my bra size, net worth, and Social Security number, or just my Facebook password? The real *you* already knows I'm not gay."

Luce shook her head. "Stop, I can't do it anymore. She is so stupid I'm afraid it will rub off."

Jo nodded toward the back door. "I have to pee."

The two women reluctantly stood up when suddenly the back door flew open with a loud bang as it smacked against the railing. Liz barreled through the doorway with a cigarette in one hand and a lighter in the other, nearly knocking Jo down. Liz stopped just inches from Jo. "Sorry," she growled, "if I don't have a cigarette, someone is going to get hurt. And I'm smoking it real slow."

Jo stepped back to give Liz room to pass. "What happened, Liz?"

Liz's hand shook as she lit up. She inhaled deeply, exhaling a rush of smoke as she closed her eyes. A long moment passed, followed by another puff that was less desperate. "If I didn't need my paycheck and medical insurance so much, I would tell him where to stuff it."

Luce looked at Jo and back at Liz. "So, this would be about Manny?"

Liz took another drag, flicking the ash to the pavement before she gazed at Jo and Luce. "You might as well use his official name, Shit-For-Brains, which in my book is generous. He made me drop everything to change the date for the Board meeting to move it up by two days, so I have to reschedule with the Boulderado and redo all the documents. I'll have to pay my babysitter overtime today."

Jo winked at Luce before turning to Liz. "You need my kidnapping service for overwhelmed and underpaid administrative assistants."

Liz paused mid-puff, eyeing Jo. "Kidnapping service?"

Jo explained in a mock-serious tone, "When he really pushes you over the edge, you push the magic pager button and I send kidnappers to take you away to a nice hotel where all your needs are served, then everyone leaves you alone. It's not your fault if you get kidnapped. But you won't be released for a couple of days."

Liz absently flicked her ashes, leveling a gaze at Jo. "I'd love to see the look on his face when he realized I wouldn't be here to do his work. Could you make it a week?"

Jo wailed, "I'll make it a month, just gangway. Now I really have to pee." She opened the back door and ran to the bathroom.

Luce followed her in, checking under the stalls to be sure they were alone. "By the way, the captions on your old cartoons are great."

Jo emerged from the stall. "Are there more captions?"

Luce gazed in the mirror, rearranging a strand of blonde hair. "You haven't seen them? They're not half bad. Check it out sometime when you get a chance."

Jo watched Luce in the mirror as she finished washing her hands. "I have to see this for myself."

Jo was first through the Tomb door. "That's funny," a grin cracking Jo's puzzled face as she read the cartoon captions. She burst out laughing, pointing to the Geek Oscars cartoon of Shit-For-Brains handing out awards. "'It's not just the plaque that counts, it's the money'. That's exactly how I felt."

Luce snickered. "It's someone who knows what a jerk Manny is."

Jo looked at each captioned cartoon. "Captain Caption has some chops. It's gotta be someone on the team, but who would come back here after work to do funny on the whiteboard when they could be anywhere else doing anything else, far away from this insane place?"

Luce frowned at the whiteboard. "What if it's not one of the engineers? It can't be Shit-For-Brains or Red Nails. They don't share a brain or a funny bone between them. They were declined those attributes."

Jo grabbed the dry erase marker, found a blank spot on the walls of whiteboards, sketched the three panels with her send-up of Red Nails' attempt to set her up, and threw the marker on the tray as she turned to Luce. "Let's call it a day."

Luce nodded and headed for the hallway as Jo turned to follow. A few minutes later, Jo leaned against Vixen, enjoying the feeling of the sun-warmed metal. "It's time to get rid of that pathetic excuse for a project manager."

The parking lot was nearly empty in the early evening. Luce shrugged. "Evil Barbie, in the no-brains model, has Manny's blessing. That's like super-glue for her job security."

Jo unlocked the Mustang. "Actually, I had a crazy thought yesterday. It's a little out there and needs work."

"How illegal is it?" Luce clicked the electronic key to unlock the Prius.

Jo threw her backpack onto the passenger seat. "It's probably legal, but a little strange. We could make her think another company is interested in hiring her."

Luce held the edge of her car door. "You mean, we could get her a job she didn't apply for?"

Jo waved her hand. "No way. I wouldn't do her any favors. I just want to mess with her, distract her with fake email from a couple of recruiters. How hard could that be?"

Luce tossed her backpack into the Prius. "Wayne could help us set that up."

Jo looked up with a happy grin. "Can we get her interested in a company in an entirely different time zone, maybe Iceland?"

Luce got into her Prius. "Let's take this one step at a time. We can't afford to get stars in our eyes just yet."

Jo stabbed her iPhone screen. "I wish she would disappear from our lives. Is that asking too much?"

The Prius hummed to life. "Tragically, probably. I'm off."

Jo got into Vixen. "Onward, girlfriend. Mañana."

12

Occupational Hazards 101

To: rookie-pup
From: Lord&Master

Trust no one, no one except me.

"Keep your friends close and your enemies closer." Read *The Art of War*, the definitive primer for how to be a warrior. You can only trust your friends to a point. You must know what your enemies are doing so you aren't blindsided by them.

Sharks cannot trust other sharks. Do not risk your future as a power broker for something as frivolous as a friendship. Live in secrecy, hyper-vigilant, planning your next moves and countermoves.

Never reveal our strategy, not even after we have achieved our goal. You will be tempted to brag about our plans and later about our victories, but it is your secrets that ensure your lifetime of power.

Get used to swimming alone. Your success depends on constant contact with those who will either feed you useful information or do your bidding. Learn to beguile both categories of dupes into needing your approval so they will gladly dance to your tune.

Bite hard and fast to render them stunned, disoriented, and completely unprepared to do anything but move on, leaving you to enjoy the pile of money and greater power you have accumulated at their expense.

~Sent from my iPad

13

Operation Red Aloha

AFTER DINNER WITH Grandma, Jo sank into the chair at the desk in the quiet of her bedroom, gritting her teeth for another late night. She forced herself to check on the results of the GuardShark tests to spot any patterns in the failures. At 10:30 PM her iPhone sang out "R-E-S-P-E-C-T" for Luce's ringtone. Jo picked up the call. "Hey, night owl, what's up?"

Luce's voice had an annoyed edge when she asked, "Jo, aren't you sick of this? We're never going to finish everything Shit-For-Brains wants by the deadline, so what's the point of killing ourselves?"

Jo's anger rose with a sudden choking sensation. "You're right. We're always pushing another impossible boulder up a mountain. I hate this."

Luce's voice sharpened. "So why don't we get new jobs and blow this stupid pop-stand? I'm so mad. I started looking online and I found some good positions at local companies."

Jo started laughing. "So instead of wishing Red Nails would leave McWare, we could get away from her and be free of Manny. Now that's an Operation Red Aloha I can get behind. What did you find?"

Luce mumbled, "Just a sec, let me organize the list and send it to you."

Jo opened her electronic resume file. "My resume isn't too out of date, but I could punch it up with hard-hitting keywords. Boy, can I write."

Luce's voice was more playful. "You can write *lies*. You made the medical software company where we first worked together look like we were doing world-class technology instead of cleaning up a truckload of scary bugs. OK, I just sent the list. Let the job search begin."

Jo zinged back, "Hey, it's a gift for fiction, very important in resume writing." She opened Luce's email. "Good list."

Luce snickered. "What we *really* need is a list of companies run by people who are even more stupid and self-absorbed than Shit-For-Brains. We have to steer clear of them."

Jo used her free foot to massage Gizmo's head, smiling as the purr revved. "And we should get Red Nails interested in the bad companies. That's genius, Luce, but how do we find those gems of corporate idiocy? I guess we could use negative networking." Jo displayed the list of engineering friends, former colleagues, and their contact information.

Luce cooed through the phone, "Oh, I get it. We can use our network to find companies with idiots in management. Genius, yourself."

Jo saved the file. "Any company that would hire her has to be so idiot-prone that when she left McWare for the new job, it would raise the level of intelligence at both companies."

Luce's sudden angry tone startled Jo. "She makes women look bad, and that really pisses me off. Women in high-tech and other professions have worked so hard to gain respect for our expertise and leadership."

Jo felt her own anger at Red Nails rising. "I hate her too. When a brain-dead kewpie doll has power, things never go well. OK, double-check me, Luce. Let's get this right." Jo called out each website, waiting for Luce's confirmation.

Luce said excitedly, "Hey, it's like finding a buyer on eBay. An established company might be our best bet, stay away from start-ups from now on."

Jo disengaged her feet from Gizmo to sit crossed-legged in the chair. "Operation Red Aloha has officially commenced. Break out the champagne! Well, maybe tea for now."

Luce's voice was muffled. "I like job-hunting in my pj's with my pint of Ben and Jerry's. Let's save the cork popping until *after* we've said adios to Shit-For-Brains and Red Nails."

Trying various Google searches, the conspirators added a few more companies to the spreadsheet and took a break when the list of twenty businesses checked out with the type of job openings that matched their skill set and experience. Jo and Luce quickly scanned the list of jobs and companies to whittle down the keepers.

Jo sat up suddenly. "What about those job search websites like monster.com?"

Luce's response was instant. "No, I blame them for my first job in high-tech."

Jo teased, "Are you still bitter? 6figurejobs.com. Now there's one worth checking out."

Luce's high-pitched laugh pierced Jo's ear. "Get serious, that's gotta be for consultants and sales reps."

Jo made notes on her spreadsheet. "Yeah, it's got e-scumbag written all over it. I think we've got a good list, but I need to get back to work. This was a fun break, but you know as well as I do that we'll have more leverage applying for jobs with GuardShark on our resumes. I need a paycheck to help Grandma pay the bills her Social Security doesn't cover."

Luce sighed. "I know, I have a mortgage and car payments. I just needed a back-up plan to survive the next month in case our plan to be heroes with GuardShark falls through. Besides, we wouldn't bail on the team, and it's easier to find a job while you still have one."

Jo reported, "Wayne set up that faceless account for me and I used it to send Red Nails a couple of fake emails from direct mail and telemarketing companies. He created a script that forwards a copy of her email to you and me so we can see if she takes the bait."

Luce applauded close to the phone. "That's brilliant. I dream of saying aloha to the red menace." She yawned. "Job hunting is exhausting. I'm ready to call it a night. As soon as we're close to finishing GuardShark, we should start applying for jobs."

Jo gave in to her own yawn. "Good plan, and we'll get our team to apply with us. OK, gotta get back to work before I crash. I'm going to check my email every hour."

Luce's voice was again engulfed in a yawn. "Knock yourself out. My bed is calling."

Jo blinked her eyes, willing them to focus on the computer screen. "I'm already dreaming about a beautiful life without Shit-For-Brains and Red Nails."

14

Mutiny At the Shipwreck

THE TEAM OF engineers noisily made their way down the hall to the Tomb, where Jo and Luce waited, the projector ready to display the PowerPoint slides created moments ago. Jo stared at the wall clock, imagining it was 6:15 PM instead of 8:15 AM.

This is it, no way to escape, nowhere to go even if escape magically presented itself. Jo nodded at Luce. "Do it."

As the engineering team took seats, popped open laptops, and settled in, Jo was grateful for the Tomb's unadorned sense of sanctuary, safe from senior management who wouldn't be caught dead entering such a functionally utilitarian room.

Luce looked around the table. "We reviewed the project schedule, and the good news is that we should be able to finish GuardShark in a month."

Jo sat down in front of her computer and displayed the first PowerPoint slide. "Management won't accept any delays."

Lonnie Schuster's tall, heavily muscled frame barreled into the room, gesturing at the slide projected on the screen with his sleeve-tattooed arm. "Is that the good news in this little story?"

Jo gritted her teeth, thinking, *Count on Lonnie to hit the nail on the coffin.*

He grabbed a chair and sat with a bang, fixing his bad-ass buzz-cut glare at Jo. "Look, I don't know why I was assigned to work with this team. I have my own projects, so don't count on me long term."

Lonnie was oblivious to the stunned looks on the team's faces, reminding Jo again that denial can be a beautiful thing. She willed herself to ignore him and clicked to display the next slide. "Every feature of GuardShark has to work, every time, in any order, and we have to prove it before management will agree we're done."

Luce looked around the table. "That means the product must be thoroughly tested every night. Unfortunately, the Test team is over-booked on another project."

Jo looked up from her screen. "We have to do our own testing, so we'll test each other's software. Any questions?"

Lonnie's alpha Type A venom spewed in a megaphone voice. "Yeah, I've got a question! What kind of nimnos are you, thinking I'M going to test software?" No one moved. Lonnie smacked his hand down hard on the table as his voice lost all control. "Look at my face! I'm Manny's technical specialist, NOT a tester. Testing is done by people who aren't good enough to be software developers!"

Luce focused on the projector screen. "Calm down, Lonnie. We'll get through this."

Lonnie face corrugated with anger. "The rest of you can be good little corporate bunnies, but read my lips. I'M NOT TESTING! I'm outta here."

He ejected himself from his chair, propelling it to roll until it crashed into the nearest wall as he stormed out of the Tomb. The little wheels continued to spin in place, the only sound in the eerie quiet.

Jo sought Luce's eyes as every engineer breathed audibly.

Wayne leaned back in his chair, stretching his long legs that ended in hand-tooled cowboy boots. "That boy missed his rabies shot."

Jo laughed but could feel her skull beginning to expand on a one-way path to a full-blown migraine. "I suspect the rest of the meeting won't be quite as entertaining." *God, don't let this place kill me. I have to keep Grandma in drill bits.*

Luce took a deep breath and looked around the table. "Are you willing to give the test exchange thing a shot?" All heads nodded in assent.

Jo smiled in relief. "Thanks. We have an even number without Lonnie. We'll find another way for him to carry his part of the load."

Sherm's mouse clicks drew attention. "If we're done, Vijay and I have something to show everyone." At Luce's nod, he said, "We did a little espionage. Watch my screen." His computer case sported a 'Climbers Rock' decal. Vijay locked the Tomb's door as Wayne and Jim rolled their chairs next to Sherm. Jo and Luce exchanged what-the-heck looks as they stood behind Sherm's chair.

The title 'Artist at Work' displayed on the screen as the engineers applauded. The film opened on the empty, dimly lit Tomb. Light suddenly flooded the room at the sound of the door opening. A broad-shouldered figure in hooded sweats walked quickly into the room and stood in front of a cartoon of bobblehead dolls. The figure stepped back, appearing to consider the work before writing a caption under it. The film cut to the empty room again.

Jim jostled Sherm's chair. "Hey, we didn't get to see who it was. Your spy skills need work."

Wayne grinned. "They're toying with our curiosity."

In the next clip, the Tomb lights came on again, and the same hoodie and jeans-clad figure sauntered across the room with an athlete's graceful stride to stand in front of a four-paneled cartoon with lots of red in the exaggerated hair and nails. As the figure reached for a dry erase marker, it fell to the floor and rolled toward the door. Bending down to retrieve the marker, the hood fell off, revealing a strong chiseled face and a mop of thick black hair.

Jo gasped, "Oh my god." She stared at the screen. "I think that might be the guy who was with Lonnie late one night."

Luce frowned. "Did you tell Lonnie it's a security violation to show visitors any of our work when they haven't signed a non-disclosure agreement?"

Jo shook her head. "No, I hid when I heard them coming. They didn't see me, and I only saw the sleeve of his friend's sweatshirt, but Lonnie called him Seth. He must have some engineering chops because he recognized all the problems we were working out on the whiteboard."

Steve stared at the computer screen's frozen image of the dark-haired stranger. "But how did he get into our building late at night?"

Jo grumbled, "Crap, Lonnie offered his friend Seth a key to our building. Sorry, I just fled as soon as they were gone. So much has been happening that I forgot to mention it."

Steve crossed his arms. "This smells bad. I'm concerned about what those two are up to." He turned to Wayne. "Can you put an electronic sniffer on all the changes Lonnie makes to any of the GuardShark code files?"

Wayne nodded. "No problem, I'll do it now. I'll put a watcher script on all his email too, and automatically copy everything he receives or sends to Jo and Luce."

Jo grumbled as she packed her computer into her backpack, "Let's check out any email Lonnie trades with this Seth guy. Lonnie's lucky we don't have enough evidence yet to bust him and his buddy. Oh, shoot, don't forget the mandatory training session tomorrow morning in the executive conference room."

Luce snickered. "Red Nails will be there, perfectly color-coordinated, no doubt."

Wayne's ambling gate matched his easy drawl. "That lady is wound up tighter than a two dollar watch."

Steve held the door open for Jo with his long arm extended from a yard away, and Jo sauntered under his arm with a beaming smirk as the team exited the Tomb, banter echoing down the hallway in their wake. Luce grabbed Jo's sleeve, pulling her back into the Tomb as the rest of the engineers continued toward their cubical offices.

Luce closed the door after Wayne and Steve, and turned to Jo. "How much love do you feel for Lon-Scum right now?"

Jo closed her eyes, massaging her temples. "What is the scientific definition of absolute zero?"

Luce gazed at her best friend. "I'm glad he's not working with the team. I wonder if we can trade him?"

Jo frowned, eyes still closed. "For what, two peanut butter and jelly sandwiches and a Snickers bar? What fiction would we fabricate about his usefulness?"

Luce dramatically waved her hand. "That's our choice, lying to another team or working with him?"

Jo spun in a dizzying little circle in the empty room as she chanted, "Fuck, fuck, fuck, fuck, fuck!" She stopped, steadying herself against the door. "That felt good. OK, I'm back. So what did we decide about Lon-Scum?"

Luce laughed with her frustrated friend. "We lack fondness for him."

Jo leaned against the door, crossing her arms. "What if we came up with a project for him that was a critical component of GuardShark's success and could be done by a single person?"

Luce pulled out her iPhone to take notes. "Every possible combination of uses of GuardShark has to be tested. We could have him build an automated system to do that."

Jo watched Luce's iPhone screen. "He hates testing, so we need a shiny-sounding name. How about SharkNet? It's the net that catches sharks before they bite you."

Luce grinned as she typed. "That's the shiniest bullshit I've heard today."

Jo pulled out her iPhone and sent a text to a mobile phone number. "We need someone with authority to sell it to him, someone exactly like Steve."

The ukulele ringtone signaling the arrival of Red Nails' email copies created a duet between Jo and Luce's iPhones. Jo grinned. "Operation Red Aloha strikes, and the lucky company that contacted her first is … drumroll."

Luce frowned. "Who is CJ? The sender's email address isn't from a company."

Jo squinted at the little screen. "Why would he want Red Nails to give Manny an offshore bank account number? That's weird."

Luce pointed to Jo's iPhone. "Look closer at the emails' to and from addresses. CJ sent this to Red Nails' personal email, but she copied it to her McWare email address when she forwarded it to Manny."

Jo looked at Luce. "If she hadn't copied herself, we wouldn't have seen it. She doesn't realize all McWare email is stored on a computer server that we can access using GuardShark."

Luce tapped her iPhone on Jo's phone. "Let's ask Steve. Maybe he knows who CJ is. I don't have to know what this is about to smell something rotten." Luce shouldered her backpack and opened the door.

Jo's voice trailed Luce into the hallway. "I can't think anymore. I wish I could put Vixen on automatic pilot straight to Grandma's house. It is a magical place with hugs, and every screw driver and repair manual known to mankind."

Luce walked through the double doors to the cubical area. "We can dive into Red Nails' email later to figure out who CJ is. You know, you should let Grandma know that a lot of old books, articles, and manuals have been scanned and made available on the Internet."

Jo stopped automatically at her cube office. "She's more into manual systems, but having access to every old repair manual would be heaven for her."

An hour later, after a run-by to the break room for more coffee, Jo and Luce set up their computers in the Tomb just before Steve sauntered through the door.

"I was about to ask how my two favorite engineers are doing, but from your faces I fear that question would add insult to injury. What's up?" Steve pulled a chair out.

Luce twisted a strand of hair. "We've always been able to count on you to rescue us from certain disaster. We need your superpowers."

Jo rubbed her forehead. "Lonnie mutinied when we told the team they have to do all the testing."

The strand of Luce's blonde hair was getting quite a workout with her anxious fingers. "Can you sell him on the idea of creating an automated test system? We're calling it SharkNet."

Steve clasped his hands behind his head, stretching his neck and shoulders. "That's a great idea. The next time we have a pile of cash, remind me to start a company with you two."

Jo shrugged her shoulders with a mock look of dejection. "If only we weren't booked until two days after hell freezes over and thaws again. We'll need a way to track Lonnie's work."

Luce looked at Jo. "We can get that from a full set of reports for each night's test results. I just wish we had something less interesting for him to do, but we need this."

Steve nodded. "We could run the new test system on GuardShark every night and have reports ready when we come in each morning."

Jo opened an Excel spreadsheet to capture their ideas for SharkNet. "The reports will tell us how much he has accomplished and will also give Shit-For-Brains, Red Nails, and the Ken dolls the final proof that GuardShark is ready to ship."

Steve grinned as he stood up. "That's good thinking. I need to find Lonnie to snag him for lunch at the pub. I'll catch up with you later this afternoon."

Luce stood up, grabbing her Mac. "Thanks, Steve, and I don't mean just for your willingness to have lunch with our resident jackass. You saved us, probably saved GuardShark."

Jo finished typing the notes and saved the file. "I suspect you saved Shit-For-Brains, Red Nails, and the Ken dolls, but I guess we'll just have to live with that." She grabbed her Mac, following Luce and Steve through the Tomb door. The Tomb returned to its cocoon-like state of dim-lit silence.

Jo and Luce worked through lunch at their cubes until Steve's text message alerted them to his arrival at McWare. They hurried to the back hallway as Steve opened the Tomb door. "That guy can sure put away the beers, but he bought into doing SharkNet." They sat down at the table and opened their computers.

Jo massaged her temples, trying to stall a migraine. "Thanks again for selling it to him."

Steve sat down, looking directly at the two project leads. "I learned something interesting."

Luce looked up from her Mac. "What might that be, Steve?"

"Lonnie probably said more because he was drinking." Steve winked. "Lonnie and Manny were in the same fraternity at CU/Boulder. That seems to be the sole reason Lonnie was hired by Manny."

Jo put her head in her hands. "I don't think I've called him Shit-For-Brains in front of the team, just with you two. At least I hope not."

Steve sat back and crossed his arms. "What do we know about Lonnie's level of expertise from the work he's done over the past four years?"

Luce thought for a moment, gazing absently at geek notes and cartoons on the whiteboards. "He worked on projects for Manny and the Ken dolls."

Jo peered through her fingers, covering her face. "I don't remember seeing any software he's written."

Steve leaned on the table. "So your first time working with him was when he was assigned to GuardShark yesterday."

Luce clicked her mouse and frowned. "I can't find any software he's written. Why does this suddenly feel all cloak and dagger?"

Steve rolled his chair next to Luce, staring at her screen as Jo rolled her chair over. "What has he been doing on GuardShark since yesterday? Have you seen any software he's written?"

Luce typed and clicked. "He installed new software tools. I can't find any software he's done so far this week. Let's take a look at the software he wrote for Manny." Three pairs of eyes glued to her computer screen. "What do you notice?"

Jo pointed to specific text lines. "This software doesn't use our standard template. There is no copyright text and it doesn't use our naming conventions. It's as if whoever wrote this has never seen or worked with any of our software files."

Steve looked directly at Jo. "What if the person who wrote this has never worked at McWare?"

Luce's mouth fell open. "What?" she asked; a split second ahead of Jo's, "What are you talking about?"

Steve used Luce's mouse to display the file properties. "I think Lonnie hired someone to do his work. Lonnie Schuster is the son of Bill Schuster of Schuster Enterprises. Our Lonnie is a rich kid who is heavy on attitude but light on skill set."

Jo threw a marker at the nearest whiteboard. "That explains a lot."

Luce sat back with a disgusted expression. "If Lonnie paid someone to do his work, that would fit right in with his reptilian personality."

Jo massaged her skull as she stretched her neck. "If this is true, what is our next move?"

Luce hunched over her computer. "Convincing Manny that Lonnie should be fired is out."

Jo studied the software file displayed on Luce's screen. "There's another reason we should be careful. The engineer who wrote this software is clearly talented, maybe too talented," Jo said, sitting down. "Maybe we could get his help to finish GuardShark. We have to find Mystery Geek, but without Lonnie knowing."

Steve frowned. "Be careful. Talent and ethics are two different things. Talent is the easier one to verify."

Jo nodded. "You bet it is."

Luce propped her chin on her hand. "How do we find this evil or angelic genius?"

Jo replied, "We can use Wayne's scripts and GuardShark's security features to pinpoint the software the system identifies as written by Lonnie, since we can be pretty sure if it's good, Mystery Geek wrote it."

Steve shook his head. "No need to go ninja, Jo. We can just let him do Lonnie's work, watch them carefully, and wait for our next move. It's ironic that we need Lonnie to keep Mystery Geek working on the SharkNet tests so we can deliver GuardShark on schedule."

Jo stopped spinning. "Ironic and crazy. Whatever happened to logic?"

Luce shrugged. "It's Dilbert, Theater of the Absurd, and Mission Impossible all rolled into one."

Steve sighed as he stood up. "It's also risky dealing with an unknown. After this is over, maybe we could just write software and leave the espionage to James Bond and Tom Cruise."

Luce stood up. "We should only communicate with each other in face-to-face meetings, no using McWare email or IMs. I sound paranoid."

Jo closed her computer with one hand and rubbed the back of her neck with the other. "Paranoia might save us. Our personal email and iPhones block unknown senders and callers, so they're safe enough."

Luce followed Steve through the Tomb door. "So we will string Lonnie along, decide what to do about Mystery Geek, and not piss off Shit-For-Brains, not necessarily in that order. I need a vacation so I can get in shape for my spy career."

A sharp bleep sounded simultaneously from each of their three computers, announcing the arrival of an urgent email from Shit-For-Brains. Jo stopped to open her Mac, frowning at the screen. "Are you kidding me? Red Nails is calling a meeting for us with Manny now, at 3:00 PM? What is this about adding new features to

GuardShark?" Her annoyance echoed off the cinderblock walls in the back hallway.

Steve read the email, looking down over Jo's shoulder. "I've got a bad feeling."

Luce sighed. "Another opportunity to spend time with Red Nails and Manny. The hits just keep coming."

Jo snapped her Mac shut. "We'll be imprisoned with the two biggest idiots on the planet for at least two hours. At least we'll have the best view in Boulder. Oh, Steve, have you ever heard of someone named CJ who might have done some consulting for Manny?"

Steve slowly shook his head. "Doesn't ring any bells. It's Cinda Janx's initials. Why?"

Jo laughed. "Wow, I didn't even think of that. Maybe she has an angelic twin."

Steve stared at Jo. "If we didn't have to go to this meeting, I would want a full explanation."

Luce stopped walking. "Can I pay you to cover for me while I hide in here?"

Jo nudged her friend's shoulder. "What, and miss all the fun? Let's get this over with. Shall we meet at Ozo's tomorrow at 7:30 AM and down here around 4:30 PM?"

They looked at each other and nodded in reluctant agreement before flying up the back stairs to face the inevitable.

15

Messaging 101

To: rookie-pup
From: Lord&Master

Sharks are adept at delivering the unpopular, unhappy message. It can be one of your most valuable assets for keeping your underlings on the leash without giving them a clue their days are numbered. Learn to do it well. Take your time, but not too much time, since time is money and money is power.

Messaging is all about the show. You are like Hollywood producers who use effective messaging to build anticipation of a film's release. Damage control is something we can discuss later since it is a more advanced aspect of business strategy and the complexities of lying to your advantage.

Find ways to cause more problems and you will be delightfully surprised how much pressure engineers can handle. Just sit back and watch the underlings pull together, pulling out all the stops like a good little band of soldiers who believe they are winning the good fight.

This little adventure is just a means to an end, so keep that end in mind every day without ever letting anyone else know our secret plan. You can learn to message effectively, to twist the knife at just the right time and take all the money and power in one brilliantly orchestrated move. Well-honed treachery takes time, and conveniently, being heartless is a time saver.

~Sent from my iPad

From the Desk
Of The
CEO

Entrepreneurs' Mantra

We don't have time
To do it right
The first time
But we always have time
To do it
Over

16

The Perfect Storm

MANNY AMBLED INTO the executive conference room twenty minutes late, golf-ready in Armani black attire and suede loafers. He was absorbed in his iPhone until he caught Cinda's look of rapt adoration, her leggy stride, and her red plaid mini-skirt. Neither acknowledged their tardiness, let alone the existence of Jo, Luce, or Steve.

Manny checked his iPhone, announcing to no one in particular, "You need to add password security to GuardShark."

Jo crossed her arms as she gathered her confidence, turning to face Manny. "Do you mean password strength checking and secure password recovery? If GuardShark has to be ready in a month, we won't have time to add new features."

Manny barked without looking up from his iPhone, "Do whatever it takes to get them done. The marketing guys decided GuardShark won't be competitive without them."

Luce white-knuckled the armrests of her chair. "We're already working overtime."

Cinda beamed as if Manny had given her a new Porsche. "Just do less testing."

Steve shook his head at Manny. "If we don't test everything every night to make sure all the new things we've added are working correctly, GuardShark won't pass the certification tests."

Manny's iPhone shrieked, and he glanced down at it before looking up angrily at Steve. "Do what you're being paid to do. I can replace you and that engineering team anytime."

Jo resisted the urge to throw something. "Why are we hearing about these new things now? The schedule—"

Manny cut her off with a sharp, "Quit wasting my time with your whining and get back to work."

Red Nails brushed a speck of lint from her silk blouse, distracting Manny. Jo wanted to scream, *He is where logic and reason go to die.*

Manny fished his keys from his pants pocket. "I've got to run. Steve, figure out how to deliver the product on time. I can't do all the work to keep this company in the game." Red Nails stood as if on cue.

As Jo's fist clenched hard, Steve put a hand on her arm. "We're going to have to pull testers off other projects to help Jo and Luce's team."

Manny gestured a brush-off in Steve's direction. "Not happening. Just make do."

Jo clenched her hands tighter around the armrests. "Make do?"

Shit-For-Brains was already heading for the door, but he turned back to glare at the engineers. "If you three can't get the job done, you are of no use to this company."

Red Nails, trailing Manny, glanced over her shoulder at Jo. "We will work out any problems at our daily 8:30 AM meeting." She scampered after Manny out the door.

Jo grumbled to the departing duo, "Thank goodness for your leadership." Jo's head throbbed, reminding her to calm down.

The bobbleheads moved out of sight, leaving the senior engineers sitting at the gleaming expanse of the executive conference room table in stunned silence. Jo's fists clenched on the table. "I'm pissed. 101 things to do with a dead CEO won't be enough." Her iPhone emitted the ukulele ringtone, followed a few seconds later by the same sound from Luce's phone.

Luce powered down her computer. "We've done what we can to redirect her career focus." She checked the messages on her iPhone.

Steve stared at Jo and Luce. "Redirect her career focus?"

Jo checked her iPhone texts before grinning at Luce and Steve. "Operation Red Aloha."

Steve stood up. "Did you tie Cinda to a raft and float her out to sea wearing a poinsettia lei?"

Jo zipped her Mac's backpack. "We would have used anthuriums so she wouldn't get lonely."

Luce shouldered her pack. "That is so rude. I wish I'd said it."

Jo grinned at Steve. "Luce and I adjusted our priorities temporarily to entice Red Nails to look for a job elsewhere. I sent her a few fake email messages from other companies and recruiters."

Steve headed through the doorway. "I'll pretend I didn't understand anything you said." Jo and Luce followed, and the three hurried down the hallway to the back stairs.

Thirty minutes later, with the engineering team assembled around the Tomb's table, Jo spoke as the list projected on the screen. "Manny insisted we add the strongest password security to GuardShark by the deadline. That's management-speak for 'do more in less time.'" She looked around the group for their reactions.

Luce leaned on the Tomb's conference table, anxiously twisting a lock of blonde hair. "He threw this in our laps with no discussion."

Vijay looked at Jo. "Can Lonnie help with this?"

"We can definitely assign Lonnie more work." She nodded and closed her Mac. "Let's dive into this in the morning. Rats, the training class is tomorrow."

Luce froze. "Shoot, guess we'll get started after class."

Jim nodded at Sherm. "We'll start looking at the old Rhombus software."

Wayne looked up from his Mac. "I just found several published algorithms and JavaScript examples for a password strength checker. Vijay, want to help me code it up?"

Vijay rolled his chair next to Wayne. "Sure thing, just IM me the links. What if we added a visual password score to give the user feedback on how secure their new password would be?"

Wayne grinned at Vijay. "I'm buying stock in you, buddy." Vijay typed and clicked, working alongside Wayne.

Sherm looked at Jo. "Can you let Lonnie know about adding tests for the new features?" Jo nodded and started typing an email to Lonnie.

Jim walked to the spot on the whiteboard where Sherm had written '101 Things To Do With A Dead CEO.' Jo asked, "Are you going to give me competition?"

Jim picked up a dry erase marker and wrote 'Roadkill' and 'Crash test dummy' under the title before waving the marker at Wayne. "I need to let off some steam before I blow. Anyone else want to brainstorm?" Wayne ambled to the board, taking the marker from Jim, and wrote 'Trash compactor test material' before turning around to the rest of the team with a big grin.

Sherm grabbed the marker from Wayne, writing 'Scarecrow' and 'Doorstop,' while Vijay grabbed another marker and wrote at a lower spot 'Cricket stumps' and 'Garden gnome.'

A cacophony of puzzlement circulated around the team. "What's a cricket stump?"

Vijay faced the team with his hands on his hips and attempted a stern expression. "Evidently no one bothered to read the Cricket For Dummies website. How will you Westerners ever learn?"

Sherm threw up his hands. "We would be more motivated if cricket were funny."

Vijay explained as he walked to his computer, "A stump is a post. Three stumps stand side-by-side supporting two bails, cross pieces, and together they form the wicket at the end of the pitch." He sat down and typed in a Google search. "I'll send you the link for the website MyCricketGame, in the spirit of broadening your humor repertoire."

Sherm shook his head. "You might be pushing your luck."

Vijay grinned. "No, if I sent you the link for the website with jokes about people who don't understand cricket, *that* would be pushing it."

Jo skimmed down the list of ideas on the whiteboard. "How close are we to 101 ideas for cartoons? I don't do sports, so I'll go with wind chimes and a mobile. Unexotic is the best I can do." Jim added Jo's ideas to the growing list.

Luce offered, "I'll raise you two unexotics. Add landfill and trail markers."

Steve walked to the board and wrote above the rest of the list, 'Decoy' and 'Lawn chess set.'

Sherm threw his marker on the tray. "The list is only for inspiration. Keep your cartoons safely tucked away until we finish GuardShark."

Jo's grin covered her whole face. "I've corrupted all the minors. I'm so proud."

17

Google Me This

LIGHTS GLOWED IN neighboring windows as Jo opened the mailbox in front of Grandma's house, grabbing envelopes and flyers. As she closed the gate behind her, she noticed a strangely shaped object had taken up residence on the wide front porch. On closer view, Jo realized it was a small vintage motor. *Grandma's saving the world again, one antiquated piece of small machinery at a time.*

Inside the house, her eyes went to the dining room, where Grandma stood before a sea of manuals, many dog-eared and falling apart. Grandma picked up a couple from the jumbled pile, read the title pages, and placed each one on a small stack.

"Hi, Grandma. That's a lot of manuals. I don't think I've ever seen this table when it wasn't covered in parts and tools. What are you up to?"

"Hi, honey. Grandpa liked to have all our manuals filed by the manufacturer, but I'm re-organizing them by the type of equipment. I have to fix Frank and Addie's VCR and Caroline's canister vacuum."

"Can I help?"

It was Grandma's turn to grin. "You know, Grandpa and I used to get a kick out of watching you stack things. You even had to organize your Legos before you would start building something."

"Born to be a geek, that's me."

Grandma picked up another manual. "One time you re-stacked every pot, pan, plate, and utensil in the kitchen, so we photographed your handiwork."

"I remember those pictures. You taped them to the refrigerator." Jo hugged Grandma, looking over her shoulder at the table. "What can I do to help you?"

Grandma pointed to the nearest pile of dog-eared manuals. "I have a stack for each type of appliance. I've got lawn mowers, VCRs, vacuum cleaners, one blender, a couple of music boxes, and one price-less manual for a player piano."

Jo held out her hands. "You hand me some manuals and I'll stack. This is like the Land of Lost Electronics. Oh, that reminds me of something Luce said."

Grandma was absorbed in her armload of manuals. "How is Luce? She is such a sweet girl."

Jo put a manual on the VCR pile. "She's great." She waved one hand over the stacks and piles on the table. "Luce said lots of old manuals have been scanned into computer files. If you ever need a repair manual, I could Google and print it out for you."

Grandma looked at Jo with a puzzled face. "What is Google?"

Jo ducked her head to hide her grin. "Google is a website where you can search for information on anything. I use it all the time."

Grandma stared at Jo. "I could find any repair manual? That's amazing. Please tell Luce thanks for me. How are you two doing with your new project?"

Jo placed a manual on the lawn mower pile. "The CEO gave us more work, so the team has to put in more overtime. We have a class tomorrow, so we have to work evenings and weekends to make up for lost time."

Grandma frowned as she handed Jo another manual. "That's ridiculous. Do you ever wonder what would happen if you and Luce told them it couldn't be done?"

Jo stared at Grandma. "You mean 'Just say no'? I have that fantasy every day."

Grandma put her hand on Jo's shoulder. "I'm sure you and Luce are doing your best. I believe in you."

Jo put her arm around Grandma's shoulder. "Thanks, that feels good to hear. Do you want me to fix dinner?"

Grandma smiled at her granddaughter. "There are fish fillets in the freezer."

Jo placed two manuals on the vacuum cleaner pile. "Fish sounds good. I can throw a salad together." She headed for the kitchen.

Grandma called after her, "Where did you learn how to make a salad?"

Jo yelled over her shoulder, "I Googled it." She was rewarded with Grandma's melodious laugh.

18

Lying 101

To: rookie-pup
From: Lord&Master

Lying is our most valuable tool. Get comfortable with it, pace yourself, try it out, enjoy it.

There are so many different kinds of lies, and there is definitely an art, possibly even a science, to knowing the best type of lie for any given situation. It's tricky, even dangerous, and there is so much to learn, so take your time.

Lies are the *lingua franca* of sharks. For us, there is no such thing as a bad lie, only lies that are more convenient, effective, or enduring. The best lies are the ones that keep on giving, feeding off their own misinformation without requiring additional effort.

I have homework for you.

1. Tell a truth as if it is a lie, and enjoy the confusion it invokes.
2. Turn a small lie into a huge lie, and notice who takes the bait.
3. Sit back and enjoy the show!

~Sent from my iPad

19

Only One Lie

Red nails. Four-inch black stilettos, a mustard-yellow mini-skirt topped with a black silk blouse that rippled with her every move. The length of bare legs commanded the stares of nearly every engineer seated in the executive conference room. She walked briskly to the lectern, where she arranged her laptop and tested her laser pointer. The silence was broken by the loud pop of Red Nails tapping one long talon against the microphone.

Jo and Luce, latecomers, watched Red Nails from the doorway before they headed to the far end of the table. They sat in wordless unison, faces barely masking disgusted resignation. Laptops open, commencing hand-to-mouth lattes, five minutes down, a lifetime before they could go back to the brain-food of technical problem-solving.

Jo stared at Red Nails, grumbling, "What is she doing here?"

Luce stared at her laptop screen, whispering, "Please God, make this go by fast, or just kill me now."

Jo took a long slow swig of her latte. "I used to like Wednesday mornings."

Cinda's long nails made an annoying click with each contact on plastic or metal. Then she spoke. "This is my first time teaching the

Quality Process course. I modified the course materials developed by Steve Scott." She beamed her win-win smile at Steve, a guru of quality processes, who sat off to the side. Several engineers shifted in their seats, stealing looks at Steve.

Jo and Luce made the mistake of looking at each other, which sent them laughing into their cups. Luce dropped her pen so she could hide her face and stop shaking while she retrieved it. They knew it wouldn't be safe to talk to each other, at least not until the break. They couldn't sit together if they were disruptive, but they needed each other to survive the farce.

Jo scooted her chair away from Luce, leaned her right elbow on the table to the left of her laptop, and used her right hand to prop her face and shield her right eye from seeing Luce, forcing her to caffeinate with her left hand in an awkward but workable stop-gap tactic. Luce mirrored the move so she couldn't see Jo. When Jo glanced around the room, she caught Steve trying to hide a smile at the not-so-subtle acting ploy of the feisty engineering duo.

Session One ticked through useless introductions and an overview of the course, with a couple of Dilberts thrown in for effect. Jo perked up at the Dilberts and kept her electronic copy of the PowerPoint on the Dilbert slide. At the first break, after barely an hour, a path was nearly ground into the carpet as the room cleared out of desperate need for bathrooms and more caffeine.

Luce looked at Jo as they lingered by the coffee pot. "Where's that kidnapping service when you need it?"

"How long does it take to chew off your own leg?" Jo asked. With the silliness gone, the boredom was a gaping void where every brain cell begged to become a veritable lemming.

Luce filled another cup. "I just wish I could go to sleep until it's over."

Jo filled her cup. "I haven't seen anyone dress like that since I became an engineer. I wonder if she ever met an actual engineer before working at McWare."

Luce grumbled, "Shit-For-Brains probably lets her think he's an engineer. She wouldn't know the difference, but then neither would he."

The trouble started after the break. It wasn't the topic, nor the lack of depth Red Nails brought to the material. It was the collective annoyance that she had never used Quality Processes. Jo winced at her chirpy, "Welcome back, now we're going to play a little game."

Groans were heard around the room. Sherm folded his arms across his lean-muscled chest, muttering, "We have real work to do. We don't have time for games."

Red Nails adopted a cupie-doll look. "I find games are a great way to relieve stress."

Sherm tried valiantly to follow her train of thought. "How can you tell when you're stressed out?"

Red Nails adjusted the projector focus. "I notice that I'm saying weird things. I guess that might not work for most of you."

The room erupted in laughter, with Jo and Luce practically spraying their respective mouthfuls of caffeine. It took a few minutes for the engineers to realize Red Nails had simply made an observation about the group of geeks, no comedy intended. Moments ticked by as several geeks tried to control their reactions to the absurdity of the situation.

Jim put down his coffee. "We're just doing sittin' around comedy, riffing off each other. It's our way of coping with all the stress of working under so much pressure."

Sherm yawned, leaning back in his chair. "Yeah, all the geeks I know do it. It's the funny stuff that just comes out when we're trying to work through all the technical problems and stay on schedule without losing our minds."

Jo nodded. "It's like improv comedy, but we're just playing off each other."

The engineers looked back at Red Nails but she had already turned her back on them. She snapped on the projector to display the next game, 'Only One Lie.' *What now?*

The slide displayed the rules that Red Nails read as she passed out blank white index cards and pens.

1. On one side, list three things about yourself
2. Make one of them a lie
3. On the opposite side, write which one is a lie

Luce quickly jotted on her card. Jo started to write something, but paused in thought as she gazed over the wasted landscape of her colleagues' hunched backs, landing on those red nails. Her face held a satisfied grin as she began writing.

When her turn came around, Jo read the list from her card:

> I'm tall.
> I'm blonde.
> I'm rich.

Puzzled stares delighted her as various engineers mumbled to no one in particular.

"I've never seen blonde on that head, does she keep it dyed?"

"She's a KSP, a Known Short Person."

"She has to reach up to swipe the badge reader, so tall is out."

"A rich person wouldn't live here day and night, killing herself for a deadline."

"We know she blew her extra cash on the Mustang's metal flake paint job."

Jo traded a wink with Luce before proceeding. "Give up?" She looked around the table in giddy anticipation and read, "The only lie here is there is only one lie here. They're all lies."

The class erupted in cheers and applause as Jo bowed. Luce gave a whoop-whoop as Steve sat grinning, shaking his head.

Red Nails stared silently, dumbfounded. "There is no reason for applause. You didn't follow the rules. Only one thing on the list can be a lie. Can't you even play the game right?"

The engineers' faces turned to disgust at Red Nails as Steve stepped in to rescue her from the silent verdict. "Jo took the game to a higher level. She played a better game."

Red Nails glared at him for a second before growling to her computer screen, "Let's take a break. Be back in fifteen minutes."

Steve grinned, giving Jo a big wink as the geeks quickly disappeared from the room. No one noticed that Red Nails stood in stone-faced silence, glaring at Jo's retreating back as she high fived Luce. When they were safely in the hall, Jo sighed, "How do you stay so calm?"

"I'm turning the idiocy into jokes. We can't play with her mind since that's clearly MIA. So every time she says something stupid, I make little notes, have some fun at her expense." Luce's even tone barely neutralized her venom.

"I like that, use her stupidity for our fun. That's like my cartoons. We could do a video of the Dumbest Best of Red Nails."

Luce shook her head. "That would max out a 600 GB iPhone."

Jo deadpanned, "Bummer." They ran down the back stairs to the bathrooms next to the Tomb but stopped when their iPhones sang out with the ukulele ringtone. Jo beamed at her phone screen and held it high as she spun in a circle. "She contacted a recruiter. Dance with me!"

Luce grinned but it morphed to a frown. "Uh, Jo, she's getting a lot of flak from that CJ person about telling Manny to pay up."

Jo scrolled through the message. "He's really giving her grief about keeping her phone on and checking in. 'Don't you dare lose focus now that the end is in sight.' What are they up to?" They re-read the messages as they slowly walked back to class.

Jo and Luce were the last engineers to return to the executive conference room, both grinning. Red Nails glared at Jo, her jaw barely moving as she handed a box filled with small folded papers to Steve. "We're going to play Quality Process Trivia Bowl. Each person will pick a question from the box."

Steve picked one of the folded papers and passed the box to Sherm. One by one the rest of the engineers followed his lead. When each of them held a lifeless folded question, Red Nails said, "So, the way this works is you will come up front one at a time and try to answer your question. If you can't answer your question, the rest of the class has a chance to answer, and the first person to answer gets a point. Let's start with Steve."

Steve read and answered his question about the definition of quality metrics, and it went downhill in usefulness from there until Vijay's question, "Name an early quality process pioneer." Mystified looks, then Red Nails prompted, "Answer?"

Silence.

Jo looked at Steve. "Henry Ford and Edward Demming." She felt a sting as Red Nails flung a blue plastic Q that bounced off her forehead. "What's going on?"

Red Nails beamed triumphantly. "You won an extra point."

Jo automatically grabbed the blue Q from the table and threw it back in Red Nails' direction. "I didn't come here to get plastic letters thrown at me, so why don't you quit wasting our time? We've actually been using quality processes for years. Your class so far is a joke." Six pairs of startled eyes fixed on the blue trajectory as it glanced off Red Nails' lectern.

Red Nails stood as stiff as her hair, staring at Jo. A few awkward seconds passed before she rallied, "I hear you saying this isn't very challenging for you. But let's finish off the questions as a little review for everyone else."

As Jo sat fuming, the rest of the engineers went through the motions in a desperate attempt to kill the rest of the morning. Luce completed her turn a split second before Jo shut down her computer, filed it in her backpack, and calmly walked out the rear door of the room. She hurried down the back stairs, through the hallway, past the Tomb, and made a bee-line for Vixen. She waited in the parking lot for Luce, the minutes ticking by as an autumn breeze whispered across her skin.

Moments later, Luce walked through McWare's back door. "You OK?"

"I just had to get out of there. Can you believe this waste of time when we have so much to get done?"

Luce looked at Jo and shrugged. "I have worse news. Red Nails announced a mandatory all-hands meeting tomorrow morning at 8:00 AM in the Boulderado meeting room. Right now, we have to meet with Manny and her in the executive conference room. Steve's already there."

Jo gazed at her friend, breaking into a smirk. "Let me guess, they're not serving us lunch."

"No chance."

"With all the fun I've had with Red Nails today, they'll probably serve me on a platter. We should have started Operation Red Aloha way earlier."

20

Lying 102

To: rookie-pup
From: Lord&Master

Be careful who you involve in your lies, and be especially careful about trusting stupid people. So far your lightweight lies have been somewhat useful, which is a good way to practice.

It is time to step up your game. Today you will learn to pull off The Big Lie.

The art of lying is about manipulation on a wide scale. This level of lying is more like a performance. Put on a show that will convince the underlings all is lost unless they follow your dictates to the letter.

Be patient. First, you need to understand what makes The Big Lie work, and where and with whom you have to be careful.

It is a good day to be a shark, so swim fast. You never know who might be gaining on you.

~Sent from my iPad

21

90% Confidence

AN HOUR LATER, Jo watched Steve close the Tomb door, feeling her head throbbing. "Did he actually use the word 'confidence'? Are we sure he didn't say SWAG or maybe LOL?"

Steve lost the battle to keep a straight face. "Yes, Manny wants a 90% Confidence Schedule this afternoon. Let's use the project plans you two put together for GuardShark to create a high-level schedule with just the target dates for completing each of the unfinished features of the product."

Jo felt the sheer futility of trying to find a new thread to hang onto. "Red Nails. I'll bet it was her idea."

Luce focused on her screen. "Using our project plan makes sense except it doesn't include the new work for fingerprint recognition and password strength checker."

Jo stared at Luce's screen. "We don't have enough engineers to finish the work on schedule unless sleep and meals have become optional."

Luce started typing. "Shit-For-Brains, Red Nails, and the Ken dolls will sleep and eat just fine."

Jo rubbed her forehead. "Okay, let's do the schedule so we can get back to real work. Here's the list of features, and I will just add password strength checker and secure password recovery to the list." The threesome spent the next half-hour fine-tuning the project schedule.

Luce triumphantly clicked to save the project plan file. "Now comes the hard part. Imagine we are Shit-For-Brains, Red Nails, and the Ken dolls. What is our reaction to this?"

Jo feigned choking. "Thanks for that image. Now I'll have to shower in battery acid to get the scum off."

Steve grinned. "There are occupational hazards in every profession. I think we need to add marketing spin."

Luce opened a PowerPoint template file. "Here we go, Scum-speak 101."

In another thirty minutes they were satisfied with the simply worded bullet points on the three-slide PowerPoint. Jo counted on her fingers. "Isn't there a rule about seven or five being the right number of key points in a presentation?"

Steve chuckled. "Given our target audience, even three might be pushing the limit of their attention span."

"Right," Luce said, "we wouldn't want to encroach on their tee-times. What could possibly be more important than that?"

Jo looked at Luce and Steve. "I'm afraid they will reject this because it's the truth. They will just dictate their own dates and fire us when we can't deliver."

Luce's face fell. "This is the best we can do working even more overtime than on the Rhombus project. The only schedule they will love is one I would have 10% confidence in."

A Cheshire cat grin spread over Jo's face. "Can you imagine what a 10% Confidence Schedule would look like? OK, I'm doing this! I'll just make a copy of the PowerPoint for the 90% schedule and do a little rocket surgery on it. Here, I'm sharing my desktop."

Luce shook her head at her best friend but the grin was contagious. "You are beyond crazy. Are we calling it the 10% Confidence Schedule or The Miracle Pixie Dust and Snake Oil Schedule?"

Jo was typing fast. "I'm going with 10% in the title, but the miracle thing gives me an idea for the fingerprint recognition and password strength features."

Steve grinned. "I'm sure bribery and lying could work but we have a little too much class to go that low."

Luce shook her finger at him. "We have a *lot* more class than they do, plus we have actual brains. What if we translated each work week into a work day?"

Jo clicked and typed. "Done. Each miracle milestone gets zero time since delusion occurs instantaneously. There, now we have a delivery date for the whole software product one week from Friday."

Steve shook his head. "Only an idiot would believe that's possible."

Luce clicked. "The 90% schedule is on its way." She frowned when Jo suddenly walked to the whiteboard. "What's the matter, Jo?"

Jo stared at the long list of 101 cartoon ideas that covered a section of the whiteboard. "Look at all these new ones. I love working with weirdos." Luce and Steve joined her at the board to read through the new entries.

Shrunken CEO earrings
Shrunken CEO matching pendant
HOV lane seat filler
Parking place holder
Slasher film extra
Mattress tester
Coffin tester
Elevator door safety sensor tester
Research on heartless organisms
Wall insulation
Quilt batting
Doormats
Decoy for mob hits
Bonsai for Christmas tree ornament

Christo could use a million to cover a defunct tech-park
Test material for trebuchets and flingers
Mannequins for Men's Warehouse

Jo walked back to the table as Luce and Steve gathered their things. "Dead or alive, Shit-For-Brains is one CEO who will always be useless." Dueling ukulele ringtones sang out from Jo and Luce's phones. Jo quickly stuffed her computer into her backpack before the three exited through the door, grinning at each other. Hurrying to their cars, they raced each other out of the parking lot, horns honking.

Jo drove on autopilot through the familiar streets of Boulder, wishing she could outrun her worst fears. The breathtaking colors of early fall that dotted the trees along Pine Street, 19th, and Bluff bathed her senses in the solace of effortless beauty.

By the time Jo climbed the stairs to the porch, the sky was awash in the fiery orange hues of a September sunset, but fatigue made weights of her Nikes. *I can't believe we have to live through another all-hands meeting with Shit-For-Brains tomorrow.*

Opening the front door, she heard voices from inside and perked up with curiosity. Grandma stood in the doorway of her workroom, delivering a series of instructions to three of her senior friends from the neighborhood.

Mike's tall lean frame wore a shirt with the faded logo of the San Diego Fire Department from his pre-retirement days. "Jo, we can use your advice." He leaned down to hand a box with a variety of batteries to Addie, a small older Portuguese lady with a rounded torso and thin arms and legs that reminded Jo of a little bird.

"Hey, Jo. Noah and I were just wondering about you the other night." She handed the box to her husband, a balding gentleman whose white beard and rotund shape made Jo imagine him as the perfect Santa Claus.

Jo set down her backpack and walked to the group. "Hi, Mike. Hi, Addie, Noah. It's good to see you. Are you helping Grandma rearrange her workroom?"

Grandma turned around, her face lit with a delightedly animated grin. "Oh, honey, I'm glad you're home. You can help us make sure we get this right. We're moving my computer in here, and we need to make sure everything is connected properly."

Jo stared at Grandma, struggling to comprehend the planetary shift in Grandma's sudden embrace of high-tech. "You want your computer in your workroom instead of the bedroom? That's new."

Grandma was giddy with excitement. "I was wasting time going back and forth between here and my bedroom, losing my train of thought and getting tired. That Google you showed me is a miracle. I found so many repair manuals, and all kinds of places to get parts for old machines, some of the places are even close by. I can get what I need when I need it instead of having to keep old parts on hand."

Jo grinned at Grandma's discovery as she focused on the contents of the room. "You've actually got the important things figured out. But it's pretty crowded in here."

Grandma grinned. "I got ahead of myself. I wanted everything I use in my workroom, but I needed help."

Addie's smile beamed. "She called us. Now we can finally do something to help her after all the things she's fixed for us. But we don't really know what we're doing."

Mike looked up. "I think Jo might be right, Illyena. I didn't measure yet but I don't think you will be able to walk around."

Jo did a mental survey of the room's dimension. "I think Mike is right about measuring. Let's keep the things you need and move the rest out. I'll bet we can free up enough space in here to make room for your computer and printer and still be able to maneuver."

"Oh, that's sounds good, honey. My measuring tapes are all on the second shelf in that corner bookcase." Grandma was practically dancing with excitement.

Grandma, the Google Goddess, who knew?

22

Power Structure 101

To: rookie-pup
From: Lord&Master

Being a shark requires a singleness of purpose, a laser focus on finding the contacts that are sources of vital business information. Act as if you belong to that herd while secretly using them. Never betray *your* ideas and methods for business success. Parse every situation to pinpoint those we can use to our advantage vs. the debris to dispose of.

I must warn you of something that could cause miscalculation, even downfall. Normally underlings pose no threat since they have no leverage. On the rare occasion, an underling will arise as a worthy opponent who might jeopardize our strategy.

The best antidote for a bad surprise is to lead the victim into a trap with no way of knowing when, how, or by whom it was designed and set in motion. It is a true coup, one to be savored.

Your evolution as a shark to the higher echelon of ruthless strate-gist must always be motivated by the reality of the rapid demise of all species that fail to adapt to the challenge of change. That is the essence of the power structure.

Some people believe power isn't everything, but for us, it will just have to do.

~Sent from my iPad

From the
Desk
Of The
CEO

To Do Today

- Justify delay to the Board
- Pursue mergers in Aspen
- Enforce unpaid overtime
- Exercise stock options
- Rest on laurels

23

10% Confidence

Jo maneuvered her to-go cup and her computer as she and Luce took seats in the back of the meeting room in the Boulderado Hotel. "Nothing good ever happens on Thursday mornings, especially not at 8:00 AM. Why would he have the meeting today instead of Friday?"

Luce positioned her latte and computer. "Thursday might be better for his golf priorities. I guess that's redundant." Luce waved to Liz as she hurried toward the podium uncoiling a black cord. "Looks like Manny forgot his power supply again." Liz finished setting up the computer, testing it with the projector before making her way quickly to a chair just in front of Jo and Luce.

Liz winked at Jo as she sat. "You cartooned me. I love it! Can I put that on my resume?" Red Nails led Manny and a tall reed-thin gentleman in a pinstripe suit to the stage, and stood in front of the microphone, surveying the audience with a cold eye.

Jo whispered to Liz, "If they don't get the joke, you might not want to work for them." Liz grinned and turned around. Jo set her latte on the carpet and popped her Mac open. "What brand of fun could Shit-For-Brains Manny have for us now?"

Jo noticed Red Nails' icy glare fixed on Luce and her in the back of the room. She nudged Luce. "Careful, the Ice Queen is sending an evil cold front our way."

Red Nails switched on the microphone. "We're going to dispense with announcements today to give Manny the full hour." She clapped as she backed away from the podium and sat down in a chair on the dais as Manny strode to the podium. He was followed by the Chief Financial Officer, Mackintosh Rielle. 'Mackerel' to the engineers, his suit was impeccably tailored for his trim physique, and with his salt-and-pepper hair, he epitomized Wall Street.

Jo searched her friend's face for solidarity against Red Nails but realized Luce's face had turned to stone, staring at the wall-sized screen. Jo's gaze followed Luce's, reading the words displayed as the room began to spin: '10% Confidence Schedule.'

The words blazed like neon tentacles reaching for Jo and Luce. Shock stopped Jo's breathing as her heart beat with resounding thuds. It felt like she was looking through a thick shield of glass, not hearing anything or anyone, unable to comprehend the abject violation of her and Luce's company computers.

Luce choked out her words, as quiet as a death rattle. "How could this have happened? I copied you two on the email to senior management, and it only had the 90% schedule attached."

Jo hissed back, "We can't talk here. IM."

[Jo: We've been hacked]

[Luce: How? Who? Need Steve and Wayne's help.]

The two friends settled in for the rest of the horror show.

Manny described the 10% Confidence Schedule as "the top 10% of everyone's confidence." The engineers shook their heads in disbelief. When Manny thanked Jo and Luce for their stellar work in finalizing the 10% Confidence Schedule, Jo couldn't look at the team members, fearing their disbelieving stares of betrayal.

[Luce: Red Nails? Lonnie?]

[Jo: Red Nails stupid Lonnie stupid, Mystery Geek? CJ?]

[Luce: gotta find out NOW!]

Jo gave a tiny nod but her face had the intensity of the Furies. Jo stared at the idiot at the podium, praying the meeting would end soon.

Manny went through three slides that looked a lot like the 10% joke schedule Jo, Luce, and Steve had thrown together as therapy, but key sections of the content had changed. The only thing unchanged was the shrunken schedule.

Manny displayed a second PowerPoint entitled 'McWare Business Forecast—Confidential,' and introduced the CFO. Mackerel reported in his steel wire voice, "McWare has reached a critical point. We will miss our revenue targets unless GuardShark is delivered in one week. McWare's investors would have the right to declare bankruptcy and sell McWare to make back their investment." He nodded at Manny and sat down beside Red Nails on the dais.

[Jo: 1 week? Mackerel lost his mind?]

[Luce: Manny is lying]

The room held a collective breath as the employees absorbed the sobering news. Manny stepped to the podium. "In light of the seriousness of our situation, I will end the meeting now so we can all get back to work. I'm sure many of you have questions, but the answer to all of them is to deliver GuardShark on schedule. Otherwise, our next all-hands meeting will be handing out boxes to pack up your offices."

Manny switched off the microphone, turned as Mackerel and Red Nails stood, and the three strode off the little stage and out the door of the meeting room in lock step. Stunned silence fixed the employees to their seats. Slowly people began rising, a few talked in worried words to nearby colleagues, but the sense of shock held court. The engineers were uncharacteristically silent, stealing looks at Jo and Luce that spoke volumes.

Jo looked around the room. She found Steve, the third musketeer, seated on the outside aisle a couple of rows away, caught his eye and pointed to the door. The Boulderado Hotel's conference center offered numerous exit routes, and they made their way to the double doors that opened onto Broadway. Jo leaned against the historic brick façade. "Fuck. Someone hacked into the computer files. We need to find out who did this and how they did it, pronto."

Steve held up his iPhone. "I sent Wayne a text message to meet me back at the office. He's the most knowledgeable about system access."

Luce adjusted her backpack. "We've got another problem. Our team thinks we came up with that schedule for Manny. We've got to talk to them right away."

Steve pocketed his iPhone. "You're right, you need to set things straight and make a plan to deal with this ridiculous delivery schedule. I'm going to meet with Wayne. Call a meeting this afternoon so we can talk to the team. Something really bad is going on."

Jo clenched her fists. "Red Nails really hates me. Manny has to be using her to screw us."

Luce wrung her hands. "My money is on Seth the Mystery Geek or CJ. What if they're the same person? We've got to find them, or him. I don't know who to mistrust anymore, let alone who to trust. Besides us, I mean."

Steve headed toward his car. "Let me work with Wayne on finding Mystery Geek. The best thing you can do is work with the team to figure out exactly what's left to finish on GuardShark."

Jo started walking toward her car. "Do either of you buy this thing about McWare going out of business if GuardShark isn't done in a week?"

Luce slowed her pace to match Jo's. "I think Manny has something else up his very expensive sleeve. He's certainly not hurting for money and neither are Mackerel or the Ken dolls."

Steve turned to Jo and Luce. "Manny would sell us out if he found a way to cash in."

Jo's silent fuming suddenly combusted. "I wish we could find a way to show the Board of Directors how bad he is for business." She got into the Mustang and rolled down the window.

Steve turned around. "Meet at 10:30 AM in the Tomb? I'll let you know what Wayne finds out."

Luce angrily clicked open the Prius. "How much do you want to kill him right now?"

Jo started the engines and said over Vixen's hum, "This is going to drive me crazy until we figure it out. Something rotten is going on." Her iPhone sang another ukulele ringtone as Luce got into her Prius and drove away, Steve's car right behind.

Jo stared at the phone, turned off the engine and scrolled through the messages Red Nails had received and sent in the past hour. She stared at the subject line of the most recent one and slowly read the entire message. *I have to talk to Luce and Steve.* She laid the phone on the passenger's seat and restarted the engine.

24

Lying 103

To: rookie-pup
From: Lord&Master

Congratulations, you orchestrated your first Big Lie.

But it is not enough to do something successfully. You must understand what worked and why, and most importantly, what you can do better next time. Trust no one else with our plans or with any details after our big win. You never know who might be an adversary or a competitor.

Conning the engineers to believe they could easily lose their precious jobs is classic manipulation. Once engineers are committed to a burn-out level of stress, they will kill themselves completing the project with brilliance and teamwork. It is a goldmine for our purposes.

You have many Big Lies in your future. It will be one of the best days you'll ever have as a shark when you walk away with a big pile of money at their expense. I'm going to be so proud of you.

~Sent from my iPad

25

Shoveling Sand Against the Tide

Jo opened the Tomb door in answer to the quick knock, letting Steve in. "Jim's rounding up the team for a noon meeting so we can set things straight." She sat down next to Luce.

Luce looked up from typing. "That gives us an hour and change to pull together the information we have and make a plan for where we go from here. Can you order pizza?"

Steve tapped on his iPhone. "I've got Proto's on speed dial." He rang Boulder's thin-crust haven. "Take out order for Steve Scott for 11:45 AM, one large Atomica and one large Traffic Jam. OK, thanks." He clicked off the call. "I'll make the pizza run while you two start the meeting."

Jo focused on her screen. "I have something to tell you both, but first, what did you find out from Wayne, Steve?"

Steve set up his Mac next to Luce. "That's one perceptive guy. He smelled a rat when Manny announced the 10% schedule and saw your faces. He was already investigating when I went to his cube. He'll let us know as soon as he's found something."

Jo looked up. "I found something in Red Nails' email. She got a message around 4:30 PM yesterday from someone named CJ with our

10% schedule attached, and forwarded that to Manny around 5:30 PM with her changes for the version he presented in the meeting."

Luce sat back in her chair, crossing her arms. "Wait a sec. Remember that weird email where CJ told Red Nails to get Manny to wire money to an offshore bank account? She must be the go-between."

Jo started clicking on her Mac. "Sounds like she's willing to do whatever it takes to stay on Manny's team."

Steve looked at Jo. "We should have Wayne monitor Manny's emails." Steve's iPhone signaled a new text message. "We might have been wrong about Mystery Geek. Wayne found out the IP address that Lonnie and Seth used wasn't the one that gained access to our files. How can we be sure that Mystery Geek Seth isn't CJ? Hackers can use different IP addresses."

Luce frowned. "What did Wayne find out about how our computers were hacked?"

Steve typed and clicked on his laptop. "Our computers weren't hacked. Wayne showed me the warnings from GuardShark that the backup of our files from yesterday evening were accessed by someone from an IP address that wasn't on the list of approved IP addresses from employees' home ports."

Jo's hand smacked the table. "We've been testing that feature of GuardShark by activating the hourly automated backup of everyone's work systems."

Steve put down the iPhone. "Exactly. He retrieved the 10% schedule and emailed it to Cinda."

Luce looked at Jo and Steve. "How long have the backups been hacked?"

Steve shook his head. "Wayne couldn't find any other suspicious IP addresses that have accessed our systems, so he believes this is the first time. No one knows that we know, so we can use that to our advantage."

Jo massaged her throbbing head. "OK, so are we ready to hunt down Mystery Geek to talk with him? If Wayne found the IP address for Lonnie's communications with Seth, please tell us he found an email address for the brilliant one."

Steve turned his Mac screen toward Jo and Luce. "Wayne used his magic to find Seth's email address by searching every unique email Lonnie has received for the past year. I'm sending it to you."

Jo read the display. "I wonder if Mystery Geek is the same guy who likes to put captions on my cartoons late at night. We could trap him and confront him to see if he's bad news, or turns out to be someone we want on our side."

Steve turned his laptop back around. "We have to be careful about contacting Seth. If anything got back to Lonnie, he would burn us with Manny in a second."

Jo rubbed her temples, closing her eyes against the throbbing. "Seth is working for scum, but he's the only one with brains."

Luce stretched her neck, breathing deeply. "Maybe he's doing it for the money."

Jo propped her chin on her hands. "We have to find out if Seth is CJ the hacker and was smart enough to use a different IP address. So we're agreed we have to track down Seth, talk with him, and figure out if he's the bad guy or someone who can help us fight the bad guy. How do we know who to trust?"

They debated options and re-read the latest information until Steve's iPhone buzzed an incoming text message. "We'll think better with pizza," he said.

Luce yawned. "And pizza will give us the energy to work forty hours a day on GuardShark to finish it in a week."

Jo massaged her forehead. "I hope the team still trusts us."

As Steve headed into the hall, he left the door open for the approaching team. The rustling hustle of footsteps nearing the Tomb was not accompanied by the usual mile-a-minute chatter. Worried and curious about the team's mood, Jo welcomed them with eye contact as they entered the room and sat down at the table.

After everyone settled, Jo looked around the table at each engineer. "Luce and I would like to apologize in advance for that false schedule and the way Manny blindsided you."

Wayne smiled at Jo. "Maybe you should wait until *he* apologizes to you two. I brought everyone up-to-date on the hacker ripping off your files from the backups."

Jo grimaced. "We were so stressed out after we sent off the 90% schedule. Just for fun, we put together the 10% Confidence Schedule." Jo glanced around the table. Four horrified faces looked back. "As a *joke*!"

Luce turned on the projector. "Manny is convinced this is reasonable. We need to go through the whole list of tasks so we know what's left to finish, and have a minute to lick our wounds before we get back to work."

Jo clicked open an electronic file to display it on the screen. "This is the schedule we created using the estimates you gave us, with extra time as a buffer in case of problems or if Manny added another last-minute feature."

Sherm stared at the projector screen. "I finished the tests for suspicious email and attachments, so I can work on fingerprint recognition."

Jim looked at Jo. "I finished testing the social media sites from my personal computer and iPhone, so I can team up with Sherm on fingerprint recognition."

Vijay looked at Wayne. "Want to team up on the password strength feature?" He turned to Jo. "I finished the tests for the firewall and password hacking."

Wayne nodded. "That would be great, I can finish testing parental controls at night. Jim and Sherm, can you point us to the work you did for password strength that didn't make it into the Rhombus product?"

Sherm nodded as he clicked and typed on his Mac. "I'm way ahead of you. I just zipped up all the software files and the tests we wrote for it. OK, the zip file is on its way to you and Vijay." Wayne pantomimed a high five to Sherm.

Jo finished capturing everyone's updates and turned to Jim. "Anything left to do on backups?"

Jim shook his head. "No, they are working great. I can get a copy of the certification tests and start automating them in our nightly testing, but I could use some help."

Steve came through the door with two large Proto's pizza boxes to the rousing cheers of the engineers. Jo looked at him with a grin. "What if we help Steve with all that pizza, and he helps Jim with the new testing?"

Steve set the boxes in the middle of the table, grabbing a large slice of the Atomica. "I'm happy to do anything for pizza." The team quickly made a dent in Proto's thin-crust slices.

Luce picked Italian sausage off her Atomica slice. "Six hands are better than two. That's it, that's everything we have to finish, in a week."

Sherm was halfway through his first Traffic Jam slice. "Wayne, how did you track down the hacking of our backup files?"

Wayne threw a pizza bone into the trash. "On a hunch I checked the log entries for all accesses to the backup files. It looks like someone from an unrecognized IP address copied them using the administrative password. I found just the one break-in, time-stamped for 3:42 PM yesterday."

Jo nodded at Wayne. "At first we suspected some sort of industry spy, but it's worse."

Sherm frowned. "What's worse than an industry spy?"

Luce looked around the table. "Our computer files were hacked by someone named CJ, who was hired by Manny and Cinda. She knew the 10% Confidence Schedule was a joke, but she convinced Manny it was reasonable. She had to know that by encouraging him to announce it at the company meeting, he would be forcing us to finish GuardShark in a week."

Sherm shook his head. "That doesn't make any sense. McWare can't sell a security product until all the features are complete and it has passed all the testing required for certification."

Jo clicked open another electronic file. "We haven't figured out what Manny is up to, but if we get GuardShark out to the market as a rock-solid computer security product, we can use it as a terrific reference for getting new jobs even if McWare tanks. Good products build careers for engineers."

Luce looked around the table at each engineer. "If Manny is up to no good, we'll all be better off working somewhere else, hopefully together."

Steve grabbed a slice of Traffic Jam and looked around the table. "We think it's safer to keep in touch via our personal email and cell phones to avoid getting our team communications hacked by whoever is up to no good. Everyone OK with that?"

Nods rippled around the table in a happy geek wave. Luce collected each team member's personal contact information and emailed the list to their personal accounts.

Jim typed as he asked, "Is anyone else coming in this weekend? Unless my wife goes into labor, I'm going to get the Twitter privacy bug fixed and the certification tests in shape on Saturday instead of sitting at home worrying."

Sherm looked up from his computer. "I'll be here early morning, but I'm going climbing in Eldorado Canyon at noon."

Wayne nodded. "Yeah, I'm coming in tomorrow."

Steve tossed his pizza crust into the waste basket. "Two points. I'm in."

Jo deadpanned, "I'll be in as soon as I've been to Ozo's. You know what happens if I don't have my caffeine."

Luce matched Jo's look of horror. "Don't even think about showing up without an empty latte cup."

Jo nodded, wiping her mouth with a napkin. "Deal."

26

No Place Like Home

Jo realized she had been standing on the front porch for several minutes. She felt suspended in time, space, completely lost in the early evening's darkness. Too many unanswered questions swirled around her, giving rise to so many more.

How long have I been standing here? What was I thinking about? I don't remember a thing. How often do I do this? Am I crazy?

Her keys were still in the front door lock. It required a momentous effort to move her right hand to grasp them and remove them from the knob. She took a deep breath and slowly walked toward the only safety she knew.

Closing the front door, she heard Grandma in the kitchen. She dropped her backpack and went gratefully toward the pungent smell of Grandma's beef stew. Watching her tend to the pot on the stove in a plaid flannel shirt, Jo was relieved beyond words to be standing in that place, in that moment. Jo stood next to Grandma, nuzzling her head on the soft shoulder. "How are your computer and printer doing in the workroom?"

Grandma hugged Jo. "Great! I looked up the manuals for Addie's VCR and figured out that I don't even need a new part for it. I can just clean and adjust the take-up wheel."

Jo grinned despite her fatigue. "That's great. Can I help you with anything?"

Grandma looked at Jo. "Honey, you look awfully tired. Did you have a rough day?"

Jo crumpled into the nearest kitchen chair. "You wouldn't believe what happened."

Grandma leaned over the table, patting Jo's hand. "You left early for your meeting. How was it?"

Jo squeezed Grandma's soft, strong hand. "Manny announced that our team has to deliver the whole project at the end of next week instead of a month from now."

Grandma frowned as she returned to stirring the stew. "That doesn't make any sense. How can he expect your team to finish everything if you don't have enough time?"

"He said the competition will beat us in getting their product out first and will ruin McWare's chance to make enough money to stay in business. The Board would have to declare bankruptcy and sell off the company to repay the investors."

Grandma's frown deepened. "It doesn't make sense that a few weeks would make such a difference."

Jo rubbed her forehead. "Things don't add up. Anyway, I'm exhausted, and I don't seem to have any brains left."

Grandma set a bowl of fragrant stew in front of Jo. "We've both had a big day. I just wish yours could have been as fun as mine was."

Jo inhaled the mélange of herbs carried on the curls of steam rising from the ceramic bowl. "It's great to see you having such a good time with your Google miracle. Your stew is the high point of *my* day."

* * *

12:33 AM screamed in scarlet from the digital clock face. Jo felt the clock taunting her hope for peaceful sleep. Black fears gathered from the fringes of darkness like hungry wolves with menacing red eyes, and her heart fought them with its fran-tick fran-tick panicked beat.

Breathe, slow. Itching, scratch my leg, stop itching! Stop, breathe, slow. God, I hate this, hate being so afraid. Even the rain isn't helping me tonight. Neck itches, back itches. 12:47 AM. There's still six hours before I have to get up to go for a run. That would still be enough sleep. God help me, I can't stop this, I'm so scared.

Jo went to the bathroom again, every nerve jangling an evil dance. Bed was no longer comforting. Bed was home to the enemy of terrorizing thoughts. Jo went to the closet, pulled down her father's large flannel shirt and put it on, swimming in the sea of its soft warmth. Tonight, in the dead time of the world, when no one would ever know what she had to do to fall asleep, she removed her mother's cream-colored shawl from her closet shelf and carefully draped it around her shoulders, the double layers of warmth melting her anxieties.

Jo stepped into the dark hallway and made her way carefully downstairs to the kitchen. Night whispered its soft hush across her skin as her hands brailled the room's topography, half-closed eyes conjuring sense memory of her home's inner face. She trusted the conversation between her hands and the walls, doors, railings, and stairs, translating the feedback to careful directions for the next step and the one to follow. Savoring the slow passage through night's delicious tunnel, she breathed in the freedom of solitude in the secret cloak of darkness, her journey unobserved.

The living room couch was a mecca for sleep. Jo unfolded the hand-knit throw. Quietly, so no steps or sounds awoke Grandma, she lay down on the couch on her side, her back to its back, letting the couch spoon her. The blanket enveloped her like a soft warm cloud. She burrowed the side of her face into the old embroidered pillow, and sighed as the moon came out from behind the clouds to bathe the porch in silver outside the living room window.

Then the best magic of all happened. She heard the bounce of the rocking chair, followed by Gizmo's low slow purr coming closer on soft paws crossing the carpet. The furry face gazed at Jo for one aloof moment before leaping, landing expertly on the ledge of the couch just in front of Jo's stomach. The kitty nosed Jo's hand until she opened the blanket for Giz to crawl underneath, nuzzling close to Jo's warm body.

Jo waited, hoping, and in a few minutes Jig jumped up on the arm of the couch by Jo's feet, then walked daintily up over Jo's legs and hip with a delicious acupressure sensation. The graceful feline nestled into the crevasse between the blanket and the couch along Jo's back.

Enveloped in layers of warmth from Dad, from Mom, sandwiched between kitties, held in the safety of Grandma's couch, Jo sighed. Peace, at last, and sleep, in the safest place on Earth.

* * *

The next morning, Jo sat at the kitchen table staring into a half-eaten bowl of Shredded Wheat. She jerked back to reality when Gizmo suddenly attacked the laces of her Nikes, and reached down to bat the kitty's paws.

Grandma's soft hand patted Jo's knee. "Honey, are you still worried? Did you sleep OK?"

Jo sighed as the kitty swatted her outstretched finger. "I had a nightmare that everything in the new software product stopped working. I'm worried our CEO is lying about a lot of things."

Grandma sipped her tea. "What do you know about your CEO? Do you know where he worked before your company?"

Jo crunched another spoonful of cereal. "No, but if one of our engineers did their job as bad as he does, we would drop him like a bad habit."

Grandma grinned as she stood up and walked quickly to her workroom. "Let me show you what I learned how to do." Jo followed Grandma to the computer, where a Chrome browser displayed Google. Grandma sat and poised her hands over the keyboard. "What is his full name?"

Jo tickled Grandma's shoulder. "Google, that's a great idea. Manny Wimple, no, Manfred Wimple. Put Colorado in front of his name."

Grandma typed and clicked, displaying a list on the screen. "That's a lot of golf tournaments."

"That's him all right, Mr. Golf. Replace Colorado with CU Boulder." Grandma typed and clicked.

Jo's hand moved the mouse a bit as Grandma read from the screen. "Tennis champion. What is an interdisciplinary major in Organizational Communications?"

"It means he wrote his own major so he could graduate by doing as little as possible. He graduated five years ago, so he's around twenty-eight. Replace CU Boulder with LinkedIn."

Grandma typed and clicked. "No matches."

Jo pulled a chair up close to Grandma. "That means Manny probably had no work experience before becoming CEO of McWare. That is known as a meteoric rise."

Grandma gazed at the screen. "What does McWare's website say about him?"

Jo shook her head. "It won't say anything. McWare is privately funded by a group of investors, so they don't have to publicize their corporate officers or anything else. Click on the link for McWare's website and see if you can find any useful information."

In a few keystrokes, Grandma was busy clicking through the handful of tabs and hyperlinks on McWare's website. "Manny put his picture on the home page, but there are no details about the company. It might as well be wallpaper."

Jo hugged Grandma. "That's a good one, wallpaper."

Grandma crossed her arms and frowned. "McWare must be making money or the investors would be upset with him, right?"

Jo stared at the vapid photo of Manny. "I can't imagine the investors are OK with McWare stumbling along, releasing one new software product each year that brings in just enough money to cover our expenses. This doesn't add up, unless the investors are using McWare as a financial loss to lower their taxes."

Grandma shook her finger at the photo. "How would they get away with it? That burns me. Grandpa and I had to account for everything in our business and pay taxes every year. Are you saying McWare is allowed to lose money so rich people can cheat on their taxes? That's not right."

Jo shrugged her shoulders. "There are all kinds of ways wealthy people keep from paying their fair share, Grandma. What I really hate is that all the great work our team does could go down the drain just to line the pockets of people who don't need to worry about having a job."

Grandma reached for Jo's hand. "I don't want to see you and Luce and your friends get hurt after all your hard work."

Jo squeezed Grandma's hand. "We'll figure out what's going on, and try to get as much done as possible by the new deadline."

Grandma stood up and hugged Jo. "You and Luce are smart enough to figure it out. And you are good people, never forget how important that is, honey."

Jo hugged Grandma close. "Thank you, thank you so much for helping me."

Grandma held Jo's shoulders and looked into her granddaughter's face. "I love you, honey. You go get 'em."

Jo gave Grandma a little wave as she headed toward the front door.

27

Career Path 101

To: rookie-pup
From: Lord&Master

Being a shark is a career choice. You might have heard the expression, "Your career chooses you." Forget that. While you are in training, your every move will be carefully orchestrated. You must marry yourself completely to your singular goal, and do whatever it takes to win. When you play with acid, the acid doesn't change; the acid changes you.

Create your own career, one conquest at a time. Dedicate yourself completely to doing whatever is necessary to prevail, no matter the cost. Find the most vulnerable business environment for reaping financial gain. Learn to zero in on those who have power, discerning how best to manipulate and divert that power to your advantage. Do your homework and patiently perfect your strategy.

Beware the giddiness of that first big score. The beauty of experience lies in the ability to learn and adapt far more quickly than those who dwell in the pitifully self-centered gratification of the neophyte.

Do not let a problem or even a failure throw you off your game. Remember, there are no mistakes, only opportunities to improve.

Learn from the best, but keep the best for yourself. You don't win by being a fool.

~Sent from my iPad

CEO Ten Commandments

I. The Board thy God is one Board;
Thou shalt have no other Boards before them.

II. Thou shalt not commission a statue of thyself for the Corporate Headquarters;
A full-size portrait is always appropriate.

III. Thou shalt not take the company name in vain, nor that of its founder;
Any other company is fair game.

IV. Remember to show up for dinner on the Sabbath to keep your wife from walking out.

V. Honor thy Father and thy Mother, or whoever bankrolled your rise up the Corporate ladder, that thy days may be long at the helm.

VI. Thou shalt not kill anyone who helped you get to the top or helped you stay there;
The Quality Process auditors are fair game.

VII. Thou shalt not commit adultery with a Board member's wife or girlfriend;
Their sisters, mothers, and cousins are fair game.

VIII. Thou shalt not steal from an account twice;
Never hold more than $2 million in laundered money.

IX. Thou shalt not give false testimony about anyone who helped you get to the top or helped you stay there;
Faking the Quality Process is fair game.

X. Thou shalt not envy thy neighbor's house, or his wife, staff, cars, dogs, riding lawnmower, wine cellar, full gym, or Italian shoes;
Make him envy yours.

Engineer Ten Commandments

I. The CEO thy BOSS is one CEO;
Thou shalt have no other CEOs before Him.

II. Thou shalt not follow the CEO's every order;
You know how to interpret what he really means.

III. Thou shalt not take the name of the CEO in vain in the presence of management.

IV. Remember the Sabbath day, since you will be working on it.

V. Honor thy Father and thy Mother;
No one else will talk to you after those 80-hour weeks.

VI. Thou shalt not kill;
But you can always start a rumor or hack the email of someone who desperately needs a wake-up call.

VII. Thou shalt not commit adultery with anyone in Sales and Marketing; Real Engineers just don't do that.

VIII. Thou shalt not steal;
Why would you want anything to remind you of the office?

IX. Thou shalt not give false testimony;
But the false rumor thing is fair game.

X. Thou shalt not envy thy boss' house, his wife's wardrobe, his cars, bank accounts, wine cellar, stock options, servants, dogs, riding lawnmower, full gym, or leisure time;
It just leads to suicidal thoughts.

28

Good Teams Are Like Complementary Protein

"**I** HATE IT WHEN Happy Friday has a week's work to finish." Jo opened the Tomb door, flipped on the light switch and pulled her Mac out of her backpack. "Why does it feel like we're doing full-time guerilla warfare and working on GuardShark in our spare time?"

Luce set up her Mac at one end of the table and sat down. "Because it's not just a job anymore. It's survival."

Jo angrily typed and clicked. "Between working a killer schedule and protecting our work from getting hacked, we're in a warzone. When do we get to focus on our jobs for an entire day?"

Luce fumed at her keyboard. "We're burning energy we should be devoting to finishing GuardShark. And I can't even remember the last time one of us had time to date, let alone meet a guy. God, people, do the math!"

Jo smacked her forehead. "*That's* our problem. *We* can do math. By the way, Grandma helped me find something interesting about Shit-For-Brains."

Luce stared at Jo. "Grandma?"

Jo grabbed her latte. "I'll explain later. I hear the patter of engineers' sneakered little feet."

Jim walked into the Tomb, followed in silence by the rest of the team, everyone taking chairs as Steve closed the door and said, "Thanks for working late last night. The test results for GuardShark look good. We wanted to share a few things we discovered."

Jo pushed her Mac to the side as she looked around the table at each engineer. "We suspected Manny was up to something, so we used GuardShark to snoop his email. He's hot to sell McWare."

Luce thoughtfully ran a finger around the rim of her coffee cup. "I have a sick feeling that Manny and his creative accountant are trying to make McWare look attractive to a potential buyer by releasing GuardShark in a week with numbers for its projected revenue. The market is clamoring for software security, and GuardShark has all the features the customers want."

Sherm gestured with his coffee mug. "Manny is such a lame CEO, so the new owners could be a lot better for us. But why would he hire a hacker to undermine our work? Oh, crap."

Vijay handed him a water bottle to douse the coffee spot on his precious 2010 Bolder Boulder tee-shirt, smirking, "Cricket shirts don't stain easily."

Sherm feigned horror. "Hey, man, it's a classic."

Jo drained the last of her latte. "Aren't they all?"

Sherm dabbed the stain with a wet corner of his tee-shirt. "Hey, it's a limited edition, only 100,000." He turned to Steve. "What do you think Manny's up to?"

Steve pulled a chair out and sat next to Luce. "In buyouts of small high-tech companies, the buyer often lays off most of the engineers, keeping a small number for a few months with incentive money to train the new owner's teams to take over the products."

Jo's eyes locked on Steve as she set her cup back on the table. "So if Manny's planning a fire sale, that would be his excuse to fire most of the engineering team to lower McWare's monthly expenses." She closed her eyes, propping her forehead in her hands as she muttered,

"What a nightmare." She shook it off and looked at each engineer around the table.

Jim sat back, crossing his thickly muscled arms. "We'd lose everything we've worked so hard to finish."

Wayne sighed. "If we don't finish it, we won't have a great software security product to put on our resumes for the job hunt we'll be starting in a couple of weeks. That's what I call bein' stuck between a rock and a hard place."

Luce's tone reflected the grim line of her mouth as she said, "Finishing GuardShark will be a ton of work, but that's not all. We expect the hacker to continue attacking."

Jo grinned at Wayne and Jim. "That's why your friendly team leads did some brainstorming last night."

Vijay looked at Jo. "What's our move?"

Jo took a breath before carefully phrasing her reply. "We believe our best bet is to tell the truth to the Board of Directors since they have to approve McWare's sale or future funding. I've never been much for confronting honchos, but this time it feels like all or nothing. We have to get their full attention for a demo."

Steve walked to the whiteboard. "We need to show them how well GuardShark is working and give them a clear plan for us to complete all the features." He wrote the date and each date after that in a line across the whiteboard, ending with Thursday 9/26, leaving room to list tasks to be completed.

Luce smirked. "The poor geek's project scheduler."

"We're a DIY crew," Jo quipped as she joined Steve at the whiteboard, uncapping a marker. "McWare's Board is responsible for ensuring the company's financial dealings are legal. They can't risk being investigated, or having their own finances scrutinized by the IRS and SEC."

Vijay set down his mug of tea. "How can we get the Board to listen to us without Manny finding out what we're up to?"

Jo looked around at each team member. "We're going to have to crash the Board meeting and convince them to watch us demo GuardShark. Manny will be there, but the Board and investors make all the decisions."

Wayne laced his fingers behind his head. "Getting the Board to listen to us should be as easy as finishing GuardShark by Thursday." He gave his long legs a satisfying stretch. "Oh, what the heck. Count me in."

Vijay nodded. "Me too."

The room was silent, each engineer on pause as they considered the consequences of Jo's idea. A moment, and another, ticked by until Sherm spoke with quiet resolution. "I don't want Manny to kill GuardShark and our team. I'm in too."

Jim looked at Sherm, at Jo, at Luce. "I'm in. What have we got to lose?"

Jo walked to the board. "We'll divide up the work. Steve will find out everything he can about the Board members and investors. Luce and I will map out our demo of GuardShark. The rest of you can focus on finishing GuardShark in less than a week. Take breaks, go home when you need to, get as much done as you can but don't die. Is everyone OK with that plan?" All heads nodded. "Thanks, I think we've got a good shot at this."

Jim set down his coffee. "What about Lonnie? Isn't he working on that super test system that exercises all of GuardShark's features in all the different ways customers will use it?"

Jo exchanged looks with Wayne. "Wayne's sleuthing found that Lonnie has been paying someone to do his work at McWare, likely from the start of his employment here."

Wayne clicked open a file on his Mac and pointed to the screen. "The IP address of Seth the Mystery Geek isn't the same one that accessed our backup files, and given the negative tone of his email to Lonnie, we are less worried that he is the hacker."

Luce walked to the table as shock registered on the engineers' faces. "It isn't all bad news. This Seth guy has done amazing work, so there's a chance he could help us finish GuardShark."

Jim frowned. "Wouldn't a brilliant crook be worse than an idiot crook?"

Steve returned to the table. "We know Seth is talented enough to create SharkNet in record time and that he told Lonnie to take a hike. But Jim is right that we need to figure out if he is the hacker, or if we can trust him to work with us and help find the hacker."

Sherm stared at Steve. "If he's a good guy, how would we get him to work with us?"

Jo looked around the table. "As soon as we track Seth down, we'll find a way to talk with him." She clicked her computer mouse, opened a file with the list of GuardShark's features, and sighed. "OK, enough espionage. Let's get back to work and see which features still need attention."

Luce leaned toward Jo. "Good, something we were trained to do. I think we need to review all the online Help content to make sure brand new users are never confused."

Steve guzzled from his water bottle before responding, "That's a good idea, Luce. Too many software products have cryptic instructions. We should also review the error messages to make sure the how-to-correct steps are clear."

Jo sighed, but quickly captured the new tasks. "Those are great ideas. I hope it doesn't feel like punishment to ask you to take responsibility for your own suggestions. Agreed?" Luce and Steve both nodded.

The engineers quickly compared notes to help Jo update the list of remaining work tasks. She clicked the button to recalculate the remaining work hours and started laughing. "Microsoft Project thinks we have three weeks' work. Does anyone in high-tech work forty-hour weeks? Isn't Microsoft *Sleepless In Seattle*?"

Steve grinned as he popped open his Mac. "Redmond, not Seattle. Let's work smart and be realistic. If we can show the Board all the important features of GuardShark, they will see its merits for themselves."

Wayne said dryly, "They don't get rich by bein' fools. They must have had an off day when they hired Manny." His crinkled eyes twinkled in his weathered face as the engineers smirked in agreement.

After the meeting, Jo waited as the happy herd moved down the hallway toward the double doors to McWare's cube farm. She quickly closed the door to the Tomb, turning back to Luce and Steve. Steve moved his chair next to Luce. "What's up, Jo?" he asked.

Jo sat on the other side of Luce. "Actually, Grandma helped me find some information this morning on Shit-For-Brains Manny."

Luce mimicked a stern tone. "Manny had better watch out. Grandma looks sweet but she would do anything to keep him from hurting you, Jo."

Steve looked down at Jo with a bemused grin. "So what did you and your grandmother find out?"

"McWare is probably Manny's first job."

Luce frowned. "I wish we could find out who is on McWare's Board of Directors. It's gotta be illegal to knowingly operate at a loss to give investors tax advantages."

Jo looked at Luce. "I also suspect Shit-For-Brains misappropriated McWare's funds. A year ago, right after the early version of the Rhombus product got such great press, he bought a Porsche 918 Spyder. Those wheels cost about $850,000 to drive off the lot."

Steve began typing and clicking on his Mac. "We know the Rhombus product made money. Manny could have written several checks for bogus expenses in amounts under his spending limit."

Luce shook her head. "That could move enough funds to him to make it look like McWare was losing money. That's fraud."

Steve sat back and looked at Jo and Luce. "One reason to do that would be to use McWare as a tax shelter."

Jo clenched her fist angrily. "Doesn't he already have enough? That money could have been used for our team, for new data servers so we could work more efficiently. We could have hired more engineers to build and run tests. How do we get proof?"

Steve closed his Mac. "Let's just hope Seth is someone we can trust to help us. Wayne and I will work on finding him."

Jo snapped her Mac shut. "I'm bringing Shit-For-Brains down before he does any more damage to our team." As her and Luce's phones rang out the ukulele twang, she said, "That could be the sound of Red Nails disappearing over the horizon."

29

Multitasking 101

To: rookie-pup
From: Lord&Master

Sharks have three jobs—the cover, the scam, and the long-term shark life.

The straight job is the cover, the job everyone else thinks you are doing. It provides camouflage, your backstory, and since we are clever, complete control of our mission and our prey. You are in a perfect position to see all, know all that is happening.

Our strategy is virtually foolproof, but we must stay focused and on schedule. It is more critical than ever to maintain secrecy. We have to win everything without our prey ever knowing how they were fooled and how much we have profited.

Look over your shoulder on a regular basis since you never know who might be watching you, and worse, learning to beat you at your own game. If you are not aware of every aspect of your plan at all times, your career will nosedive to an early end.

The most successful sharks are constantly observing and making adjustments to achieve the goal. There is a way of watching that is not obvious, committed to the singular purpose of achieving the goal.

Stay focused. We must always ensure that we do not ever become a target. We are not victims, but we are not just winners either. We are champions.

~Sent from my iPad

30

Spy vs. Spy vs. Spy

Jo YAWNED AS she closed the Tomb door after Luce and Steve sat down, her to-go cup warming her other hand. "Saturday mornings at work should be outlawed. What's our plan for Lonnie and Mystery Geek?"

Luce popped open her Mac. "Steve, what did you and Wayne find out about him?"

Steve pulled up a text message. "Wayne found the name Seth Ackley in Lonnie's old email. Wayne's on his trail."

Jo leaned over to read Wayne's message. "How could anyone with brains put up with Lonnie?"

Steve opened a file on his Mac. "From the tone of the email they exchanged, Seth is intelligent and barely tolerates Lonnie."

Jo sipped her latte. "Why would such a talented engineer work for scum when he could get a real job or a consulting contract?"

Luce looked at Steve and Jo. "Maybe he doesn't want to work full time. He could be making a lot of money under the table."

Jo grumbled to her screen, "That option has the advantage of being free of management crap. Sign me up."

Steve sat back in his chair. "We need Seth's talent to add the tests to SharkNet for the password security features, so we have to keep Lonnie on the hook."

Luce nodded. "Until we talk to Seth and decide if we can trust him, Lonnie has to think we still believe he's doing the work."

Steve slapped the table, looking at Jo and Luce. "I've got it. We should give Lonnie a compliment. Lonnie craves attention, and what would aggravate an intelligent engineer like Mr. Ackley more than someone else taking credit for their work?"

Jo felt something cave into her stomach, flashing on a fleeting glimpse of Shit-For-Brains zooming off in his Porsche while the engineers worked overtime. "I think we know how that feels. I'll send Lonnie a sweet-as-pie email."

Luce shook her head, muttering, "I can't believe all the stuff we have to deal with. I used to have fun on Saturdays."

Jo idly played with her iPhone. "Hey, just because we're working at the office on a Saturday morning doesn't mean we can't have some fun." She pressed the video icon on her iPhone, pointing it at Luce. "Smile for the camera, Ms. Actors' Studio."

Luce made a face for Jo's video. "Are we making a little goodbye video for Red Nails?" She closed down her Mac.

Steve looked confused. "Did Operation Red Aloha land her a job?" He stood up with his Mac and a to-go cup of tea.

Jo laughed as she deleted the video. "She contacted a couple of companies and recruiters." She iPhoned her own selfie. "This is me daydreaming about Life After Red Nails." Jo closed down her Mac and packed it away.

Luce shouldered her backpack. "I'll check on email to Red Nails from addresses outside McWare."

Jo tossed her empty cup in the waste basket as she headed for the Tomb door. "I wish we could just donate her to another company, or another country. But I'm afraid they might retaliate."

Luce grumbled, "They might clone her and send both back."

Steve laughed. "*That* one I can remember to tell my wife. I can never remember all the funny stuff you two say by the time I get home. She thinks the 101 Dead CEOs contest is hilarious." He led them through the Tomb door to return to their cubes and the next mountain of work on their virtual plates.

Jo yawned. "I'm going to try to make a dent in all the work I didn't finish yesterday."

Luce nursed her latte. "Come and get me when you take a lunch break. If you don't see me, look under my desk."

Steve took a healthy pull on his tea and followed Jo and Luce down the back hall toward their cubicals.

A few hours later, Jo pulled her hoodie close against fall's chilly fingers as she and Luce hurried through the back door of McWare, their stomachs growling for the hot soup from the to-go bar at Sprouts Farmers Market. "What could make Steve so anxious to meet us in the Tomb ASAP?"

Luce shrugged a cashmere-covered shoulder. "He must have a good reason, or a really bad one."

They opened the Tomb to the grinning faces of Steve and Wayne. Luce sat at the table, shivering as she popped the lid of her tomato bisque soup. "So, have you two found Mr. Ackley?" Jo sat next to her and opened her insulated container of steaming cioppino.

Steve's grin grew, threatening to overtake his whole face. "He definitely knows Lonnie."

Luce gaped at Steve, Jo, and Wayne. "A friend? Just how crazy or desperate would that make him? I don't get it."

Steve handed a printout to Jo and Luce. "Friend might be a strong word. Seth Ackley's resume from five years ago says he graduated from CU/Boulder in three years and finished Harvard graduate school in Electrical Engineering and Computer Science. He worked for Mitre Corporation for less than two years before disappearing from the high-tech job scene. He's only twenty-nine and they hire only the brightest engineers."

Jo frowned and shook her head. "Someone like that working for lame-o Lonnie isn't logical."

Wayne sat back and crossed his arms. "There's something to be said for cash with no strings."

Steve nodded at Wayne. "If Lonnie pays him in cash, Mr. Ackley can live off the grid. We need to know what he's up to."

Luce nudged Jo. "How do we know we can trust him?"

Wayne flipped the printout to the last page. "We don't, but it might be a simple matter of circumstances. Mitre has two primary locations in Virginia and Massachusetts. I found an obituary for Celia Ackley, wife of Seth Ackley, of Waltham, Massachusetts and Boulder, Colorado. She died of cancer the same year he stopped working for Mitre, over three years ago. She was a toxicologist working for the EPA in Massachusetts."

Jo's heart plummeted. "That must have devastated him."

Luce watched Jo's face. "That is so sad. But I still don't see how we can find him and get him to talk to us so we can decide if we can trust him."

Jo suddenly turned to Wayne. "Don't we have the capability to track every change to every file in GuardShark and SharkNet, down to the IP address level?"

Wayne grinned. "I'm on it. I'll set up an automated job to detect every access to our files from that IP and the email address for Seth, and for the IP and email address of the hacker. If it's the same person, we will find out sooner or later."

Luce sighed. "That makes me feel a little better, but how do we find Seth?"

Jo's face lit up like sunshine. "Oh my god, I've got it."

Luce waited in the seconds of silence that followed, fixing a frown on Jo. "Earth to Jo, don't just think the thought, *say* it out loud."

Jo grabbed Luce's shoulder. "I'll bet real money that Seth Ackley is the wise-ass who puts all those captions on my cartoons, which makes him a smart mouth engineer who is as snarky as I am. I know I'm right about this, and snarky trumps money, power, and all the rest of it for an engineer."

Steve laughed, nodding. "You nailed it, Jo. If he's the one ridiculing people like Lonnie and Manny, that's exactly what every frustrated engineer in the world does, sooner or later."

Jo was giddy with excitement. "And what do frustrated engineers crave most? Other frustrated engineers to riff with against idiots. Leave Seth to me."

Luce put her hand on Jo's arm, her voice no-nonsense. "No, Jo. You are *not* talking with him alone."

Steve leaned toward Jo. "Luce is right, Jo. We talk to him together or not at all."

Jo swallowed before saying, "OK, I guess you're right, but do you really want to be here that late at night? Sherm's videos all show him here around 10:45 to 11:00 PM."

Luce's hand stayed on Jo's arm. "No problem. This is important. We might as well give it a shot tonight. Steve, are you OK with that?"

Steve grinned, running his big hand through his short hair. "My wife thinks she's heard it all about this crazy place, but I can't wait to see the look on her face when I tell her what I'm doing tonight to keep my job."

* * *

Jo checked the time on her iPhone, Saturday 10:30 PM. *Great, now I'm cartooning against the clock. Where's the fun in that?* The late night quiet of the Tomb gave her the calm she craved, whispering of peace and secrets. Pondering the choices for the remaining components of the cartoon, she Googled the Porsche Boxster to find an image she quickly rendered with exaggerated headlights.

This looks like something out of a Pixar film. Hey, John Lasseter, have I got a storyboard for you.

She listed caption options under the cartoon with a big question mark.

1. Hey, I always said I was a hard-charging, make-it-happen kind of guy.
2. I don't remember if they promised this would be the end of the beginning or the beginning of the end.
3. I love getting paid for a job that requires absolutely no expertise whatsoever.
4. Hey, everyone's good for something, even if it's just as a bad example.

OK, the trap is set. Now it's time to launch Operation Capture Captain Caption.

Jo rolled a chair to the wall space next to the door, where she would be hidden from view when the door opened. She turned off the light. The late night cool air in the Tomb touched Jo's face as the dim light and resolute silence calmed her. As soon as her eyes adjusted, she made her way to her chair and sat down to wait.

Jo considered her options for initiating a meeting with Seth without causing a defensive reaction. She grinned, intrigued by the myriad of secrets and the critical juncture for the team, GuardShark, and McWare's stability. *Great, no pressure.* She glanced at the wall clock, 10:45 PM. *Almost time.* She felt the adrenalin rush of fear of the unknown. *Be careful. Don't screw this up.*

Jo gripped the armrests. She gazed at the whiteboards, where notes from various engineering discussions were interspersed with her cartoons and the list of ideas for the contest. 'CEO-in-the-snow paperweight' made her chuckle. *Crazy weirdo engineers.* Her eyes paused at each cartoon. *We've been collaborating for a while.* How many nights had he come into this room looking for a new cartoon to caption? *Focus. You have a job to do here.*

She texted Luce, "Can you see me on the Tomb-cam on your Mac in the dim light?"

Luce texted back, "Yes, and Steve and I are standing just inside the door to our office area, ready to high-tail it to the Tomb as soon as Seth goes inside the door."

Jo heard the growl of a high-powered motorcycle rumbling to a stop, the engine suddenly quiet. She texted Luce, "I think he's here, that must be his killer bike I just heard from out back."

Jo read Luce's acknowledgement at the same time she heard the back door open and the sound of approaching footsteps that stopped abruptly outside the Tomb's door. Jo's heart threatened to beat its way out of her chest. *He's here. It's time. I don't know what to say. I don't remember how to talk. I can't breathe.*

The door opened and a crisp click flooded the room with light, startling Jo with its abruptness. The door's angle shallowed as it came within inches of her chair. Time froze in the seconds that marked three footfalls as the back of the broad-shouldered sweatshirt moved into Jo's full view.

The door closed with a soft thud. The six-foot tall dark-haired man walked slowly to the whiteboard. His athletic physique stood facing the board. *He's looking for a new one.* Jo grinned, trying not to laugh out loud. She was still smiling as he turned around in the direction of the wall clock and froze mid-step, staring at Jo sitting in the corner. His deep blue eyes contrasted with the warm honey color of his skin. He stared at her, unmoving.

Seth's gaze shifted, startled as the Tomb door opened. Steve and Luce stood in the doorway, inspecting the young man.

Jo willed her voice to a tone of quiet warmth. "Hi, I'm the artist. I thought we should meet. My name is Jo Galvan. This is Luce. We're the lead software engineers. Steve Scott is our quality manager. You're Seth, right?" She smiled as she stood and closed the short distance between them, her right hand outstretched. *Please don't be afraid of us.*

Seth's gaze shifted back to Jo, and his large warm hand closed with firm gentleness around her petite one. "You surprised me, but it looks like you meant to." His voice was even warmer than his hand.

Jo realized she was staring at him, and said quickly, "Yes, but we come in peace. We've wanted to meet you for a long time. Your stuff is really funny. You have fans here." Jo was relieved to see Seth grin as he looked down at her, still holding her hand.

"Thanks. Seth Ackley. Your cartoons are great. How did you know it was me who did the captions?"

"I wish I could take credit for being a super sleuth, but the truth is some of my team rigged a spy-cam to catch you." She reluctantly removed her hand from his.

Seth's warm laugh relaxed Jo. "I've been cam'd," he said. He looked back to Luce and Steve. "But why?"

Jo took a breath and stuck her verbal toe in the water. "We wanted to talk to you about something. Why don't we sit down?" She turned around to grab the arm of the chair she had used to hide and wheeled it to the table. Luce and Steve each took a seat.

Seth sat down next to Jo, looking from Luce to Steve and back to Jo. "What?" He waited.

Jo felt time stop in the silent room. It was now or never. She folded her hands on the table, trying desperately to seem casual. "We need two favors. First, hear us out, and second, don't tell anyone what we talked about."

Seth looked at her with a gaze that relaxed into a smile. "You can trust me to keep a secret. This is way too intriguing to walk away from. Are we doing espionage?"

Jo laughed, feeling her tension evaporate. "I know your email is commando2010@gmail.com and you authored all the SharkNet software. We need your talent to help us finish our most important product yet."

Seth's grin faded to a blank stare that morphed quickly to sheepishness. "Looks like I'm a lot better at writing software than covering my tracks. I guess I wouldn't make a good criminal."

Steve shook his head. "Lonnie's absence of brain cells was our main clue that someone brilliant was his ghost writer. Finding you has been quite a challenge."

Seth exaggerated a sigh. "Well, thank you for that. What software do you want me to write?"

Luce grabbed her backpack and pulled out her Mac. "We need help analyzing a truckload of electronic data, but Lonnie can't know what we're up to."

Seth's face hardened. "Lonnie is an idiot, but I've been in a situation where I needed to make enough money to pay my bills without having to work in a stressful environment for crazy management."

"We all envy you," Luce said as she opened her Mac. "We have to analyze a bunch of electronic messages and various documents to assemble a timeline for specific information and possible illegal activities." Seth rolled his chair to look over Luce's shoulder as she scrolled through a list of computer files. "Calling it data is like putting lipstick on a pig."

Seth pointed to the screen. "Who are we spying on?"

Jo exchanged a look with Luce and Steve before turning back to Seth. "We're spying on whoever is spying on us. Someone has been hacking our files and sabotaging our MAWM software. We need to find out who it is and solve this before noon on Thursday." She watched him carefully, looking for any sign of a lie.

Seth winced. "That's insane. What's Mom?"

Jo grinned. "Sorry. It's M-A-W-M, for Make-A-Wish Miracle. My version is Make-A-Wish, Motherfucker. It's our codename for GuardShark."

Seth chuckled. "Good one. How do we get started?"

Jo explained, "We have all the email messages in a password protected directory. We can give you the directory location and the password on a piece of paper."

Seth nodded with an amused smile. "Using a manual system, smart move. Who else knows about this?"

Jo felt Luce and Steve's eyes join hers in a laser focus on Seth's body language. "We're keeping it to our team. We suspect the hacker was hired by our CEO Manny. We found email proof that he wants us to fail to deliver GuardShark so he can sell McWare. That will cost us our jobs."

Seth frowned. "Maybe Manny's working a deal under the table with a competitor. Security software will make big money."

Steve cocked his head at Seth. "Or he's working with someone who would benefit when McWare loses money. He can manipulate the costs of building the product to put McWare in a financial loss situation."

Seth sat back, crossing his arms. "If GuardShark, sorry, MAWM, just has errors, McWare would sell for a fire sale price. That's a cheap way for the new owner to acquire the hot new security product that could make them rich."

Jo shrugged. "We need to find out what's really going on, but we also have to finish everything by Thursday morning so we can go directly to the Board members and investors at their meeting Thursday afternoon to show them that GuardShark works. Are you in?"

Seth looked from Jo to Luce and Steve. "Sure, but you know hackers can be hard to find and identify. And you have to keep them from knowing you're on to them."

Jo gave him a snarky grin. "We found you. Are you really working with us?"

Seth laughed and stood up. "You're giving me the chance to do really complex, dirty stuff so we can track down a sleaze-bag who wallows in evil deeds? I'm in."

Luce looked up from her Mac. "That's how we all feel. We want you to work with our team without any of the bad people getting wise to our plan."

Jo kept her voice at an even tone as she asked, "We can set up an office cubical for you, or do you need to work remotely?" *I hope he doesn't pick up on our suspicions.*

Seth winked. "I've got Lonnie's key, so I can just work in this room anytime. No one will notice me because I'm just another geek. We're invisible."

Jo pulled out a pad of yellow sticky notes. "OK, before we call it a night, let's trade contact information. We can give you our information. Wayne is the engineer who is in charge of our systems. He can create an account for you to log in to our secret stuff."

Seth grabbed the pad. "I'm writing as we speak." He dealt the little yellow sheets to Luce and Steve before writing his information on three pages from the pad.

Jo grinned. "Me too. Manual systems rule." The ukulele sound sang out from her phone.

"What's that?"

Jo checked Red Nails' email. "Just another little spy thing." She held out her yellow sticky as Luce and Steve handed theirs to Seth.

Seth handed Jo the yellow pad and passed out the three copies of his information to her, Luce, and Steve. "And I thought geeks were boring."

31

Lying With Data 101

To: rookie-pup
From: Lord&Master

There are three kinds of lies: lies, damned lies, and statistics.

Mark Twain gave Benjamin Disraeli the credit, but the phrase is not in Disraeli's writings. Twain lied about lies. It's beautiful. The best lie has enough truth to sell itself.

Statistical data can be manipulated. Political pollsters are paid to select data to predict elections. Ironically, what actually matters is how the predictions themselves influence the voters, and more importantly, the campaign contributors. It must be an amazing rush to ride that rocket.

There is a type of data that is of particular interest to us in achieving our plan. Our spy found evidence the engineers are testing GuardShark constantly. They fix every problem and retest immediately to make sure they haven't introduced errors. It is the most disgusting display of accountability I've ever seen. That just doesn't work for our business model.

Sabotage is the best option to achieve our strategy of failure. Carry out the plan no matter the cost, and stay focused on the goal. We're in the most critical stage of this venture.

~Sent from my iPad

32

The [Next] Perfect Storm

Jo ROLLED HER office chair past Luce's cubical and into Wayne's, carefully skirting the giant poster of the Cheyenne Frontier Days Rodeo. "What's going on, Wayne? I've always counted on Mondays being safe and boring. I'm starting to believe in gremlins." She carefully took a bite of a chicken Caesar wrap.

Wayne played absently with a small plastic wind-up bucking horse but his focus was fixed to his computer screen. "All of Sunday night's tests failed. It's like GuardShark has suddenly died." He pointed the horse at his monitor, half a bacon burger in the other hand. "Look at this mess."

Error messages scrolled relentlessly down his computer screen, rolling fast like a digital tsunami of software failure. Several minutes later the error list vanished from his screen, replaced by a huge text message: 'GuardShark FATAL ABORT: 257 Critical Failures.'

Jo took a breath to get a handle on her rising anxiety. "Open the error log file. We need to research each test failure. How could everything go wrong?" She took a healthy bite of the combination of chicken, Caesar'd romaine, and a whole wheat tortilla.

Wayne clicked his Windows File Explorer window to show Jo the location of the error file, and opened it to display the contents as he finished the burger half. Luce joined them, looking over Wayne's shoulder, picking up a stuffed toy pig. "This is new livestock." Wayne shot Luce a grin as he reached for the uneaten half of his lunch.

Jo leaned closer to the screen, talking through her mouthful of food. "They are all the same type of error, 'unmatched data result.' We need to hurry if we're going to figure this out before Cinda's status meeting at 8:30 tomorrow morning. She would love to convince Manny that testing and product quality aren't important to making money."

Luce put the pig back on the desk and nibbled at her pita with baba ganoush. "Cinda sent a cancellation for the meetings for the rest of the week. She must not have enjoyed our last meeting."

Jo snickered as she took another bite. "Maybe she's got something more important to do. Let's look at the errors from last night and compare them to the results for the same tests that passed the night before."

Sherm stood up in the cube next to Wayne's, talking over the divider while licking salsa from his fingers. "We've all been careful to test our software code changes, so it doesn't make any sense."

Jim leaned his stocky body against Wayne's cube wall, holding a half-eaten Subway meatball marinara sandwich. "Hey, Sherm, I didn't see the fixes for the Twitter privacy bug. I thought you were going to get them in yesterday."

Sherm's tone had an edge. "I tried all Sunday morning to debug the Facebook privacy code you put in on Saturday so I could re-use some of the common features, but it kept hosing up. I couldn't get you to answer my text messages, so I blew it off and went climbing in Eldorado Canyon."

Jim slumped, taking a long breath. "Hey, man, sorry about that. My wife thought she was going into labor, so we were at the Birth Center until 2:00 AM over Saturday night. They have a rule that cell phones have to be turned off, and I was so tired by the time we got home that I forgot to turn it back on until this morning."

Sherm's faced tensed. "I get how important that is, but I'm doing most of the work that we're supposed to do together."

Jim nodded. "I know, I should have remembered to text you. I'll debug the Facebook errors this afternoon. I'm sorry I messed you up. I'll do better." Sherm gave Jim an off-handed shrug.

Wayne swiveled his chair around to talk to both Sherm and Jim, his weathered face wearing a kindly smile. "Babies come when they come. Sherm, I can help fix the Twitter privacy errors. I've almost got the Help system done, so my buddy Vijay gets to have all the fun of testing it for a while. But I don't think that's what caused last night's test errors."

Vijay joined the group on hearing his name, talking amid forkfuls of red lentil masala, the enticing aroma spicing the air. "I'm ready anytime, Wayne." He looked down at Jo. "I've been going through the timestamps on our software files, and there are two new ones that were added just before SharkNet would have kicked off last night. They're both from Lonnie."

Jo could taste her anger. "Of course, he's the one engineer who doesn't follow the rules. Vijay, could you figure out what is wrong with his files and fix the problem?"

Vijay waved his fork. "Sure, I'm on it."

Wayne nodded to Vijay. "Just let me know when you have it fixed and I can re-run SharkNet."

Jo rubbed her forehead before taking another bite. "It's way too early for this. Wayne, can you change the system password and let us know so we can all write it down? I'll email Lonnie to just email his files to Luce and me from now on because we're worried about a virus."

Wayne nibbled a french fry with mustard as he nodded. "You bet. Say, do you want to tell everyone about Seth?"

Jo's eyes opened in surprise. "I can't believe I forgot about him. Luce, Steve, and I talked with Seth Ackley last night and he's ready to work with us. I asked him to meet us at 1:00."

Wayne tossed his burger wrapper in the trash. "He's definitely got engineering chops. I just hope we can trust him, and he can hold his own in the joke department."

Jo said evenly, "We'll be keeping an eye on him. He doesn't know how tough this crowd is."

The team worked through lunch, moving among each other's cubes. They talked over the five-foot cube walls, asking questions, checking on details, and proposing options to fix problems. At 12:50 PM, Jo walked down through the office area's door to the back hall and settled at the table in the Tomb. The rest of the team drifted in and seated themselves haphazardly around the table just as the low rumble of a motorcycle came from the parking lot. Jo's iPhone chimed the arrival of a text message. Moments later, Seth ambled into the Tomb, laying his helmet on a corner of the table.

Jo stood up to greet him, surprised by the flutter in her chest. "Hi, Seth. Let me introduce you to the team." She gestured in turn to each engineer around the table. "Wayne manages our systems; he will set up all your computer accounts and show you how to use our systems. Jim is our lead software designer, Sherm is an ace software engineer who has been studying the certification testing for our security product, GuardShark. Vijay is our intern. And you've already met Luce and Steve."

Seth's face held an easy grin as he traded nods with each engineer. "Hi, good to meet all of you. Jo texted me a little while ago that the SharkNet tests all crashed last night."

Jo waved him to a chair next to Luce's open Mac. "Luce says the re-run of SharkNet still has all the same errors. So Lonnie's bad files weren't the problem."

Seth scanned Luce's computer screen. "Lonnie is an idiot, but he wouldn't be able to do real damage. Wait a minute. I think someone tampered with the test database."

Jo stood behind Luce, next to Seth, leaning in to get a closer look at the screen. "Why would anyone bother doing that? Test data has to be more boring than watching paint dry."

Seth tapped the screen. "The test data includes the expected results of the basic tests, and if any of those test results fail to match, SharkNet automatically reports a critical error status. I know the data I created, and this isn't it. Jo, can I use your Mac for a second?"

Jo slid her computer to Seth, grumbling angrily, "Anyone who can access our file system can access our test data. Someone is trying to make us and GuardShark look bad. How do we find out what specific data was changed so we can correct it, and who did it?"

Seth clicked and scrolled on Jo's laptop. "Can one of you restore the test data from the backup a couple of nights ago, and re-run SharkNet with it? That should prove GuardShark is good."

Wayne nodded as he began typing. "Sure, and I'll copy the correct test data and the good test results to a secure computer storage area so this doesn't happen again." He clicked and typed in a torrent.

Jo sat up suddenly. "Seth, if you notice something wrong like this in the future but you can't tell one of us in person, don't use our company email accounts. The hacker can see that. We text each other's personal iPhones, and we'll get you that information for the rest of the team."

Seth nodded, sliding Jo's Mac back to her. "Good plan. What's this critical email from Cinda?"

Jo frowned at the screen. "She's accusing us of negligence because of all the errors from SharkNet this morning."

Seth read over her shoulder. "Look at the timestamp on her message. It was sent before the system would have emailed the test results that have all the errors."

Jo stared hard at the message header. "Red Nails sent her message more than an hour before the test results were emailed."

Seth's grin was triumphant. "Red Nails is Cinda, right?"

Jo grinned back at him before turning her Mac around to show the team. "Look, that proves she is working with CJ the hacker."

Jim slapped the table. "I'll bet she went by the timestamp on the test results from the day before, when we were only running the short list of tests. She wouldn't have a clue about our strategy of running different permutations of the suite of tests and for various lengths of time to emulate as many variations of customer usage as possible."

Vijay shook his head. "Wow, that's GuardShark 101. Can she read? Or what if she is CJ?"

The team stared at Vijay for a second in stunned silence before Sherm laughed. "C'mon, man, you've seen her in meetings. She really doesn't know anything about GuardShark or SharkNet."

Wayne said quietly, "Or much of anything else."

Steve said slowly, "I'm not so sure. What if Vijay is on to something and she has just been playing dumb? Her initials are CJ, and she seems pretty close to Manny. Let's keep an eye on her."

Luce turned to Jo and Seth. "Whoever CJ is, we have to collect the bad test results and the email from Red Nails so we have proof of the sabotage."

Jo turned her Mac back around. "I'm creating a folder with all the evidence to build a case against Red Nails and protect us from being fingered as negligent."

Wayne nodded to Jo. "We have a spare backup computer that I've never put on our corporate network. I can load a copy of all the good files we need there from a fat USB stick. I mean, all the good stuff before the sabotage."

Luce turned to Wayne. "What would it take to implement more secure access to our systems?"

Wayne grinned and winked. "Forty-five minutes and some of your homemade banana bread."

Luce grinned. "I would be overjoyed to bring you banana bread. In fact, I'll bring a loaf for each of you. I over-bake when I'm worried."

Wayne looked around the table. "I will give each of you a sticky note with the new login information on it; you can keep it in your wallet."

Steve nodded at Wayne. "Anything electronic is vulnerable to hackers, no matter how good the security software."

Luce texted herself to bring banana bread. "I love that manual systems will save us from someone else's evil cyber-attacks."

Wayne eased back in his chair. "Done, SharkNet is re-running with the good data." He called in Seth's direction, "Hey, buddy, it's time for your group interview, but no pressure." The rest of the team focused on Seth.

Jo nodded at each engineer. "OK, who wants to go first?"

Jim crossed his arms over the Dartmouth logo of his sweatshirt. "How did you figure out the cause of the test errors?"

Seth explained to the team, "I compared the data that was used to check last night's test results with the data I created for SharkNet for verifying the expected test results. It turns out the hacker put bogus data in the database that was used for last night's testing so the test results didn't match the expected results. Wayne just had to restore the good test data and re-run SharkNet to give us good test results."

Jo closed her Mac. "OK, who's next?"

Seth sat back in his chair. "Inquisition me."

Sherm started laughing, extending his hand to Seth. "I think you passed."

Jim was next to shake hands. "With flying colors."

Vijay and Steve congratulated Seth. Luce shook his hand. "We have to celebrate. We're pizza people."

Jo put her hands on her forehead as she turned to Seth. "We forgot about the important stuff! We didn't ask you if you can handle Proto's pizza or if you knows any good CEO jokes."

"C'mon, I could eat Proto's five nights a week. What's the difference between God and a CEO?" Seth looked around the table. "God doesn't think He's a CEO."

Jim gave a whoop as he beat a little drum roll on the table to accompany the snickers from the rest of the team, who stood up to congratulate Seth.

Jo extended her hand to Seth. "It's official, you're one of us now. Let's take Manny, Red Nails, and CJ down." The warmth of his large strong hand felt comforting around Jo's smaller one, but a warning thought prompted her to release his hand. *We've got lots of work to do, and we're still not sure we can trust him.*

33

Strategic Blame 101

To: rookie-pup
From: Lord&Master

Blame is a key element in our business strategy. Failure in the business world is forgotten when unimportant people are the cause of the failure. Powerless underlings are the perfect culprits to take the fall. We can easily spin that move as clean-up of a mess made by arrogant engineers.

The best way to design the blame scheme is to play on the prey's weakness and use it to our advantage. Listen carefully. Engineers' greatest weakness is ultimate belief in logic and expertise. Our blame strategy capitalizes beautifully on that flaw.

It is critical that we maintain constant focus and guard against the effects of diminished energy on our ability to plot, reason, evaluate, and be both physically and mentally nimble.

That's why we need to enjoy this. This is our kind of fun. Otherwise, it would just be a job and we might as well be legit. That's funny. Why? Sharks wallow in the pleasure of taking advantage of the little fish by striking without warning. Go legit? Don't make me laugh.

~Sent from my iPad

How To Tell If You Are the CEO or An Engineer	CEO	Engineer
QUALIFICATIONS	Company founder is Father	BS and MS in EE/CompSci, 20+ years of experience
KNOWN BY	Last name	First Name
HIT ON BY	Every woman in marketing	Every man in Sales
WORST NIGHTMARE	Drop in stock price	Network crashes
HOURS WORKED PER WEEK	35 including golf games	80 with a cold or flu
NICKNAME	Chief	Sweathog
CAN PERFORM SIMULTANOUS ACTIVITIES	Walk and chew gum OR Chair a meeting and calculate net worth	Database migration, Lead Engineering task force, Write a new software product NOTE: Female engineers can also give birth
CANNOT RECALL	Engineers' names	An example of the CEO's gratitude
LAST YEAR'S BONUS	$1 Million	A stuffed replica of the corporate logo
NEXT YEAR'S VACATION	Las Hadas	Workshop on security research
FAVORITE LITERATURE	Comic books and Golf Digest	Security theory
STRESS RELIEVER	Porsche purchase	Yoga video
MOST FREQUENT QUESTION	What have you done for me?	How can I help you?
RECENTLY PAID OFF	$15 million for private island retreat	College loans
JUST ONCE BEFORE I LOSE THIS JOB, I WISH	To make a killing in the stock market, be on the cover of Golf Digest and see my name in lights	To leave work by 5:00 PM

34

When the Going Gets [Really] Tough

As Jo PLOPPED the bag of Dairy Queen Buster Bars on Vixen's passenger seat, her iPhone chimed a call from Luce. "Jo! You need to look at the email Seth just sent us, now!"

Jo eased into the driver's seat. "Can't, I'm on a DQ run for a treat for the team, but I'll be back in ten minutes. What's up?"

Luce's voice pitched higher with each sentence. "Wait a second until I get outside to the parking lot. OK, Seth went through Manny's and Red Nails' files and email to find the agenda for the Board meeting on Thursday the 26th. Manny is planning to announce that we didn't finish GuardShark, and filing for bankruptcy is the next thing on the agenda."

Jo erupted into the phone, "But that's not fair! Manny's the one who demanded we finish GuardShark by Friday the 27th, a whole day later."

Luce's voice was angry venom. "Right, we have proof of that from the 10% Confidence Schedule that Manny presented our all-hands meeting last Friday. Manny set us up. He's been setting us up all along."

Jo closed her eyes as she gripped the Mustang's steering wheel and breathed slowly against her rising panic. She focused on this new entry in her mental list of hurdles to pull off their coup at the Board meeting. *One fire at a time, one fire at a time.* After one more breath, she opened her eyes as she shifted into first gear and started the engine.

Jo fished in her backpack as she talked to Luce. "I need to get back to the office. Talk to me while I'm driving." She put in her iPhone earbuds and pulled onto 28th Street.

Luce's voice was frantic. "I can't think. Help me, Jo. Everything is riding on the Board meeting."

Jo was grateful for the parade of red light stops that usually annoyed her. "Luce, we have two major things to finish. First, the team has to finish fingerprint recognition and password strength checking so all of SharkNet's tests pass. Second, we need to find out from Wayne and Steve what errors SharkNet is reporting so the team can fix any last problems."

Luce spoke more slowly, breathing audibly. "Right, I'll set up a meeting with the team as soon as I talk to Wayne and Steve."

Jo pulled into an empty parking space at McWare. "OK, that's good, Luce. The other thing we need is evidence that Manny is behind the sabotage and has been trying to undermine our team's work on GuardShark to sell McWare down the river for his own gain. Seth is working on that in the Tomb."

Luce's laughter had an anxious tension. "I forgot Seth is working in the Tomb. I'm so panicked, I'm certifiable. My yoga calm wore off around 8:15 this morning."

Jo laughed. "Hey, think of all the times you've kept me from imploding. Go talk to Wayne, Steve, and Seth, in that order."

"OK, see you in a few. But, Jo, read the whole email and talk to Seth and Steve about it."

Jo hurried through the back hallway to the Tomb. The surprise of the empty dark room shocked her nerves into a sudden panic attack. *Where is Seth? Did he leave to do some hacking from another IP account?* Fear washed over her again as she began setting up her Mac and suddenly remembered the ice cream.

Jo grabbed the bag and sprinted out of the Tomb, down the hallway, through the double doors and around the perimeter of the office cubicals to the break room, quickly depositing the Buster Bars in the freezer before hurriedly retracing her steps back to the Tomb. She made a mental note to retrieve the frozen treats for the afternoon team meeting.

Jo sat and quickly popped her Mac to launch her personal email. She opened Seth's 'Critical—Read Immediately' email, talking back to its author out loud. "It's the agenda for the Board meeting and the list of people invited. Are you kidding me?" Jo's gaze froze on the screen. "The last topic of discussion is the sale of McWare?"

She read on. "Contingent on delivery of GuardShark. Failure Options: Chapter 7 vs. Chapter 11." Jo Googled 'Chapter 11 vs. Chapter 7' and read the top hits as her heart raced. "Chapter 11 and Chapter 7 are two legal forms of bankruptcy proceedings for businesses. Chapter 11 allows a corporation to continue doing business but with a plan to repay creditors. Chapter 7 means all assets are sold immediately so the proceeds can be distributed among the creditors. Crap, this is really serious. It means McWare is in very dire financial trouble."

The Tomb door opened suddenly, startling Jo, followed by the relief of seeing Seth's warm smile. "Hey, I wondered where you were. I was just reading your email."

Seth pulled a chair next to Jo and set up his Mac. "I had to go home to try the login Wayne set up for me and bring my computer here so we could work together. It's more efficient. But he needs to verify my home IP address so all the traffic from it into the files here is clearly identified as being from me."

Jo's voice betrayed her frayed nerves. "I just read the agenda item for McWare's sale or bankruptcy discussion. Is this the list of Board members? What about investors?"

Seth pointed to Jo's screen. "Scroll down. The list of investors is on the next page, and look whose names are on it."

Jo gasped and turned to Seth in shock. "The list of investors isn't in alphabetical order, so it must be in order of percentage of ownership, and their names are across the top at the same level. I'll bet you real money Glaston Wimple and Bill Schuster each own more than 25% of the company."

Seth nodded. "Together they probably own a controlling interest."

Jo sat back and crossed her arms. "Wouldn't they be the first to find out if Manny and Lonnie are working together to screw up McWare's chances for making money on GuardShark? Or maybe they expect to use McWare's losses as business write-offs for their taxes."

Seth looked startled. "I've heard stories about underhanded tactics in start-up companies, but I would bet you a new transmission that Manny is behind this."

Jo thought for a minute. "Manny's too stupid to pull this off, at least not by himself. Calling Lonnie stupid would be an insult to stupid people. I'll bet a successful man like Mr. Schuster is tired of putting up with his son's bullshit." Jo felt Seth staring hard at her. "What?"

Seth shrugged, moving his focus to his screen. "Nothing, just got a picture of disappointed fathers. OK, let me show you what I've found out about Manny's secret plans."

Jo rolled her chair next to Seth's Mac. As the data displayed, he warned, "There's bad news here."

Jo focused on the dates and brief descriptions of email messages. "These dates are four years old. That must be the original agreement giving Manny four years to repay the investors from McWare's profits or from the sale of the company and its assets."

Seth pointed to another column. "The payback date is Monday September 30th, one business day after you are supposed to finish GuardShark, but that doesn't make sense. No software product makes money the day the software is done. It still has to be packaged, advertised, press releases created, and all the rest of it."

Jo looked at Seth. "Manny deliberately tried to sabotage us from finishing it. I'll bet he planned all along to let our team miss the window when GuardShark's revenue could have saved McWare."

Seth scrolled to the recent dates on the spreadsheet. "Here's the smoking gun. When your team kept pulling success after success to keep things on schedule, Manny and Cinda intentionally orchestrated the sabotage of your test data by working with CJ."

Jo stared dumbfounded at Seth. "Do any of the emails give us a clue about why Manny would undermine his own potential gold mine?"

Seth nodded as he answered, "Manny rants all the time in his email about his killer business strategy, but he has to be working with someone really savvy to plot McWare's downfall."

Jo leaned her elbows on the table, rubbing her throbbing head with both hands. "The agenda for this Thursday's Board meeting was Manny's plan all along. We have to find a way to keep him from getting away with this. Wayne put a monitor on Manny's email, so we should take a look in case he mentions how CJ is helping him."

Seth sat back, crossed his muscular arms, and looked directly at Jo. "Good idea. What's your plan for fighting Manny?"

"We have to show the Board that we finished their whole GuardShark product and it works. We're going to crash the Board meeting and run a demo."

Seth nodded. "You can also show them these messages as evidence that Manny and Cinda got CJ to sabotage your team's work. You might as well go for broke. Your team *is* GuardShark."

Jo put her head in her hands, closing her eyes against the rising pain. "Manny will just tell them we made this all up. Who listens to engineers, anyway? The Board and the investors don't know us, and Manny is one of them."

The Tomb door burst open as Steve led Luce and the team into the room. "If you mean the Board, we'll just have to make them listen to us, Jo. Thanks for texting us. On the way down here, I got everyone caught up." Luce, Steve, and the engineers pulled up chairs as Luce closed the Tomb door.

Luce rolled her chair next to Jo, putting a hand on her best friend's shoulder. "We all agreed that we're ready to demo the finished product to the Board. Our engineering team is as much of an asset to this company as GuardShark will be."

Sherm crossed his sinewy arms. "We know GuardShark inside and out, so who's better than us to show it to the Board?"

Jo glanced at Seth. "That's what Mr. Ackley just said. Great minds."

Steve sat up. "What if we let the Board members use GuardShark themselves? That's better than just showing it to them."

Jo blinked, staring at Steve for a split second before looking around the table. "Are you up for letting a brand new group of people try GuardShark?"

Jim nodded. "You bet. If we just demo the product, Manny could say we were showing what works and hiding the problems. But if they use it, they will sell themselves on it."

Sherm grinned. "That's genius, Steve, but I've never been in a room of rich people. What do we wear to a Board meeting? I'm limited to race shirts from 1998 through last Memorial Day, and a few climbing shirts."

Steve turned to Sherm. "Matching socks are always a good choice."

Luce flexed both hands and shook them. "I'm so jazzed and juiced about all this that I want to finish GuardShark tonight and work on the plan for the Board meeting all day tomorrow."

Jo stretched her neck, rolling her shoulders to release the tension. "I think we have a good chance of making this work, but we have to be careful that Manny and the rest of the evil ones don't find out what we're up to. I'd bet real money they have more dirty tricks to play."

Seth grumbled, "I have a feeling there's more we don't know that might make or break our approach to the Board. I'll find out everything I can on each of the Board members and investors."

Jo and Luce's iPhones sang out with the ukulele ringtone. Jo scrolled on her iPhone. "Red Nails' latest email. Luce and I have been tracking her communications for several days."

Steve stood up. "Wayne, can you pull up the test results from re-running SharkNet?"

Seth waved his hand. "I was just looking at them. Here, use my computer." He spun his Mac around and slid it across the table to Wayne. Steve walked behind Wayne and studied the screen.

Wayne clicked and scrolled, translating the results for the team. "All the tests are passing except a few errors with fingerprint recognition and three warnings for extended password security. Vijay and I can debug the password problems."

Vijay nodded to Wayne. "We should be done before tonight's big test run."

Jim looked at Jo. "Sherm and I have a couple of errors from our fingerprint recognition work, but we know what's wrong. We should be done late this afternoon. Don't start tonight's test runs until we let you know we're done."

Steve looked around the table. "I think we're ready to get back to work."

Jo sat up suddenly. "No, wait. We have unfinished team business. Don't go anywhere. I'll be right back. Tell some CEO jokes, or better yet, fill Seth in on the contest."

"Contest?" Jo grinned at Seth's question as she ran out the Tomb door. Running all the way to the break room, upstairs to give an ice cream treat to a delighted Liz, and downstairs to the Tomb. She burst through the door. "Buster Bars! We're celebrating our newest weirdo, Seth."

The team cheered, whooped, and applauded as Jo passed out chocolate-dipped heaven on a stick. Seth popped the wrapper off and took a hefty bite. "I like the way this team works."

35

Strategic Blame 102

To: rookie-pup
From: Lord&Master

Don't ever turn your iPhone off again. We have to stay in constant touch with each other.

We have critical problems. Why hasn't Cinda gotten CJ's status to us? Why isn't she at work? Why am I just finding out about this now? We have to use her to handle charging those two geek girls with gross negligence and fraud.

Cinda is the designated scapegoat. We need her to keep in touch with CJ. As long as she is the go-between, our part in this can never be traced. She must handle all the payments and passing all the hacked files back and forth. You must stay on top of things with Cinda.

Make sure CJ has destroyed all the evidence from every computer system. I won't involve you in this because you are not yet ready to do what may be necessary.

Above all, do not panic. We have an excellent strategy, so we will fix this temporary glitch and wait until it's time for our next move. We have one clear objective, so adjust, refocus, and stay the course toward that goal.

It's zero hour now. Everything is riding on this. Game on! Get this done right, and get it done now!

~Sent from my iPad

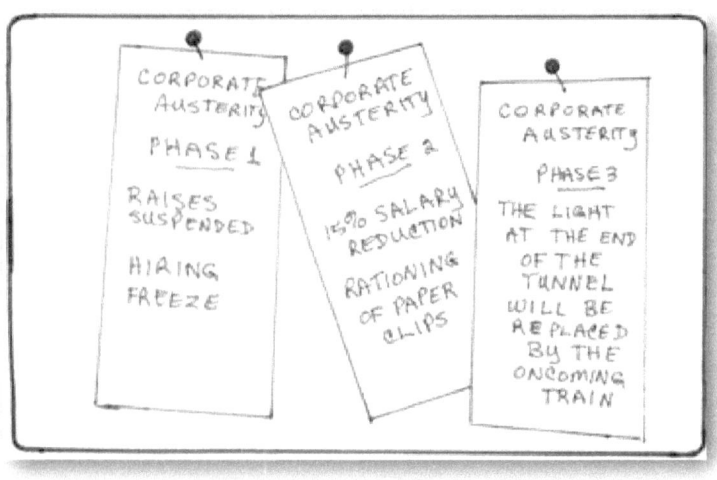

36

The Bad News Is Worse Than We Thought

THE LATE AFTERNOON sun slanted through the windows of Ozo's as Jo waited with Steve for her decaf latte. A growling rumble from outside turned her attention to the front windows in time to see a black Norton Commando 961 SF motorcycle in pristine condition wheel to a stop on Broadway, waiting to make a left into the coffee house parking lot. The leather-jacketed rider held the powerful machine with a long, muscular, denim-covered leg. Jo was transfixed by the bike's craftsmanship, but was startled when she noticed the rider was waving at her.

Jo took a quick breath, willing herself to wave back in what she hoped looked like a nonchalant gesture of greeting. Her thoughts spun. *He's a gear head. I can't get distracted by this guy. Focus. Think about GuardShark and the Board meeting.* Seth's leather-gloved hand gripped the handlebar as he deftly made the turn, moving out of Jo's view.

Seth removed his leather gloves, put them in his helmet, and cradled the helmet in his arm as he and Wayne came through the door and sidled up to Jo and Steve at the counter, both grinning at Jo. Seth unzipped his black leather jacket. "Hey, Jo, Steve. We've got a lot to talk about." He ordered a decaf americano with room.

Jo turned to Seth and Wayne. "That doesn't sound like a casual chat."

Wayne pulled out his wallet. "I just hope these nice Ozo's people are good at cleaning high places 'cause you're gonna hit the ceiling when you hear what we found."

Jo grabbed her latte and took a grateful sip. "Can't wait to hear about it. Luce is holding a table for us." She walked over to Luce, who was setting up her Mac.

Luce looked up as Jo pulled out a chair. "What's up?"

Jo's eyes locked on Luce's. "Seth and Wayne found something else that's bad. Is it me or do things just keep getting worse?" The three guys made their way to the table and settled in. Jo put down her latte. "So, what have you got?"

Seth looked at Jo. "It's about you and Luce." As Jo started to ask the obvious question, he continued with urgency, "Let me get this out before either of you say anything. At the next Board meeting, Manny is planning to charge you two with gross negligence in performing your jobs, fraud for committing to the list of features you promised to deliver in GuardShark, and announce to the Board you're being fired for cause."

Jo angrily slammed her cup to the table, spewing a little geyser of latte foam. Wayne put a weathered hand on the table next to Jo. "Wait, let Seth finish. You need to hear the reason Manny is planning this move."

Seth pushed his Mac in front of the two women. "Here's the smoking gun email where Manny and someone he calls Lord&Master plan to get you and Luce off the team just before he sells McWare. That move would eliminate your combined compensation from the monthly expenses, and give the new owner less chance of success with GuardShark."

As Jo and Luce stared again in stunned silence, Steve frowned. "Lord&Master? That's creepy. Manny's making some sort of power move with this person, and he's willing to sacrifice the two most expert engineers to do it."

Jo grinned. "He underestimates our team, no surprise there. They would make any high-tech company successful."

Luce looked at Jo and Steve. "Do we know how to get everything we need for Thursday's Board meeting?" As they nodded, she picked up her cup. "Then let's stick to the plan to crash the Board meeting, let them see that GuardShark works, and take Manny down."

Seth slouched in his chair. "What, I don't get to have any fun?"

Jo nailed him with a knowing look. "You get to track down the hacker. I have the worst feeling that creep has more evil planned."

Seth teased, "What revenge are you planning for the sleazebag?"

Jo growled, "If I had my way, hackers would have to work for telemarketers."

Seth closed his Mac. "You're scary, Jo. I sure hope I can stay on your good side."

Jo fought the sudden flush that travelled through her body as she toasted, "Down with the sleazebags!" Ukulele sounds chimed from her and Luce's phones. She scanned the text and looked up at Luce with a big grin. "Take a look. Red Nails is busy trading email with that company where we walked out of the interviews."

Steve squinted down at the screen on Jo's phone. "Don't they do direct mail marketing?"

Jo waved her phone as she did a little dance. "Red Nails is all excited about working for that scummy company." Another ukulele sound sang out on the two phones. "Whoa, check this out. Look at the message she sent CJ. 'Manny is acting funny and I'm getting scared he knows about us, so I'm going to make up a story and leave tomorrow.'"

Luce scrolled down her phone's screen. "She sent a message to Manny that she needs to resign because her grandmother is very ill and needs long-term help. Wow, who isn't she lying to?"

Seth looked over Luce's shoulder. "Do we know anything about her relationship to CJ?"

Jo looked up at him. "He made a comment in an email a few days ago that he expected her to finish the job he taught her to do. It sounds like they've been working together for a while, but how can someone as stupid as Red Nails be useful to an evil genius like CJ?"

Seth stared at Jo. "In my experience, the idiot and the brainy one are usually using each other. We all know I'm not guiltless."

Jo stared back. "There's a big difference. You didn't demand a lot of money wired to an offshore account as payment for sabotage. And you laughed at our jokes."

Steve looked around the assembled group. "Before we all head home or back to the office, let's review all the people we need to check on, the tasks to finish, and the team's priorities for tomorrow."

Jo muttered, "If only we had time to write the software to give us twenty-four more hours in a day, we would have a fighting chance of finishing GuardShark and getting quality sleep. I've decided that, at least for tonight, I'm going home in time to have dinner with Grandma."

37

Change of Plans

Jo CLIMBED THE familiar stairs in the early evening darkness and crossed the wide front porch of Grandma's house. She stopped for a beat, frowning at the front door that stood ajar. *It's not like Grandma to leave the door open.* She slowly entered the house, closing the door behind her as she called out, "Hi Grandma, I'm home." No answer, but Gizmo bounded up, insistently meowing and pawing Jo's leg.

Grandma wasn't in the living room or kitchen, and the bathroom off the hall was empty. Jo gently pushed Grandma's bedroom door open, breathing a sigh of relief to see the sweet elderly lady lying on her bed. Jo walked softly to the bed and reached out to put her hand on Grandma's hand. Cold, clammy skin. Grandma's breath seemed shallow. Jo's heart skipped a beat.

"Grandma, are you OK? It's Jo. Can you open your eyes?"

Grandma struggled, her voice weak. "Honey, I need help. Cold … hard to breathe."

"OK, I'm calling for an ambulance, but I'm going to stay right here with you." Jo pulled out her iPhone, punched 911, quickly answered the dispatcher's questions for the address and Grandma's symptoms. The dispatcher stayed on the line for what seemed like an eternity before the sirens announced the ambulance's arrival seven minutes later. Jo led the EMTs to Grandma's room as her heart raced.

"Grandma, the paramedics are going to help you but I will be right here." Jo touched Grandma's arm before backing away. The crew gently moved Grandma onto a stretcher and into the ambulance, efficiently setting up an oxygen mask and saline line. Grandma looked even tinier in the big ambulance.

Jo called to the EMTs, "I'll follow in my car." They nodded, closed the ambulance doors and pulled out to the street with siren blaring and lights flashing.

Jo realized she still had the dispatcher on her iPhone. "The ambulance just left to take my Grandma to the hospital and I'm going to follow them."

The dispatcher replied, "You did all the right things. Can you find your grandmother's purse with her ID and insurance information to bring to the ER at Foothills Hospital?"

Jo sighed, grateful for the lifeline. "My mind went blank. Yes, I'll bring all her information. Thank you so much."

Jo locked the house and hurried down the stairs, mentally mapping her route to the hospital as Vixen purred to life. Tears welled as she focused on pulling onto the street, driving one block at a time toward the woman who was her whole life. Everything became simple, the next breath, the next block, the next turn. She pulled into the hospital parking lot and found a spot in the second row from the Emergency entrance. *Please God, please keep Grandma safe. I can't lose her. I love her so much.*

Inside the Emergency and Trauma Center at Boulder's Foothills Hospital, Jo felt dwarfed by the chair next to the registration clerk's desk, her trembling hands searching Grandma's wallet. The soft colors in the high-ceilinged admitting area, comfortable chair, and the quiet computer equipment spelled intelligent efficiency that gave Jo a sense of trust. "Her name is Illyena Galvan, and I'm her granddaughter." Jo handed the identification and insurance cards to the thirty-something black woman whose vibrant turquoise blouse was adorned with a hospital badge for Keeshia Grantham.

The clerk read Grandma's ID. "Born January 22, 1940. I don't see any previous hospital admittance for her. Has she had any illnesses?"

Jo shook her head, her hand gripping the arm of the chair. "No, Grandma never gets sick. She gets an annual check-up."

Keeshia made electronic copies of Grandma's ID and insurance cards, and handed them back to Jo with a smile. "Let me call the nurse to find out when you can see your grandmother."

Jo waited, feeling helpless, lost as minutes ticked by. Finally the clerk re-cradled the phone. "The nurse said it would be about twenty minutes before you can go back to her room. They are going to run some tests." She nodded to Jo's right. "You can have a seat on one of the couches."

Jo walked heavily to a sofa near the double doors leading to the medical area, relieved that Grandma was getting help just steps away, grateful for the state-of-the-art medical facility. *She's all that matters. I can't believe I ever thought work or anything else was worth worrying about. Oh my God, work, Luce. Gotta call Luce.*

Jo's heart raced as she punched Luce's speed dial.

"Hey, geekazoid, what's up?"

Jo's throat closed in a sob that cried out for her best friend. "Luce, Grandma … hospital …"

"Oh my God, Jo, what happened? I'm here for you. Where are you?"

Jo choked hard on the lump of terrified grief. She breathed, swallowed, and took another breath. "I'm at Foothills Hospital, waiting in ER. I found her nearly passed out. She looks bad, Luce."

"Jo, I can be at the hospital in ten minutes."

"No, Luce. I should be able to see Grandma in a few minutes."

Luce's voice was quietly reassuring. "You're lucky to have her, and she is lucky to have you."

Jo's voice wobbled as she said, "She's never sick. She's so healthy she'll outlive entire generations." A nurse came through the double doors and nodded to Jo. "The nurse is here, so I can see her now. I'm not sure when I'll be at work tomorrow."

"Don't worry about work. Take care of Grandma and take care of you, OK? That's all that matters right now. Call me and let me know what happened, no matter how late it is."

"OK, thanks, I will." Jo waved to the clerk as she headed through the double doors, walking down the row of individual ER rooms with medical equipment that felt more comforting with each step.

Grandma was in the third room, a digital monitor displaying her vital signs, a saline drip bag hanging on its rack next to the bed with the tiny but far from frail woman resting her beautiful head on the plump hospital pillow, swathed in a sea of soft blankets. Her long hair hung loose in a grey halo on the pillow. The nurse motioned Jo to sit in the chair she put next to the bed before pulling the curtain closed to leave the Galvan family alone.

Jo's hand found the older soft one, relieved to feel its warmth. Grandma stirred and opened her eyes. "Honey, I didn't mean to give you a scare."

"How do you feel? Is it easier to breathe?"

Grandma said weakly, "I can breathe OK. I feel a lot better, so nice to be warm. Sleepy."

Jo gently squeezed Grandma's hand. "Just rest and let the people here take care of you. I can stay with you."

Grandma's eyes closed as she whispered, "No honey, you go home, rest, eat some dinner. They will take care of me. I'm going to sleep."

Jo melted into a long hug with Grandma, feeling the soft cheek against hers. Jo blotted her tears from both of their faces. "I want to talk with the doctor before I go home."

As if on cue, the curtain opened on a slim, dark-haired Asian man holding an iPad. "I'm Dr. Liang. How are you feeling, Mrs. Galvan?"

Grandma's eyelids fluttered open. "I feel better, warm. I'm so tired. Do you know what's wrong with me?"

The doctor glanced at the monitor and looked back to Grandma. "Your sodium is quite low, which has lowered your blood pressure, and you are a bit anemic. With a couple of medications and rest, we should have you back to normal in a day or two. I wrote prescriptions for sodium tablets, an iron supplement, and some instructions for checking your blood pressure. Do you have a home blood pressure monitor?"

Grandma whispered, "No, I've never needed one."

Jo held Grandma's hand. "I can pick one up at the drugstore on the way home. Is there one you would recommend?"

The doctor turned to Jo. "I recommend a blood pressure device that has an arm cuff and a large digital display. I think they run around $60 and just take a couple of batteries. Any drugstore should have it."

Jo let go of Grandma's hand and typed the information into an iPhone note. "I'll get one and set it up for you, Grandma."

Grandma's eyes closed. "Sure, honey, whatever the doctor thinks is best. I just want to sleep."

The doctor noted something on his iPad. "Sleep is the best thing for you, Mrs. Galvan. It will take them an hour or two to get a room ready upstairs for you." Grandma snuggled down into the blankets.

Jo felt her heart give way as her voice faltered. "I've never seen her like this. She's always been so healthy."

The doctor spoke quietly. "These changes in blood chemistry can sneak up on someone her age. Her tests show everything else is healthy. I go off shift at 7:00 AM, but you can check with Admissions in the morning to find out her new room number, and the nurse on her floor can get you in touch with the doctor who will be following her." He made notes on the tablet screen before disappearing through the curtain.

Jo collapsed into the chair, scooting it closer to the bed. She held Grandma's hand, watching her breathe quietly, her eyes monitoring the soft folds of the blanket as they rose and fell in rhythm. She was suddenly as hungry as she was tired, and the idea of driving home felt like an Olympic event. She kissed the familiar cheek once more and gently squeezed the beautiful hand.

The curtain opened, and Jo read 'Kathy' on the name tag of the slender blonde woman who brought in a small tray of medication cups. Kathy smiled warmly. "Her numbers are already close to normal. She's just tired from the side effects of low sodium. People sometimes forget to drink enough water or eat enough food."

Jo's voice was shaky with emotion. "Grandma gets so involved working on her projects that she forgets basic things like lunch and staying hydrated."

Kathy nodded at Jo's iPhone. "If she's comfortable using a computer or an iPhone, email services like Outlook and Gmail have a way of setting alarm reminders."

Jo nodded, willing herself to ask the right questions as her energy ebbed. "I can set that up tonight when I go home. Do you have a list of the medications she will need to take and how often?"

Kathy checked Grandma's chart. "Sodium tab three times a day, iron supplement in the morning with food, and blood pressure medication twice a day, which could be at the same time as the first and last sodium tab to make it easier to remember." Jo typed notes into her iPhone. "Will someone be with her at home?"

Jo shook her head. "No, but there are several retired people in our neighborhood who drop over to gab and bring her things to fix. They would be happy to keep an eye on her."

Kathy closed Grandma's chart. "That's great to hear. So many people of her generation and older can easily get lonely and feel forgotten. She sounds pretty independent."

Jo grinned. "She's convinced she can do what she's always done, which is everything."

Kathy checked Grandma's pulse. "Does she still drive?"

"She has a driver's license but she sold her old car. I take her wherever she needs to go, or one of her friends take her."

Kathy laid the emergency pull cord next to Grandma's hand. "She should be fine at home as long as she gets more rest for a while and takes her medications."

An orderly came through the curtain with a thick blue blanket, tucking it around the small form. Grandma stirred. *She looks so peaceful.*

Kathy's voice was quiet, soothing, as she asked, "Are you doing OK? I know this must be scary for you."

Jo was startled by Kathy's question. She suddenly became aware of her own tears, and swallowed, forcing her voice over the lump in her throat. "She's my only family."

Kathy put a hand on Jo's shoulder. "It sounds like she has quite a support system, and she's comfortable with a computer, which gives her more ways of getting help and information. That's so important for an independent older person."

Jo grinned as a yawn seized her. "She is definitely an original. I need to go home and feed me and the kitties before I fall down."

Kathy picked up the empty water pitcher. "You go home and get some rest and food. The number for the nurses' station for this part of the floor and the direct number for this room are on the whiteboard over there by the door. Goodnight."

Jo added the phone numbers into her iPhone contacts. She turned back to Grandma, looked down at the soft sleeping face, and bent close to breathe in the faint lavender scent as she gently kissed the barely lined cheek. "I love you, Grandma," Jo whispered.

Closing her eyes, Jo let the sound and feel of Grandma's quiet breathing whisper to her. When she opened her eyes, she gazed out the window as a star twinkled in the night sky just above Sanitas Ridge in the distance.

Jo gathered the dregs of her energy, found her car, and drove home in the moonlight. Later, she sat in Grandma's rocking chair, staring down at Gizmo curled in her lap, rhythmically stroking the purring kitty. The plate with dinner crumbs rested on the end table. Her recent text message to Luce displayed in its little green box on her cell phone, followed by the white box with Luce's supportive response.

A new blood pressure monitor and extra AAA batteries sat in the Walgreen's bag. She held her iPhone, staring at the phone numbers for Grandma's room and the nearby nurses' station. *I'll get up at 6:00 AM and call the nurse to see how she's doing. They will call me if anything is wrong.*

Fatigue washed over her as she stumbled barefoot from the rocking chair and up the stairs to her room. From point A to point B, Jo crashed softly into her bed, still wearing her work clothes. She pulled the flannel sheet and blanket over her body, barely noticing Gizmo jumping up next to her chest and snuggling close as she fell asleep.

2:42 AM screamed in scarlet from the digital clock face, the cool night air in the moon's soft glow lost in the clock's taunting glare. The vision of Grandma dwarfed in her hospital bed broke Jo's heart. Jo's mind whirled. *Why do I feel like I can't breathe? Breathe, slow, breathe out, slow, breathe in. Itching, scratch my arm, now my shoulder, stop itching. Stop, breathe, slow. Gotta pee again, but I just peed. God, I hate this, hate being so afraid.*

Big unrelenting red digits screamed again, 2:44 AM. *There's way too much red in my life.*

2:47 AM. Jo's heart felt like it was beating its way out of her chest in a desperate attempt to flee. Worry gnawed, with anxiety clawing its own parallel path into her nerves. She sat on the floor in the spot that gave her the best view of the moon, getting lost in it as its cool glow calmed her. "Help me, please help me." *Why does it feel so weird to say something out loud when I'm alone late at night in my own room in the dark?*

The day's troubles seemed to whirl and swirl in electric sound bites that pulsated in the strobe blinks of goblin voices echoing in her head. *I could do a cartoon of throwing those ridiculous bobbleheads off a high cliff.* She chuckled as the comic images played out in her mind's eye. Minutes later, her head jerked. She had nodded off.

She crawled back into bed, snuggling next to Gizmo and Jig, who were purring away in their respective kitty cinnamon roll poses. Sleep welcomed her.

38

Strategy 101

To: rookie-pup
From: Lord&Master

Sharks are all about strategy, something best done in advance. Reactive strategy is an oxymoron. Perfect the ability to re-strategize in response to sudden opportunities or bad surprises. Longevity in this career depends on your ability to handle even the worst surprises as opportunities.

CJ followed the two girls to a coffee shop on Broadway, where they met with three men. CJ was able to photograph them with his cell phone. One was Steve Scott, and the two girls I matched to our corporate wiki page with photos of the engineering team. Take a look. Do you recognize the young man in the black leather jacket?

We have to stop those girls. CJ emailed that the business with the blonde has been handled. CJ is shark material, wastes no time on ethics or legalities.

I have one job for you. Every night, get in touch with CJ at 10:30 PM to confirm everything has gone according to plan. Send me an update no later than 11:00 PM. Do not drop the ball!

~Sent from my iPad

From the **CEO** Diary — MY FIRST TWEET!!

Big Dog CEO @BigDogCEO

@myfans   BREAKING NEWS!!

I'm breathing in
I'm breathing out
Cool, huh??!!

Reply   Retweet   Favorite   ... More

39

Glitch, My A**

Early Wednesday morning, Jo stared out the window of hospital room 204 toward the Flatirons. The rocky faces shimmered between pink and steel blue in the morning sun. *If only I could be sitting up there.* Jo's iPhone sang out Luce's ringtone, and she gently squeezed Grandma's hand before she walked out into the hallway to answer it.

Luce's voice sounded anxious. "I know it's not safe to dial and drive, but I think I'm in trouble. My car is acting weird and the rain is making it harder to control. I'm going to the Toyota dealer to get it checked so I'll be late to the meeting. Did you look at the email Seth forwarded to us?"

Jo maneuvered around a breakfast cart in the hallway. "I read through it before I left the house. That was weird where CJ orders Red Nails to stay at McWare to finish the job." Jo navigated around the medication trolleys. "I'm at the hospital with Grandma but I'm leaving for the office in a few minutes. I can work with Seth on Red Nails' smoking gun email linking CJ to Manny. Just call me if you need a ride from the dealership—"

Luce's scream pierced Jo's ear, as did the blare of honking horns. "Luce, what's happening?" Jo's world stopped for the second time in two days.

Luce screamed over more blasts from horns, "I don't have any brakes! Oh god, I'm on 63rd and I just flew through a red light at Spine Road. Jo, I don't know what to do! I can't breathe. Jo, I can't stop the car!"

Jo erupted, "Floor the brake, pump it, and floor it again." Jo realized she was screaming when a nurse raised her eyebrows.

Luce shrieked, "I'm standing on the brake! I don't know what to do!"

Jo's world disappeared in the horrifying vision of her best friend hurtling down 63rd in the unstoppable Prius. Her heart beat furiously and she caught her breath as she closed her eyes, envisioning the streets in the Gunbarrel area northeast of Boulder. "Luce, 63rd will start going up a hill in one more block. Pull over into the right lane. The car should start slowing down, Luce. Breathe. Feel the car slow down. Breathe."

Luce stumbled over her words. "OK, it's slowing down a little. But how do I get it to stop?"

Jo willed her voice to stay calm. "At the top of the hill you can turn right onto Longbow and right into the parking lot of the first building after the corner. Breathe, Luce. You're going to be OK."

Luce choked out, "OK, I'm turning right on Longbow."

Jo opened the door to a stairwell. "You're doing fine, Luce." Her words glanced off the angular walls and rails.

Luce whispered, "I'm letting the car roll into the entrance to the lot. Thank God it's empty."

The heavy door closed behind Jo as she pictured Luce in the Prius. "That's good. Now just let the car roll in a big circle around the lot until it slows down enough for you to bump into a curb without getting hurt."

Luce's voice quivered as she said, "OK, it's slowing down where the lot rises. I'm going to nudge my back tire on the curb."

Jo leaned against the cool concrete wall. "Be careful, Luce. You don't want to hit hard."

Luce choked, "OK, here it comes, I'm turning. The car is rolling close to the curb."

Jo gazed at the steel geometry of the angled railings that outlined the incrementing and receding hospital stairs, her hand gripping the phone. "Luce, are you OK?"

Luce sounded shaky but happy. "Yeah, I'm going to turn the wheels into the curb to stop the car."

Jo's eyes locked on the Emergency Exit instruction sign in screaming orange. "That's good, Luce. It's almost over."

Luce whispered, "I'm stopped. God, I can't believe I'm OK. I need to turn off the engine but my hands are shaking and I can't feel my fingers."

Jo commanded, "Luce, put the phone in your lap, turn off the car's power switch and set the parking brake." Hearing her voice echo off the stairwell's surfaces like a sound chamber, she continued quietly, "If you use both hands that will help you control the shaking. That's all you have to do, Luce. Just turn everything off, and keep breathing."

"OK, I'm laying down the phone." The longest minute in the world oozed at a snail's pace. Jo closed her eyes and watched the red sea of exploding stars displaying their fireworks show inside her eyelids. She realized she was holding her breath, and slowly breathed out, relaxing her grip on the hard plastic edge of the phone.

Luce sobbed, "It's off. The engine is off. Jo, I'm so scared. I can't move."

In a wave a relief, Jo realized she was crying too. "Luce, you're OK. Stay there. I'm coming to get you. Foothills Hospital is about five miles from where you are, so it won't take me long. I can stay on the phone with you until I get there, OK?" Jo hurried through the door and down the hall to room 204, the cell phone still pressed hard to her ear.

Crying, Luce replied, "Yes, I need to hear your voice."

Back in room 204, Jo put her arms quickly around Grandma, who was sitting in the hospital bed that seemed so big, and kissed her on the cheek. "I'll be gone for a few hours to do some work, Grandma, but I'll try to be back for lunch with you."

Grandma squeezed Jo's hand. "That would be nice, honey, but don't worry about coming back if you get busy."

Jo gently released Grandma's hand. "I'll call you later this morning. You rest, OK?"

"I will, honey." Grandma smiled, her face a healthy pink that made Jo's throat catch.

Jo hurried out of room 204, and swallowed hard before saying to Luce, "I'm back, and I'm walking to the car."

Luce's voice sounded more decisive. "Jo, let me call you back after I call the Toyota dealer to send the tow truck." Jo hurried through the corridors and across the parking lot through the light rain to Vixen, picking up Luce's ring as she started the engine. "It really helps that you're on the phone with me. I would really be scared without you to talk to."

Jo put in her earbuds before steering out of the parking lot. "I'm glad you could talk to me last night. Scary isn't as scary when I have you to talk to."

Luce's voice sounded almost normal. "I feel like a balloon that lost its air. I'm exhausted."

Jo felt the tears rolling down her face. "You got through a scary thing, Luce. That's why you feel tired. I'll be there in ten minutes."

"I'm going to get out of the car just to move a little. I need to shake off all these nerves. OK, I'm leaning on the car in the rain. Hey, my car is my support system, not something that's going to kill me." Luce's laugh was edgy.

Jo exhaled, the steady clip of the windshield wipers strangely comforting. "It's good to hear you laugh. I'll stay on the phone with you until I get there. How do you feel?"

Luce sounded more like her old self. "I'm breathing in, I'm breathing out."

Jo breathed and smiled. "You really should Tweet that."

"I'm not that social." Luce's voice was lighter.

Jo drove down Foothills Parkway to the Jay Road exit, and a few minutes later accelerated through the yellow traffic light at 63rd and Twin Peaks. "Yeah, that's more Shit-For-Brains' speed. I'm coming up 63rd, getting close to Longbow. I spy a sea foam green Prius and a blonde engineer standing next to it in the rain." Jo saw Luce waving.

"Hey, I see you, I see Vixen. You're here."

Jo steered Vixen into the parking lot and stopped beside Luce's Prius, turned off the engine and jumped out. The two best friends hugged each other as the soft rain fell around them.

Jo squeezed Luce's shoulder. "I'll text Steve that we'll be late. Are you sure you want to go to the meeting, or would you rather I took you home or to Toyota?"

Luce shook her damp head. "No, I need to focus on work, otherwise I'll just keep reliving the nightmare." Jo stood next to Luce, grateful for her best friend's safety, oblivious to the rain.

A few minutes later, a tow truck lumbered into view on Longbow and pulled into the parking lot. Jo waited while Luce gave the tow driver her information. Luce got in the Mustang. "Thanks for coming to get me."

Jo shivered from the sheen of water on her skin. "I'm just glad you were able to stop the car without getting hurt."

Luce bucked her seat belt. "I don't know if I'm OK or not, but I sure feel a lot safer now. What the hell happened to my car? Have you ever heard of brakes just giving out like that? I need to stop thinking about that. Let's get back to finding the hacker."

Jo started the engine. "The Toyota mechanics will fix it. So what else were you saying about Red Nails' email?"

Luce's voice went up a notch in pitch. "Oh, right, we took time out to keep me from dying. Manny and Red Nails were talking about CJ's genius skills and that he's never been caught."

Jo snickered. "Sounds like our hacker. It's funny the hacker uses the same initials as Red Nails."

Luce deadpanned, "RN? Ha, I'm funny again. Maybe she limits her friends to people with the initials CJ to give her teeny brain a break. Anyway, I just know he's out there trying to hack more of our files."

Jo looked at Luce. "Maybe it's a she. Whatever, that creep is like a disgusting cockroach, only with two legs." They continued to speculate about the villain's strategy on the short drive to McWare.

40

Brake This

As Jo AND Luce walked through the Tomb door, Steve, Wayne, and Seth got up from the conference table to greet them. Steve put a hand on Luce's shoulder. "Boy, is it ever good to see you."

Luce shook her head. "I might never drive again."

Wayne winked at Luce. "Ma'am, I think you've got four chauffeurs." The nods and quiet smiles around the little group confirmed the offer.

"Works for me." Luce sat down shakily as the others joined her at the table. "I need to think about work, not killer brakes. So, who are CJ and Lord&Master, and what are they plotting with Manny?"

Jo frowned. "I'm having trouble connecting the dots. I get that Manny has an overblown ego and would gravitate toward anyone who paid attention to him. But how does that turn into working so hard to get GuardShark and McWare to fail?"

Steve re-read the email on his Mac. "It sounds like someone invested a lot of money in McWare and agreed to Manny's leadership as CEO. Manny is all ego and no brains, easy prey for any powerful person who shows interest in him."

Luce looked at Seth and Wayne. "Did you find anything that can be used to track down CJ? He's still out there."

Wayne nodded. "Seth and I are combing through information hidden in email messages and the log from the sabotage of SharkNet's test data a few nights ago."

Jo massaged her temples. "It feels like the hacker is watching all of us. He's probably hacking us as we speak." No one disagreed with her as they each began researching a different set of email messages.

At the ukulele ringtone, Jo grabbed her iPhone. "Hey, look at this. Red Nails just emailed everyone that she has to resign to take care of her sixty-year-old, ailing grandmother. Let's review, she's in her thirties, so her mother and grandmother both got pregnant at fourteen."

Luce scanned her phone screen. "Every family has traditions."

Jo muttered, "In their case, it's flunking math." She re-read the message, frowning. "The good news is she's leaving. Something feels off. We don't know what she's really up to. None of her emails mention a new job."

Luce put down her phone. "Maybe it has something to do with that demand from CJ to 'finish the job today.'"

Jo scrolled through Red Nails' latest email. "Does anyone else get a bad feeling that Red Nails has one last round of dirty work to do before she leaves McWare?"

Steve looked up from reading the email. "It has to involve CJ and Manny since she seems to be the link between them."

Jo frowned. "What could she be up to? She can't possibly know anything technical. No one's that great at acting."

Steve put down his phone and looked straight at Jo. "She follows instructions and she is willing to do whatever she is told without knowing or caring about the consequences. That makes her very useful to criminals."

Jo snapped her fingers. "That's what she and CJ have in common, no conscience."

Seth looked at Wayne. "We should bring them up to date. We installed GuardShark on McWare's network and configured it to send a warning for every attempt to access McWare's computers by an unknown user."

Wayne nodded. "The system response will be a bit slower for opening email and saving files people might be editing, but we can live with that until we catch CJ."

Jo sighed. "Good thinking. I wish the Board could see this. The rest of us should keep monitoring email between Red Nails, Manny, CJ, and that Lord&Master creep. This war isn't over yet." Nods all around as they settled in at the Tomb's table.

Jo's stomach was already talking when they broke for lunch. She and Luce pulled out of Alfalfa's Market parking lot. Luce held the bag with their lunches, the fragrance of roasted red pepper hummus with garlic eggplant on fresh-baked ciabatta bread filling Vixen's cab. "Are you sure Grandma is up for an extra visitor?"

Jo accelerated through a yellow light. "She was so happy when I told her you were coming with me. I told her what happened with your car this morning." Ten minutes later, Jo parked in the visitor's lot at the hospital. "Grandma is anxious to go home. She misses fixing things and having her own schedule. She's being more patient than I would be."

Luce grinned. "She's all homemade soup and socket wrenches."

Thirty minutes later, as they finished eating, Grandma laid her fork on the hospital tray. "I'm feeling a lot better. I hope the doctor lets me go home today."

Jo glanced at the numbers on the monitors. "They want to make sure you will be OK at home. Did they run more tests this morning?"

Grandma sipped from her water glass. "Yes, before breakfast. I keep thinking about the last little adjustments I need to make to Don's lawn mower."

Jo said gently, "Grandma, you might want to take it easy for a few days. The lawn mower can wait."

Grandma shook her head stubbornly. "I'm stronger than you think I am. Oh, Luce, I wanted to ask you about what happened to your Prius."

Luce stopped mid-bite, shrugging. "My brakes went out as I was driving to work this morning in the rain. I was so scared, but Jo calmed me down. I've never had trouble with my Prius."

Grandma pushed her tray table away. "It sounds like the same problem Don and Rachel had with their new Prius a few years ago. It turned out to be a defective part of the brake system. You should Google for Prius brake failures."

Jo tapped quickly on her phone's screen. "Found it. Wow, it's almost always a complete brake failure on wet roads. Luce, you really are lucky that you and your car weren't hurt. Here, look."

Luce read from the phone's screen. "Some older Priuses have a braking problem when a faulty computer chip creates a lag in response between the braking system and the antilock brakes, especially over bumpy or wet roads." Luce stared at the little screen before handing the cell back to Jo. Her hand shook as she speed-dialed on her iPhone. "I'm calling Toyota. Hi Sean, this is Luce Savodsky with the light green Prius that was towed this morning after the brakes failed. Did you find out anything yet?" Her face turned to stone.

Jo stood up. "What is it, Luce?"

Luce held up a finger to signal wait-a-minute. "No, I've never had any of the computer chips in my car replaced, or had any problem with the brakes."

Jo moved closer to Luce. "What's going on?"

"The police? OK, I'll talk to the police. I can rent a car for however long it takes for the new chip to come in. OK, I'll look for your email. Thanks, Sean."

Grandma looked angry. "Does the mechanic think someone tampered with your car?"

Luce's face looked haunted. "He's convinced someone replaced my car's original chip with an old bad one." Her eyes were glassy. "He said the computer chip in my car is a defective one that was discontinued three years before my car was manufactured. He's printing out documentation I can use to file a report with the police."

Jo nearly dropped her sandwich. "Someone sabotaged your car's brake system? What kind of crooks are we dealing with?"

Grandma frowned. "Honey, you didn't tell me someone was trying to harm you. What's going on at your company?"

Jo angrily threw her wrapper in the trash. "Our computer files were hacked but no one was in physical danger, until now. Someone is trying to keep us from getting our product done on time so the company will fail."

Luce shook as she put the iPhone in her lap. "I'm really scared. They know where we live. Don't you park your car outside too?"

Jo nodded. "I wasn't home until late last night. I barely got to Walgreen's before they closed. I had to pick up a home blood pressure monitor for Grandma."

Luce's voice hardened. "What the hell are these people going to do next?"

Grandma's voice was demandingly protective. "Have you talked to the police about the problems at your company?"

Jo shrugged. "We didn't have a reason to talk to the police until now. We're pretty sure the CEO of McWare is behind all the sabotage, and our team is trying to find the hacker who is doing his dirty work."

Grandma reached for Jo's hand. "You two be careful. Someone is trying to hurt you."

Luce spewed anger. "I've had it with Manny and his nasty friends."

Jo stood up, reaching for Grandma's hand. "We need to go back to work for a meeting with our team, but I'll call you later this afternoon and also talk to the doctor to see when I can spring you out of here."

Grandma winked. "Go get the bad guys, but be safe. Just call me when you get a chance."

Jo gave Grandma a big hug. "I will."

Luce reached out to squeeze Grandma's hand. "Thanks for figuring out what was wrong with my car. You're an honorary geek in my book."

41

Surprises 101 (The Good, The Bad, and The Really Ugly)

To: rookie-pup
From: Lord&Master

What did I tell you about turning off your iPhone? We have to be in constant touch now.

You must stay on top of everything. We've had to deal with a couple of surprises, but that's good practice for you. This is the most critical time in our game plan. Our strategy is always the same. Do whatever you need to do to win.

You did a good job of getting CJ's report to me last night, but we need an update. Find out what Cinda is really up to, but don't go through CJ. It's too risky. Do not expose our vulnerability because of your unwarranted level of trust in her.

We must determine how much damage she has already done to us, or might be planning. Do not be fooled by her appearance of stupidity.

After all, she got you to trust her enough to share a good deal of key information about our plans, so she can't be as stupid as she acted.

We have set up our opponents to make wrong moves, but we must stay several moves ahead of them. There can be no mistakes now. This is war.

This is a fight to the death, winner takes all. Do whatever you have to do to win. It's all or nothing now.

~Sent from my iPad

42

Safety In Numbers

Jo MARCHED RESOLUTELY into the Tomb with Luce in step just behind her. "Grandma might be our new secret weapon."

Steve closed the Tomb door. "We got your text message. Someone must be willing to do anything to stop us from finishing GuardShark."

Luce's hand shook as she pulled out a chair. "The Toyota mechanic gave us evidence we turned over to the Boulder Police."

Jo said grimly, "CJ must be a hack of all trades if he sabotages computers and cars. If that creep knows Luce's address, it's probably my turn next."

Seth looked up from his Mac. "Wayne and I finally found the IP address of the computer used to send the messages, but we need FBI help to trace through the extra hops behind firewalls on systems in other countries. Sabotaging your car points to someone close by."

Wayne frowned. "No offense, Luce, but I'm wondering why he messed with your car? Jo's Mustang has the old kind of brakes with lines that are easy to cut."

Jo's anger was palpable. "I was at the hospital with Grandma and then at Walgreen's, so I didn't get home until late last night. But this thug is nearby."

Seth frowned. "Be careful, Jo. Can you park your car out of sight tonight?"

Luce interrupted just before Jo spoke. "Jo and I talked to Officer Alvarez at the Boulder Police station about an idea, but I don't like it because it's dangerous."

Jo waved a hand. "I'm going to be the safest little geek in the world thanks to my new friends, the Boulder County fuzz."

Steve frowned at Jo. "Don't set yourself up as a target. This jerk's way too dangerous."

Seth looked at Jo, his voice like quiet steel. "Steve's right, Jo. From the email, it's clear our villain will do anything necessary. Don't take chances with this guy."

Jo gripped the chair arms. "It's OK. Officer Alvarez made me promise to follow the plan to the letter. Did any of you see the message Red Nails got a few minutes ago? CJ's pissed at her for not using secure email."

Seth sat back, crossing his muscular arms. "Sounds like CJ could do a testimonial for GuardShark. Maybe we could do a marketing campaign for hackers."

Jo growled, "The only special version I'm doing for hackers would wreak sudden death on *their* systems." She turned to Luce. "Did you see the announcement email for Red Nails' going away lunch tomorrow? She won't be an employee at McWare after today, so she's meeting people at the Spruce Restaurant at the Boulderado. Guess who wasn't invited?"

Luce put an index finger to her chin and rolled her eyes. "Could it be anyone with a brain and an engineering degree?" At Jo's nod she beat a little cha-cha rhythm with her fists. "I love being rejected."

Jo turned to Seth and Wayne. "Besides CJ the criminal, what else have you found out about Manny's plans?"

After more discussion, Jo summarized what they knew. "So, it's clear Manny and Red Nails set us up from the beginning for

GuardShark to fail and let all the blame fall on us. They are just shining examples of consensus."

Steve stood at the whiteboard making a list. "Good thing we found out the agenda for the Board meeting. Jim texted me they will have all the results from tonight's SharkNet run by 7:00 AM. Sherm and Vijay have been practicing the demo and role-playing the questions we might get from the Board and investors."

Luce frowned. "I wonder what's in the legal papers Manny is so desperate for Red Nails to sign at McWare's attorney."

Jo cleared her throat. "That would be the charges against you and me for some trumped-up crime. I just hope we can get the Board to listen to us."

Luce crossed her arms, her face set. "Piece of cake. Manny, Red Nails, and CJ have no clue that we've got the real GuardShark software and the real test run results hidden on our secret computer. But I won't relax until it's over."

Seth nodded. "Amen to that. Those messages between Manny and Lord&Master are pretty sinister."

Steve capped the marker and laid it on the tray. "Is it me, or does Lord&Master sound perverted? That creep is evil, but also intelligent and savvy. Why would he work with Manny?"

Jo stretched and stood up. "I need to head over to the hospital in a few minutes."

Luce put her hand on Jo's shoulder. "Please promise me you will be careful, and let me know what happens, OK? No matter what time it's over tonight. Say hi to Grandma for me."

Jo grinned. "Don't worry, I want to live to see who wins the cartoon contest." She stretched her neck and shoulders against the stress of multiple worries before packing her Mac into her backpack and heading to the parking lot.

Jo drove on auto-pilot to Foothills Hospital, her mind rehearsing tonight's plan. As she parked the car near the hospital's main entrance, she brought herself back to her visit with Grandma. *Don't give Grandma any reason to worry.*

In room 2004, Jo leaned over to hug Grandma, playfully pointing at the salmon on her dinner plate. "Looks like room service at the Boulderado."

Grandma offered her fork to Jo. "Are you hungry? They gave me more than I can eat."

Jo shook her head and winked. "I'm making a grilled cheese sandwich for dinner, with onions and habaneros. I need comfort food. Besides, the nurse might report me if she saw me stealing food from a patient."

Grandma grinned. "Did the police find the crook responsible for Luce's brakes?"

Jo shrugged. "They're working on it." Jo didn't like stretching the truth, but she didn't want Grandma to worry about her part in tonight's scheme. "So are you sure about going home tomorrow?"

Grandma's voice was resolute. "Honey, I am so ready to go home I would bribe you to take me now if I thought it would work."

Jo smiled. "Let's trust the doctor on this one. Your nurse Kathy showed me how we can set up a timer on your computer to remind you when you need to take medication."

Grandma grinned. "Oh, so now my computer will nag me."

Jo laughed. "You need to rest during the day until you feel stronger."

Grandma's voice took on a stubborn tone. "Honey, I'm feeling fine, and I promise I won't overdo it. I miss seeing my friends."

Jo grinned sheepishly. "OK, I just don't want you to end up in the hospital again. It will be great to have you home."

They hugged each other close, but Jo couldn't keep her mind from racing ahead. *We've gotta get that snake tonight.*

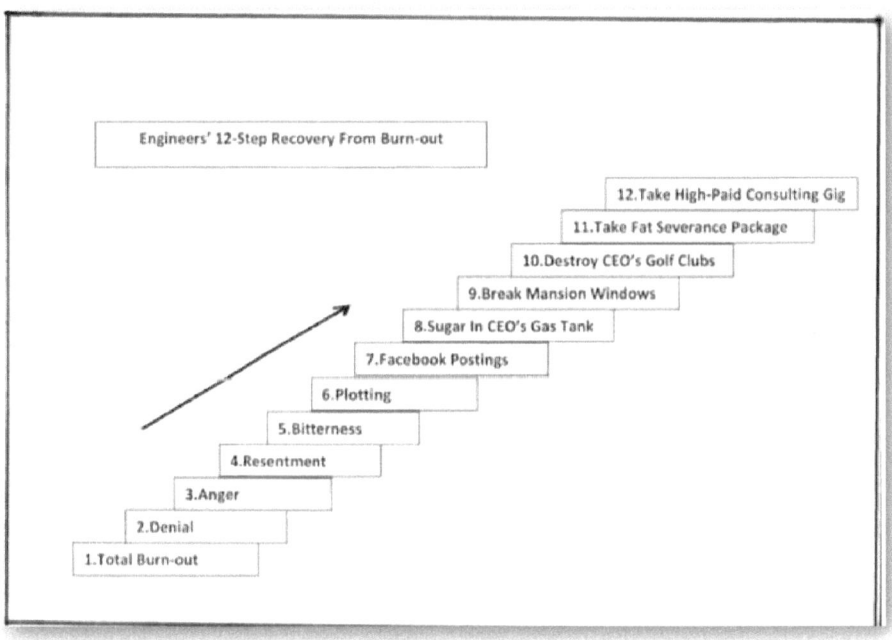

43

Bait and Switch

THE SOFT MOON cast a faint shadow of Vixen's steering wheel onto the dashboard as Jo slowly removed the key from the ignition. She sat for a moment, drinking in the sense of knowing with complete confidence that at this second it was safe, safe to drive. *I will never again take that for granted. I can feel him watching.*

Jo's hand moved to the slim device attached to the front belt loop on her jeans, pressed the button twice, waited the longest second of her life for the vibration, pressed the button once, and got out of the car, grabbing her backpack. She locked the car as usual and tried to walk as normally as possible to the front steps and across the wide porch. Her hand shook a bit in time with the pounding of her heart as she unlocked the front door. She went inside and locked the door behind her before turning on the lamp in the living room. *Step one, check.*

Jo mentally reviewed the list of instructions. She went to the kitchen to get a glass of water without turning on a light. She went upstairs to her bedroom, unloading her Mac from her backpack. In the darkness, she pulled out the large lightweight plastic object. *It feels like a weird-shaped beach toy. I wish I was at the beach instead of here.*

Jo put her mouth over the air nozzle and blew into it for five minutes, feeling light-headed. She crawled across the floor, pushing the object the short distance to her desk chair, pulled the chair out and placed the inflated object on the chair, all the while crouched close to the floor. She set up her computer on the desk, and quickly reached her hand to click on her desk lamp. She crawled slowly across the floor to the doorway and down the top three stairs before standing up. Jo carefully descended the stairs, barely making a sound. At the bottom of the stairs, she tiptoed through the dark rooms to the small back hallway leading to Grandma's bedroom.

A cool shaft of soft moonlight fingered through the old lace curtains, etching a filigree pattern on the creamy quilt that covered Grandma's bed. Jo edged her way along the wall in the dark room to the reading chair, crawled into it, and snuggled into the softness of the hand-knit cashmere throw, curling her legs under her. She closed her eyes, pressed the button twice, waited a second for the vibration, and pressed the button once. *Step two, check.*

Jo opened her eyes and gazed out the window at the quilt of stars. In her mind's eye she saw only Vixen, sitting in the carport, bathed in moonlight. *I know you're out there. Don't hurt Vixen. Don't hurt me.*

Gizmo's little meow announced her arrival in Grandma's bedroom. Jo relaxed as the grey tabby's white boots padded silently across the carpet before leaping like a graceful afterthought into her lap. Gizmo arranged herself into a lap shape, settling in as Jo automatically stroked the soft fur. She sighed, sinking into the secret little cave of cashmere and kitty fur.

Jo's heart hammered on her nerves, pulsing in waves of anxiety like an electric current. Instinctively, her hand massaged Giz's tummy. She forced herself to focus on the kitty's purr.

Breathe, rub, purr.

The curtain moved and Jo flinched, tensing until she felt the tiny breeze whisper across her face. *I can do this. I can wait as long as it takes. Grandma is safe. I'm going to be safe. God, I hope I don't have to pee until this is over.*

Breathe, rub, purr.

Fifteen minutes later, insistently repeating bongs assaulted Jo's ears, accompanied by loud banging sounds. Gizmo woke up and leapt to the floor for safety. Jo realized someone was ringing the doorbell and pounding on the front door. She stood up, shedding the cashmere throw as she steadied herself with a hand on the back of the chair, and quickly went to the hall. Making her way to the darkened dining room, she heard shouts from beyond the front door.

"Jo, police! Open the door!"

Jo switched on the dining room light, blinking against the blinding glare, and shouted, "I'm coming!" She ran across the living room, unlocked and opened the front door to a dark-haired thirty-something, physically fit female officer whose face floated in the darkness above the navy police uniform.

"We got him, Jo. He dressed in black like some idiot's idea of a ninja with night vision goggles and tools that could be used to cut your brake lines. We grabbed him as soon as he was on his back in the carport, inching his way under your car."

Jo felt her throat go dry as she choked on her fear. "Are you sure my car is OK to drive?"

Officer Alvarez nodded as she directed her flashlight toward Vixen. "Your car is fine, your house is fine, and he was alone. You did great, followed the script perfectly. CJ won't be hurting anything or anyone anymore."

Jo shook her head. "I was terrified. I wouldn't last five seconds in your job. What do we do now?"

The officer listened to a brief radio report before responding, "Could you come down to the station with me now to take a look at him through one-way glass to see if you recognize him? It won't take long and I can bring you right back home. It would help us a lot, even if you've never seen him before."

Jo's heart skipped a beat. "OK, just make sure he can't see me and doesn't even know I'm there. He has bad friends."

The officer nodded. "We won't go into the precinct until I get confirmation that he is locked in the interrogation room. I'll take you straight into the viewing room and straight out afterwards."

Jo took a breath, her voice as shaky as her nerve endings. "OK, let's go before I lose my nerve."

An hour later, Jo got out of Officer Alvarez's police car. "Thanks for everything. Let me know if I have to do anything else. Goodnight." She wearily opened the gate and closed it behind her, marshaling her energy toward the front steps.

Jo turned around at the front door as Officer Alvarez slowly drove down the empty dark street. She felt her energy evaporate, letting her knees fold as she sat down on the top step of the familiar front porch stairs. She pulled out her iPhone, selecting the second number listed on her favorite contacts. Her voice broke as she said, "Luce, the cops got CJ. You'll never guess who he is."

"I don't believe it," Luce said when Jo told her the man's identity.

They talked in relief for a few minutes before Jo warned, "Luce, the police said we can't tell anyone about CJ's arrest until they finish the investigation. There are too many unanswered questions."

"Got it, my lips are sealed."

Jo yawned. "I'm dead tired. I need to sleep."

Luce's laughter was like music. "You are a super sleuth, and darn lucky. I'll see you in the morning. Goodnight."

Jo sighed as she clicked off her phone, breathing in the soft night air. She used the railing to pull herself up and started to open the front door but stopped. Noticing the keys still in her pocket, she asked out loud, "Why not give it a try?" She walked down the stairs to Vixen, unlocked the driver's side door, and got in. Inside the car, she felt simple gratitude for the long moment of silence, broken only by her breathing.

Jo felt strength return to her voice, her body, her mind. She laughed, feeling free of the fear that had clutched her in its claws until an hour ago. She started the engine, eased off the clutch so the car rolled back in obedience to reverse gear, then clutched and applied the brake. The car instantly came to a dead stop, and everything in Jo's being melted in a sea of tears as relief washed over her.

Her chest ached from holding her body tight against days of fear, and the sudden visceral release left her feeling weightless. The free-fall juxtaposed with the immediacy of the thick leather seats beneath and behind her, and she wondered at how her world had suddenly stopped spinning. She felt suspended in one beautifully quiet moment. She realized she was no longer crying. She was home, and home was safe.

Jo turned off the engine and remembered to get Grandma's mail before going into the house. She was grateful to be locking the door for good as she left the unopened mail on the kitchen table and climbed the stairs to her bedroom one last time. She cracked up laughing when she saw the life-sized blow-up doll sitting in her desk chair in front of her personal computer. Jig jumped up on Jo's bed with a 'scuse-me-lady look.

"Jig, if I wasn't so tired, I would take a selfie with the blow-up doll for Luce. The cops can do their own work from now on. I can't handle the stress."

Jo closed her laptop, clicked off the desk lamp, and stripped down to a tee-shirt and underwear. She took the familiar five steps in the darkness to her bed, and fell asleep as her head hit the pillow.

From the Desk
of the
CEO

Seven Habits
of
Highly Effective CEOs

☑ Greed
☒ Envy
☑ Wrath
☑ Sloth
☑ Gluttony
☑ Lust
☑ Pride

44

Some Money Costs Too Much

"**M**E-OWRL! ME-OWRL!" Jo awoke, startled by Giz's yowling, her eyes targeting the screaming red digital 6:14 AM. "Giz, did I forget to feed you and Jig? What's that?"

The doorbell rang insistently, followed by a long cascade of knocking. Jo jumped out of bed, pulled on her jeans, and stumbled downstairs. The opening riff of "R-E-S-P-E-C-T" singing from her iPhone announced Luce's incoming call. "Luce, are you OK? Are you outside on my porch?" Jo asked as she crossed the living room.

Luce's voice was all high-wire anxiety. "No, the courier must have come to my place first and now she's at your place."

"What courier?" Jo coughed to clear the gravel from her throat. "What are you talking about?"

The doorbell screamed again, sending Gizmo scampering ahead, jumping on the rocking chair next to the couch where Jig was already standing up, looking intently at the front door.

Luce's voice sharpened. "Just be sure it's a woman with a brown ponytail, a denim jacket, and unbelievable make-up before you open the door, Jo."

Jo pushed the curtain aside and peered out the window. "Yep, that's her. Hold on." Jo kept the phone to her ear as she opened the front door with a defensive frown. The woman fitting Luce's description was standing on the porch holding a slim manila envelope.

"Are you Josephina Galvan? Do you have some identification?" The face was engulfed by black-mascaraed twin tarantulas in the spots usually inhabited by eyes, in high contrast with a wall of white lipstick. *Is that the prototype for lips?*

Jo intentionally sharpened her tone. "Excuse me? Where's *your* identification? You've got five seconds to give me a reason not to call the police."

"These papers are for Josephina Galvan. It is my job to deliver them to you." The tarantulas moved up and down in unison as the white wax lips opened to make little shapes for talking sounds.

Jo turned her back on tarantula eyes and lowered her phone voice. "Luce, did you get a manila envelope of papers delivered to you by White Lips? What is it? OK, did you show her ID? I don't like this, but I guess I'll do what you did."

Jo turned back to the doorway, switching to her Project Leader voice. "My ID is in my backpack, but I need your business card. I'm serious about the police. I'm working with them on two crimes and I have to keep them informed about everyone who contacts me, especially strangers."

"OK, OK, here is a business card. Geez, you and the blonde sound like you're reading from the same script." White Lips handed Jo a business card for Boulder County Courier, Tanyiaa Baskinson, as Jo held up her Colorado driver's license. The tarantula eyelashes squinted at the plastic rectangle in Jo's hand. "OK, sign here." She held out an iPad, and after Jo autographed it, handed over the envelope.

Jo took it without an acknowledgment, closed the door and turned on the lamp. The sound of White Lips' steps died away. Jo stared at the manila envelope printed with the name of Levin and McInerny, Attorneys, LLC at a Pearl Street address.

"Jo?" Luce's voice shrieking from her iPhone startled her.

Jo felt her anger's rising tide as she crashed full force back into reality. "Luce, what the hell is going on? Is this the legal stuff Manny and Red Nails cooked up, charging us with fraud and negligence and all that other phony crap?"

Luce's voice punctuated commands. "Open the envelope, Jo. Take out the papers."

Jo frowned as she followed Luce's directions. "You sound funny, Luce. Whatever this is, we'll figure out how to deal with it."

Luce's voice dissolved into tearful pleading. "Jo, sit down before you start reading. Please. We need to go through this line by line together. I'm having trouble breathing." Luce's voice broke and trailed off.

Jo sat in Grandma's rocking chair and switched on the glass-globed lamp. "It's OK, Luce. I'm sitting down. Let's see, looks like page one is a formal statement that McWare's officers have reason to investigate me for fraud, gross negligence, and theft of intellectual property. So far I see a lot of words but nothing specific." Jig and Giz nestled at Jo's feet.

Luce's voice came in short gasps. "Look at the second page, Jo."

Jo let the words on the page shape her mental images. "OK … yeah … the language is pretty threatening, but it's just words on paper. Even if McWare's Board of Directors actually press charges and take us to court, there are a hundred steps in that process, and we're on step two."

Luce gasped for breath. "I know, Jo, but it says they are planning to fire us for cause unless we resign at the attorney's office by noon today."

The photocopy of a cashier's check was printed with watermark patterns for security. Jo caught the sheet before it slid to the carpet. Her breath caught in her throat. *Twenty thousand dollars.* "Did you get a copy of a cashier's check? They're bribing us to disappear before the Board meeting."

Luce choked out, "After you called last night and told me the cops caught that CJ creep, I felt like we could do anything. But now I'm so scared. What are we going to do, Jo?"

Jo took a deep breath. "I'm scared too, and it's not even seven in the morning! Do these people also double as firing squads?"

Luce's hiccupping laugh came over the phone. "You crazy weirdo. I'm glad you're my friend."

Jo's voice surged with renewed energy. "You know what? We've got a bunch of friends who are as crazy and brilliant as we are, and damn it, *we are doing this*! Are you with me, girlfriend?"

Luce's voice was louder. "You bet I am."

Jo rocked the chair as Giz and Jig looked up at her, startled. "We're going to get that sack of doo-doo and the rest of his creepy partners in crime."

Luce's laughter invaded the phone. "Let's do it. OK, it's 6:45 in the AM. It's Board meeting day and, if we're lucky, Manny's last day as CEO. I just wish we had more proof that ties CJ to Manny."

Jo's voice took on an edge as the weight of fear fled. "We've got enough. It's time to get dressed and put on our game faces. I'll pick you up and text Seth and Steve to meet us at Ozo's. Can you text Wayne?"

Luce crowed, "Let's get that slimy idiot once and for all."

Jo yelled, sending Giz and Jig scampering, "That sleazebag is going down!"

* * *

The high-pitched whine of a well-tuned Norton Commando 961 SF made Jo smile, automatically turning from the counter at the coffee shop to check out the sleek machine Seth wheeled deftly into a parking space, the powerful black alpha bike positioned well away from the LifeSaver-colored automobiles. Her eyes caressed the lines of the beautifully powerful British bike, chrome polished to a mirror finish that glinted in the early morning sun.

Jo followed Seth out of the corner of her eye until he and Wayne walked in the door, followed by Steve. "That was fast. You must be the wash-and-wear kind of geeks."

Luce turned to the guys. "Thanks for meeting us. I freaked out when that courier showed up at my house at 6:00 AM. I just lost it."

Jo nodded. "You and me both. I wanted to sick the kitties on that bowling alley reject of a courier, but I guess she was just doing her job."

Seth shook his head. "You've been through back-to-back hell and you're still cracking jokes." He ordered a double americano after Steve ordered herbal tea.

Jo turned to follow Luce to a table, but couldn't resist tossing a response over her shoulder. "Comedy is survival."

Jo sat down next to Luce. As the three men sat down at the table, Wayne tried to read the papers in front of Luce. "What exactly did the papers from the attorney say?"

Luce took a breath before explaining, "There is a vague statement about having evidence that I committed fraud, gross negligence, and stole intellectual property. But it's really all about the check."

Steve and Wayne chorused, "Check?"

Jo pulled the manila envelope out of her backpack, spreading out three typed pages and the check in the middle of the table. "Actually, it's a copy of a check. Twenty grand, right here in big numbers and words. There's a formal agreement that I have to sign and present to the attorney by noon today to get the real check. If Manny believes Luce and I would ever sign that thing, he must believe pigs can fly."

Seth picked up his americano. "Let me guess. You would be signing away your right to pursue legal action to refute the charges, and agreeing to resign from McWare today, before the Board meeting."

Wayne shook his head. "Congratulations. You've officially been bribed."

Luce grinned. "Not until I sign the form and cash the check."

Jo held up her three pages and the photocopy of the check. "Here is what failure to bribe looks like." She tore the pages in half from top to bottom to a round of applause and cheers.

Luce's triumphant grin echoed in her voice. "Me too." She ripped her pages and laid them on top of Jo's pile. "That really felt good."

Steve ruffled the little pile of torn papers with his plate-sized hand. "And the beauty of your technique is that we can still read them. I think these documents would be very interesting for the Board members and investors to see this afternoon."

Jo sat up. "That's a good idea. Let's make a final list of what we're presenting to the Board."

Luce suddenly looked serious. "Do we know where it's being held? Can we just barge in?"

Seth put down his cup, reaching for pieces of Jo's torn papers. "It's in the Driftwood Room at the Boulderado. I doubt the door will be locked."

Luce frowned. "I didn't recognize any names except Glaston Wimple and Lonnie Schuster's father. Lonnie's probably given him an earful of crap about us."

Wayne looked around the table. "So what's our move? Do we track down email and home addresses for all the Board members and investors, and send them a packet of documents that show Manny, Cinda, CJ, and Lord&Master attempted to defraud the Board and the investors by sabotaging our team and GuardShark?"

Jo quickly replied, "We don't know which Board members we can trust, and who might be in on Manny's scheme."

Steve shook his head. "Even if we could trust them, it's too much for them to wade through on such short notice. Let's just demo GuardShark's features and show a few key email messages that point the finger at Manny."

Jo made notes on her phone. "That's good, and we'll give them copies of the bribe checks delivered to Luce and me. They will see

GuardShark is a marketable product, and we'll expose all of Manny's underhanded tactics."

Luce took another hit of caffeine. "Right, GuardShark is what the investors paid for, and Manny is the one who tried to cash in without repaying them."

Seth slid the papers back to Jo. "It's a one-two punch."

Jo set her cup down. "We need to show them the proof we found that ties CJ to Manny."

Luce was animated. "I'm texting Jim, Sherm, and Vijay to pull together the smoking gun email messages we have."

Jo looked around the table. "We've all been in this together, and we're all going to see it through together."

Seth sat back in his chair, looked down at his hands, and took a breath before looking directly at Jo. "Except me." In response to the shocked look on her face, he continued, "I'm not a McWare employee. You don't want to jeopardize the confidence the Board and the investors need to have in you and your team by trying to explain the back door way I've figured into this scheme."

Jo's eyes fixed on Seth's intelligent face as her brain searched in vain for a way to legitimize his presence at the meeting. Luce's voice shocked her back to the present dilemma. "Well, crap. That isn't fair to you, Seth. We couldn't have figured everything out without you."

Jo's words and eyes reached out to Seth. "You had so much to do with helping us finish GuardShark and finding out about CJ. I know you're right, but I really hate not having you there."

Steve looked at Seth. "You're one of us."

Jo couldn't hide a smirk. "Steve means that in the nicest way possible."

Seth grinned. "You laughed at my jokes and fed me Proto's pizza and ice cream. You've ruined me for working with anyone else."

Luce beamed. "So our plan worked. First Vijay, now you. That's our version of a one-two punch."

Jo gulped the rest of her coffee, her eyes still connecting her to Seth. "OK, but you'll be there with us in all your indomitable spirit." She stood up, shouldering her backpack. "I need to call my grandmother to see how she's doing. She is so antsy to go home that I'm afraid she's going to start repairing hospital equipment." Jo looked around at the group, breathing in their collective courage before heading for the door.

Outside, Jo leaned over Vixen's hood, running her hand across the pristine finish of the candy apple metallic red paint job. "Hi, Grandma. How are you doing? Did you sleep well?" Jo pictured Grandma holding court in the hospital. "Are you sure the doctor will let you go today?"

Jo was aware of Luce sidling up beside her. She smiled into the phone. "Eleven o'clock sounds perfect, Grandma. I'll be over a little before that, and Luce might come with me, if that's OK." Luce pantomimed applause. "I'm glad you're feeling good. See you later."

Jo closed her eyes in gratitude that Grandma was going to be OK. *My world is almost right again.* She opened her eyes to the sun glinting off the shimmering mountains.

Luce put her hand on Jo's shoulder. "Sounds like Grandma is getting liberated. We need you when you can come back inside for a few minutes to help us pick out the smoking gun email messages. And then I'm going with you to get Grandma." Jo raised her fist over her head in a solidarity salute and followed Luce back into the coffee shop.

Late that morning in Grandma's hospital room, Jo checked the little closet. "Are those all the clothes you wore when you came to the hospital, Grandma? I think we need some souvenirs, like a couple of those hospital pudding cups or a nice bag of saline." She put Grandma's personal things in a hospital bag and handed it to Luce.

Grandma's brown eyes twinkled. "I don't need any reminders. I can't wait to get home, but I told everyone who called they should wait until Monday. The doctor made me promise to have a quiet weekend."

Jo winked at Grandma. "Sounds like a good plan. OK, do we have everything?"

Luce held up the hospital bag. "This has all the copies of the discharge paperwork, lab results, instructions for her follow-up doctor's appointment, and the souvenir hospital water bottle."

Grandma pointed to her purse. "I've got my prescriptions."

Jo put an arm around Grandma's shoulder. "Home, my lady."

The orderly came through the door with a wheelchair, but when Grandma shook her head, he smiled. "Hospital rules, ma'am. I'm just going to drive you to the front door."

Grandma pouted. "They must think I'm an old lady." She reluctantly sat in the chair and put her feet on the metal rests, hugging her hospital bag on her lap with the expression of a grumpy kitty.

As the orderly wheeled the chair with Jo's most precious cargo, she put a hand on Grandma's arm. "I'm parked on the south side, so we'll bring the car around and meet you downstairs at the front door." Jo and Luce headed for the stairs, whooping and laughter bouncing off the walls of the stairwell as they made their way to the ground floor.

45

Dressed to Kill 101

To: rookie-pup
From: Lord&Master

Good looks aren't everything, but sometimes they just have to do.

Money and power are always attractive, but the kill is what we live for. Embrace it, celebrate it, dress for it. We must not give in to the desire to show off. We don't want anyone to suspect our involvement in setting up the victims.

You are about to make your first kill, and that will change you forever. You will feel the power in every fiber of your being, the surging energy of knowing that you made all of it happen. Your first victory will transform you. Can you already taste the deliciously heady thrill of winning everything?

You will live above all the silly rules and tediously boring platitudes, free of the sad little dilemmas associated with having a moral code. Our only code is achieving our objectives by any means necessary.

Can't you just taste that level of power, smell that uninhibited freedom?

It is time to get ready for your big moment. A warrior dresses for battle, but we have already won, so we're dressed to kill.

Today is an excellent day to be a shark.

~Sent from my iPad

46

Driving While Not Cell Phoning May Be Hazardous

THE CONCRETE STAIRS and high ceiling of the stairwell reverberated with the dying sounds of Jo and Luce's banter as they reached the ground floor. "You drive, Luce. I'm tired of doing all the driving."

Luce recoiled in mock horror. "You know I can't drive a manual transmission."

Jo opened the door to the parking lot. "You've been perfecting the art of driving cars with no brakes."

At the hospital loading zone, Luce hopped out of Vixen's front passenger seat and stood beside the door, holding it open for Grandma. "I can sit in the back so you can sit up front with Jo. We need lunch, right?"

Jo reviewed her travel plan for Grandma. "OK, let's pick up lunch on the way home, then Luce and I will head to the Boulderado."

Jo's iPhone screamed for attention. She pressed the button for the incoming call as Grandma carefully sat in the passenger's seat before Luce closed the door.

Jo heard Seth say, "Jo, we've got a problem."

Jo gripped the phone as Luce settled into the back seat. "Are the tests screwed up again?"

Seth's tone was distinctly angry. "The test results and the reports all look fine. We've been keeping an eye on Manny's email traffic, and it looks like he's got CJ doing more dirty work."

Jo reached over to fasten Grandma's seat belt. "Tell me exactly what you found, but hurry. We're tight on time." Holding the iPhone close to her face, she pulled Vixen up to the fifteen-minute waiting area.

Seth spoke quickly. "CJ sent a message late yesterday afternoon directly to Manny, demanding he wire one hundred thousand dollars to an offshore account in payment for hacking our files and sabotaging Luce's car. Manny refused to pay up unless CJ followed through on the plan to take down McWare's computer network. CJ emailed back that it was set to go off at 2:00 PM today." Jo felt Luce's hand squeezing her shoulder.

"Just a sec so I can tell Luce." Jo turned sideways to face Luce in the back seat. "Manny ordered CJ to bring down McWare's computer network today, in two hours. If that happens, we can't log into the network to run GuardShark for the Board meeting. CJ emailed Manny directly, didn't go through Red Nails." Jo felt her heart explode as she caught her breath.

Luce frowned. "But CJ was arrested last night." Her iPhone's insistent chime interrupted. "Hi, Officer Alavarez," she answered. Luce grabbed Jo's shoulder, staring hard at her. "Yes, we can drop by, but we're on a tight schedule to break into the Board meeting at 3:00 PM today at the Boulderado. OK, see you in a few minutes."

Jo was startled by Seth yelling her name. "Seth, sorry, but Luce and I have to make a stop at the police station. Can you and Wayne check out the network and text me and Luce what you find? Have Steve find Sherm and Vijay right away and tell them to create a zip file of the whole GuardShark software and test data, and email a copy to each of our team members so we can run it on our computers."

Jo's face suddenly looked even more afraid. "Oh, no, I forgot about them. Yes, that's good. I'm so glad you remembered. OK, thanks." Jo shook her head and turned to Luce. "Seth collected all the smoking gun email messages too. The guys are forwarding all those messages to our personal email distribution list."

Luce took a deep breath, moving her hand on the back of Jo's seat. "It's lucky that we put together that list for everyone."

Grandma looked at Jo as the car pulled away from the hospital's loading zone. "You and Luce sound really busy, honey. I have enough medication from the hospital to last me for a day or two, and I can eat lunch at home."

Jo looked at Luce's reflection in the rearview mirror. "That sounds good, Grandma. Luce, did the police find more evidence?"

"Office Alvarez needs to talk to us for a few minutes at her office on 33rd. She has something important to tell us before the Board meeting."

Jo closed her eyes and tried to stop the spinning feeling. "It feels like we're trying to swim ahead of killer sharks."

Luce put her chin on the edge of Jo's seat. "Whatever happens, Jo, we're in this together, and so is our team."

Grandma grinned. "See, you've got a village too."

Jo opened her eyes and looked at the two women. "You're right," she sighed. "OK, the police station is closer so we'll stop there first, take Grandma home after that, and on to the Boulderado. Manny has no idea he's dealing with Amazon warriors!"

Luce laughed. "If only we had learned to dress like Red Nails, we could have fit Manny's corporate image."

Jo smirked. "I couldn't handle that much shopping or shallowness."

Luce muttered, "Not without mall-wear."

Jo snorted a laugh, shaking her head as she started the engine.

At the Boulder Police Station, the three women had just sat down on nondescript chairs when Jo saw the familiar face of Officer Alvarez, who greeted them, "Hi, Luce. Hi, Jo."

Jo put her hand on Grandma's arm. "This is my grandmother, Illyena Galvan."

"Hi, I'm Officer Alvarez. We can all talk in an interview room down the hall." The uniformed woman led them to a small room with a table and indicated the six grey chairs with upholstered seats. The officer touched her iPad screen and began the discussion.

Thirty minutes later, the officer handed Jo and Luce a single printed sheet of paper each. "So that's the story, or as much as I'm allowed to tell you at this point. Hope this helps." Jo and Luce read their copies as grins slowly took over their faces.

Jo looked up to see Officer Alvarez staring at Grandma. "Thanks, Officer, this is going to be very useful at the Board meeting."

Grandma looked curiously at the officer, read her name tag and suddenly smiled. "Are you related to Juanita Alvarez?"

Officer Alvarez nodded, smiling as she gestured toward a photo of an elegantly dressed Hispanic woman standing next to a hand-somely dark man, both in their twenties. "Yes, she's my mother. You look familiar. Did you know my parents when they lived in Boulder?"

Grandma looked lovingly at the photograph. "Your father and Jo's Grandpa used to play snooker. We were all so sorry when your father died. How is your mother?"

Officer Alvarez smiled. "Mom teaches Home Ec in a middle school in Pueblo, makes sure the kids all get good basic skills. I visit the class a couple of days before school ends each term. It's a good way to let kids find out that cops aren't all scary."

Grandma patted the officer's hand. "You remind me of your mother. Please tell her hello for me." The policewoman nodded, smiling softly.

Jo's phone buzzed insistently and a few second later Luce's phone announced a text message. Her face froze. "Luce, are you reading the message from Seth?"

Luce looked furious. "Shit-For-Brains Manny, sorry Mrs. Galvan, and his partners in crime must really be desperate."

Officer Alvarez frowned at Jo. "What's going on?"

Jo felt her face harden with anger. "Our CEO, Manny, sent a company-wide email that McWare's computers have been hacked. Everyone has fifteen minutes before McWare's computer network goes down. He ordered everyone to evacuate the building, which is completely unnecessary. I told the team to take their computers with them and head over to the Boulderado by 2:30 PM."

Jo texted rapidly on her iPhone. "Seth says the corporate network is perfectly healthy."

Luce read over Jo's shoulder. "Seth suspects Manny or his hacker devised this charade to get the Board to believe that you and I sabotaged McWare's network so we could cover our tracks from stealing company secrets."

Officer Alvarez typed and clicked before scooting her chair back and grabbing her cap. "I'm going over to McWare to check on something. We're done here." She stood up and started walking to the front door. Jo, Luce, and Grandma followed her to the parking lot.

Luce called after the officer, "What's going on? Is our engineering team in danger?"

The officer's iPhone rang and she turned to face the three women. "No, I'll catch up with you two later to explain. It's wonderful to see you, Mrs. Galvan." She turned her attention to the caller.

Luce nudged Jo. "We'd better get Grandma home so we can be at the Boulderado before the Board meeting starts."

Jo opened the passenger door for Grandma. "Right. Luce, can you text the team to meet us at the hotel?" She handed Grandma the seat belt to buckle before closing the door.

Luce got into the back seat. "Yeah, that's a good idea."

Jo hurried around the car and quickly got in. "Luce, tell them to meet us at 2:45 PM on the back stairs up to the mezzanine, *not* the big staircase."

Luce finished texting. "Done. Steve will tell them."

Jo caught Luce's eye in the rearview mirror. "I just wish I knew how to show the Board that anyone can use GuardShark, even someone who's never seen it before."

Grandma turned to Jo and said mischievously, "You mean someone like me?"

Jo watched Luce's reflection light up with a grin as her delighted voice sang from the back seat, "Wow, yes, someone exactly like you, Mrs. Galvan."

Jo felt an adrenalin rush, but she forced herself to ask casually, "Grandma, are you saying you want to help us demo the product for the Board?"

Luce rested her chin on the back of Grandma's seat. "That's a great idea. You would be a big help to us, Mrs. Galvan."

Jo felt everything falling into place. "Grandma, you can show the Board members and investors how easy it is for someone who has never seen our GuardShark security product to use it the first time. None of us can do that."

Luce leaned toward Grandma. "Are you feeling up to helping us?"

Jo reached over to squeeze Grandma's hand. "You just got out of the hospital. Your doctor might not see this as a quiet weekend."

Grandma beamed. "It's not the weekend yet. I feel fine, and it sounds like fun. But I won't know any of those Board people."

Jo laughed. "That's OK, we only know our lame-brain CEO. Wow, I feel like I can breathe again." She squeezed Grandma's hand and exhaled in a grateful sigh before starting the engine.

47

Tick Tick Fran-tick

Jo PULLED VIXEN into an extra wide spot in the Boulderado Hotel's parking structure. Luce checked her iPhone. "Jo, we still have to download GuardShark and all the smoking gun email messages to our computers, and make copies of the police information before the Board meeting. We have just over an hour before we meet the team."

Jo checked the time on her iPhone. "Oh good, no pressure. Grandma, Luce and I have to do some things to get ready for the big meeting. Will you be OK with all that walking?"

Grandma shook her head. "I feel fine. I can come with you and just sit and wait while you and Luce take care of everything." She suddenly grinned, her eyes twinkling. "I'll have tea."

Jo stole a glance at Grandma. "How about some lunch?" Jo unlocked Grandma's seat belt before opening the car door, and grabbed her backpack as she got out of Vixen.

Grandma shook her head at Jo as Luce opened the passenger door to help her out. "Honey, I feel great. If I'm hungry, I'll order something with my tea. Let's go to the Boulderado."

Jo took a deep breath. "Let's go get 'em." She shot a glance at Luce. "Can you text Seth and find out if they sent the GuardShark files and Manny's email to our personal email?"

Luce sent the text message. Moments later her iPhone blared. Luce suddenly yelled into the phone, "Oh my god, Seth. What's going on? What are Wayne and Jim yelling about? Is that Sherm and Vijay in the Tomb with you?"

Jo hurried to the other side of the car to join Luce. "What's wrong, Luce? What's going on at McWare?"

Luce's eyes widened in fear, her attention glued to the caller. Jo's chest pounded as she felt every nerve ending on fire with the adrenalin of what-the-hell-now fear. Moments ticked as Jo held her breath.

"Seth, I need to let Jo know what's going on." Luce looked at Jo. "GuardShark found an electronic time bomb in McWare's network that's programmed to go off at 2:00 PM today. It will disable network access for everyone except someone with Administrator login like Wayne. They are trying to kill it before it crashes McWare's network."

Jo stared at Luce. "Didn't they already send the files and emails to us?"

"The zip file was too big to get past GuardShark's firewall because we were testing the highest level of security for attachments to email. Jim and Sherm just finished reconfiguring GuardShark to allow a bigger size file. They are going to re-send the file to everyone in a few minutes."

Jo felt her heart drop out of her chest as if a giant vacuum cleaner had swallowed it whole. She shut her eyes against the mounting fear, and finally took a breath when she felt Grandma's hand on her arm. She opened her eyes and gave a quick wink to Grandma before squeezing the warm hand back.

Jo felt her heart race as she looked at Luce in the dim light of the parking structure. "Tell them to copy all the GuardShark files to a DVD, to several DVDs, and to each of their computers. You and I can copy from a DVD to our computers if we have to. Let's talk while we walk." She led the others down the short alley to the sidewalk on 13th Street, with Luce's longer stride quickly taking the lead.

Luce continued the phone call with Seth, giving a thumbs-up to Jo as they carefully stepped aside for other pedestrians near the busy hotel entrance. "Seth, did you hear what Jo said about making several DVDs with a full copy of GuardShark? Yes, I already saw the copies of Manny's email on my iPhone. OK. Bye."

Luce sighed. "I feel like I've lost my mind, several times. I think we're ready. We can use the Boulderado's WiFi to get our personal email."

Jo gazed up at the stately brick façade of the historic hotel. "We have to make copies of the information Officer Alvarez gave us. We just need to get into their Business Center."

A chime for an incoming text from Luce's iPhone made her jump. After listening for a minute, she summarized, "Jim says Wayne and Seth were able to kill the time bomb, but the system monitor showed that another one started. It looks like that CJ creep programmed the first time bomb to look for a kill command and launch a clone before the first one died. But they were able to send all the files we need to our personal accounts."

Jo stretched her neck. "That's a relief. We've got fifteen minutes to get into the Business Center to print out the pages we need for the Board meeting, and download all the GuardShark files to our computers."

Suddenly Luce stopped, put a finger to her lips, and quickly pulled Jo and Grandma off the sidewalk to the side of a large airport shuttle van, motioning to them to stand close to the van's door with their backs to the sidewalk as if they were getting into the van. Luce mouthed, "Red Nails," to Jo, and Jo whispered in Grandma's ear, "Bad person from McWare is walking our way."

From the sidewalk on the opposite side of the van, Red Nails' chirpy voice punctuated the clickety-clack of her stilettos. "I have no idea how they found out about all my accomplishments, but I guess word gets around quickly in a small town like Boulder. So just remember that it pays to do a good job for important people if you want your career to take off. Thanks for lunch." She gave a little parade wave and tottered down the sidewalk toward the parking structure.

Jo and Luce held their hands over their mouths to keep from laughing out loud, crouching lower and keeping their faces hidden until Red Nails was safely out of sight. Luce gasped, "Oh my god! She actually believes her own hype."

Jo was out of breath. Seeing Grandma's puzzled look, she added, "She's the bad project manager who helped our creep CEO Manny and their hacker friend CJ do all the dirty work. We let some other companies know she might be looking for another job."

Luce held up her iPhone. "We have forty-five minutes before the Board meeting. Let's go." The three women straightened up and hurried back to the sidewalk toward the Boulderado's entrance.

As a formally dressed young man opened the huge glass and brass double doors that welcomed visitors to the historic Boulderado Hotel, Grandma purred, "I love this hotel, so elegant."

Jo put her hand on Grandma's shoulder. "Luce and I need to go upstairs to the Business Center to do some email and use the printer before the meeting. Do you want to stay down here at the restaurant? You can take the elevator upstairs in thirty minutes and meet us outside the Driftwood Room for the Board meeting."

Grandma gazed up at the elegant masterpiece of the stained glass ceiling. "If you're going up those beautiful stairs, I'm coming too. You go ahead, do what you need to do and don't worry about me. I'll catch up."

Jo ran up the majestic staircase as Luce rushed ahead, unconsciously reaching out to run her hand along the polished intricately carved cherry wood banister, feeling the pleasure of its silken glassiness. Jo turned to wave down to Grandma before racing to catch up to Luce, who was already in the short hallway between the mezzanine and the conference center.

They hurried across the plush carpet, passed the paintings in the ornate frames in the hallway, and came to a dead stop in front of the Business Center. Luce muttered the words from the sign on the door, "Use Room Key to Access the Business Center." Jo and Luce stared through the glass at the computers and printers inside, so near yet so far away.

Jo tried the door handle. "What do we do now?"

Grandma came up behind them. "Is it locked?"

Jo stared at the door dejectedly. "We need a room key. I can't think."

Grandma whispered, "I have an idea. Let me try something. Why don't you two go look at the art work?"

Jo and Luce looked at each other quizzically and shrugged before ambling to the far wall in front of a painting of a group of Boulderites wearing turn-of-the-century fashions and picnicking in a Chautauqua meadow. Out of the corner of her eye, Jo saw Grandma approach a young man with a blonde ponytail as he came down the hallway.

Grandma's voice was sweeter than rosebuds in May. "Hello, dear. I wonder if you might be able to help me?"

The young man's gold earring caught a beam of the Boulder sunshine gleaming through the hallway windows as his face warmed with a smile that came through his voice. It was an effect Grandma seemed to have on most people. "Sure, ma'am, what can I do for you?"

Grandma told her tale as Jo and Luce dared each other with their eyes to keep straight faces. "My granddaughter went downstairs to the gift shop and she must have taken the little plastic card for our room key. I need to use the Business Center to send an email to her mother. It's my granddaughter's first time away from home."

The young man fished in his jacket pocket and pulled out his electronic room key. "No problem, ma'am." Jo and Luce remained glued to each other's eyes as their mouths dropped open at the sound of the electronic click of a door unlocking. "Let me get the door for you, ma'am. Do you need help using the computer?"

Grandma's voice melted all over him like butter and syrup on piping hot pancakes. "Oh, no thank you, dear. I've been taking computer classes at the Senior Center. You are such a nice young man. What is your name?"

The man's voice sounded as if he were trying on a more formal tone of politeness than he might have been used to, like wearing a tux to a prom. "My name is Lyle."

Jo caught a glimpse of Grandma's hand clasping his. "It is lovely to meet you, Lyle. You have a good day, dear." Jo and Luce held their collective breath as Lyle's smiling face floated by them in the direction of the mezzanine. As his ponytail disappeared from view, they scurried to the Business Center, where Grandma stood just inside the glass door, holding it slightly ajar, beaming a triumphant grin.

Jo and Luce held on until they were inside with the door closed. They burst out laughing as Jo hugged Grandma. "I had no idea you were such a good actress."

Luce applauded. "Mrs. Galvan, you're a natural."

Grandma shook her head. "Sometimes it's easier to get what I need from strangers by playing the little old lady they expect. Now you two get to work. I didn't fib to that nice young man for nothing."

Jo pulled her Mac out of the backpack, set it up on the computer desk, and sat down. "We've got twenty-eight minutes. I'm connecting to the Boulderado's WiFi."

Luce pointed to the instruction card in a holder on the wall. "There's the current password."

Jo sighed, rubbing her forehead. "I can't believe what an idiot I was for not realizing the Business Center would be locked."

Grandma patted Jo's shoulder. "Every genius needs a human moment now and then."

Luce chuckled. "You would fit right in at our team meetings, Mrs. Galvan. I'll make the copies we need." She pulled the printed sheets from her backpack and pressed the copy button. "I made some for our team too. They'll want souvenirs from our showdown."

Jo typed and clicked. "OK, I got into my email. Now I have to figure out the printer situation." She checked the small printers attached to each of the hotel's guest computers. "This is the only one with a connector that fits directly into my computer." Jo jiggled the cable. "Are you kidding me?"

Luce looked up from stuffing copies into her backpack. "What's wrong with the printer?"

Grandma was rummaging in her bag as Jo fumed, "It's got screws for the cable. I need a Phillips. Can you believe this?"

Grandma handed Jo a small screwdriver. "I always carry a few small tools with me. No telling when you might need to fix something."

Jo peeked into Grandma's bag, grinning quizzically. "Don't tell me you have a socket wrench set in there. No, don't tell me. Just surprise me the next time disaster strikes. Here, you're the fixer, so you do the honors." As soon as Grandma loosened the connector screws, Jo pulled the printer cable and plugged it into her Mac. "OK, let's take this baby for a spin."

Jo typed a few words, clicked the mouse a few times, and thirty seconds later a page with four words printed: "Geeks rule! Grandma rocks!" The three women erupted in giddy laughter as Luce quickly popped open her laptop, logged in, and began downloading the files attached to her email from Wayne.

Jo clicked several files open and printed each one, while Luce and Grandma took turns inspecting the pages as they came off the printer. Seven minutes later, Jo said, "That's everything we planned to print out, and now we've got the latest version of GuardShark running on our systems. We just need one last critical thing."

Luce frowned. "What?"

Jo closed her Mac and looked up with a cocky grin. "Our team. We have to meet them at the mezzanine's back stairs behind the bar. The Board members and investors will be coming up the grand staircase in the next few minutes. I just wish we had some way to know when they are all in the Driftwood Room so we can sneak our team just outside the room."

Grandma nudged Jo. "Honey, what if I sat at one of the mezzanine tables near the Driftwood Room? I have my iPhone and you have yours, so I can let you know as people go in."

Luce stared open-mouthed at Grandma. "That's brilliant. Were you a spy?" She closed her laptop, quickly stuffing it into her backpack with the printouts.

Grandma grinned. "No, we've just used our iPhones as walkie-talkies at home to stay in touch with each other when we're working in different rooms."

Jo grinned. "No one would suspect you have connections to software thugs like us." She stopped and put a hand on Grandma's shoulder. "I keep forgetting that you just got out of the hospital."

Grandma's eyes sparkled. "This is fun. Besides, all I'm going to do is sit at a lovely table drinking tea while my granddaughter and her best friend get ready to kick some ass."

Jo laughed. "Are we ready to do this, Luce?"

Luce gave her hands a shake. "My heart's starting to pound and the room feels like it's about to start spinning."

Jo reached up to put her hand on Luce's tall shoulder. "So that's a yes. Forgive me Grandma, but I'm fucking ready to fight for our team's right to be respected for the work we did."

Luce raised a fist. "We're gonna take Manny down."

Grandma grinned, putting her hands on her hips. "He doesn't know who he's messing with, but he's about to find out."

Jo scrolled through her iPhone for a photo of one of her cartoons, and held it up for Grandma to see. "Manny looks something like this, but with blonde-tipped spiked hair instead of curls, and will probably be well-dressed in a nice suit. He looks dumber in person."

Luce shook her head in mock derision. "Your granddaughter, the artist."

Grandma memorized the cartoon. "If I have anything to do with it, he's never going to hurt you and your team again."

Jo and Luce stood on either side of Grandma, hugging her. "All right, Grandma! Let's go."

Jo and Luce shouldered their backpacks and Grandma turned on her iPhone, setting it on vibrate. They entered the little hallway connecting the conference center wing to the original hotel, walking toward the mezzanine.

48

Bad Surprises 101

To: rookie-pup
From: Lord&Master

We're ready for the kill. It's all going to be ours. The moment of winning is the best part of being a shark. There is nothing more delicious than the moment when we vanquish our prey.

One of the most effective techniques is leaving the victim alone long enough to allow a sense of safety to return before we strike again. Fear becomes self-perpetuating, paralyzing the victim, making the kill that much easier.

I don't know why I have to keep reminding you that CJ and Cinda no longer matter to us. When CJ decided to leave town and Cinda decided to leave McWare, they showed their true colors. From now on we will only work with underlings we can control, like the engineers.

Bad surprises are for idiots. Idiots are their own worst enemies, and you were getting dangerously close to becoming an idiot. Thankfully, I was here to ensure that didn't happen.

We are within sight of victory. Time for the kill! Can't you taste it?

~Sent from my iPad

49

Super Mobilized

Jo AND LUCE peeked over Grandma's head and around the corner of a large square column to spy on people casually ascending the grand staircase. Grandma's faded everyday clothes made her the perfect shield, guaranteed to deflect the interest of any mover and shaker in Boulder's high-tech world. Anxiety flooded Jo's nerve endings in sharp contrast to the languid ambience of the vast mezzanine lounge. "What if Manny sees us, Luce?"

Luce reassured her friend, "Manny wouldn't look twice at Grandma. All we have to do is walk across the mezz to the little back staircase. Steve sent a text that our team is waiting there."

Jo nudged Grandma, nodding to a spot across the mezzanine. "You're on. Set up watch at that little table just outside the Driftwood Room."

Grandma grinned and made her way to the table, smiling as she seated herself on the rich brocade of an antique chair. As soon as the grand staircase was empty, Jo and Luce hurried across the carpet, past the little groupings of classically refined settees and chairs to the back stairs, waving to their team.

Jo phoned Grandma. "Hi, it's Jo. Luce and I are on the back stairs with our team. Are you OK sitting there?"

"I'm fine, honey. A tall gentleman in jeans went into the room. A woman with short dark hair and a slight limp just went in, followed by a man in his forties who is wearing running clothes."

"That's good, Grandma. The dark-haired woman is Manny's administrative assistant, Liz. She takes notes at the Board meetings. The tall guy is probably Bill Schuster. Somewhere I heard people refer to him as Big Bill. He is a major investor in McWare and a Board member." Luce pointed at her watch. Jo whispered into the phone, "Grandma, Luce and I need to talk with our team now, but I'll stay on my iPhone if you have anything to report."

"Go ahead, honey. I'll keep a lookout."

Jo and Luce looked down at the team, stacked one behind each other on the stair steps. A familiar wave of relief and excitement washed over Jo as she realized how many times this very team had pulled together to resolve a crisis. *We've got to show McWare's investors and Board of Directors how great our team is.*

Jo hissed, "Are we ready to do this thing?" Various team members raised a high five and Jim pantomimed a whoop-whoop.

Wayne leaned against the railing a couple of stairs below the landing. "So we're just going to crash the Board meeting as a group and demand they listen to us?"

Jo nodded, breathing against her racing heart. "That's our plan. They need to see that we're the team that finished GuardShark and we're ready to demo it to them."

Steve stepped to the middle of the pack. "We included a chart of the final SharkNet test results to prove GuardShark has everything customers want. They'll see its potential for making a ton of money for McWare, and for them."

Jo managed a grin. "In the immortal words of one of the earliest computer geeks, Grace Murray Hopper, 'If it's a good idea, go ahead and do it. It's much easier to apologize than it is to get permission.'"

Sherm leaned on the bannister. "Manny still runs the company, so can't he fire us for breaking into the Board meeting?"

Jo grinned at Sherm. "We're going to take care of Manny, in a way he won't like."

Jim looked at his watch. "So how are we doing this? It's 2:55 PM. Doesn't the Board meeting start at 3:00 PM?"

Vijay looked around the group, frowning. "Where's Seth? Isn't he helping us demo GuardShark?"

Luce shook her head. "We're going to demo it without him. Seth's afraid Manny will use the fact that he isn't a McWare employee against us."

Jo looked at each engineer. "It's going to be fine. You all know GuardShark better than anyone. Imagine showing your friends the work you did on GuardShark, and just do that for the people in the room." She gave an air high five to the team as proud smiles washed across their faces.

Luce climbed the stairs to the landing, singing, "It's show time."

Jo raised her fist high. "Off we go!"

Luce looked down the stairs at the team readying for battle. "I'm so nervous and excited. I think my heart is going to explode."

Wayne put a hand on Luce's shoulder. "You're not the only one who's jittery. I'm nervous as a long-tailed cat in a room full of rockin' chairs."

Jo put her hands on her hips. "Who do we have to be afraid of? We're the ones picking the fight. Let's do this."

The team erupted with pin-drop quiet cheers, applause, and a cavalcade of high fives in an electric ripple of geek enthusiasm, ending and beginning with Jo and Luce. Jo and Luce nodded to each other, and simultaneously pressed send on their iPhones to deliver identical pre-written text messages. Jo felt for the device on her belt, pressed the button twice, waited for the acknowledging buzz, and pressed the button once more.

Vijay grinned at Jo. "If we get fired, can we still have the cartoon contest? I don't want all that work to go to waste." Sherm quietly pummeled the Miracle Intern's arm.

Jo shook her head. "That's our team, rude comics to the bitter end. OK, I guess we're ready."

Luce put a hand on Jo's arm. "We don't really know what's going to happen once we're inside."

Jo hip-bumped her friend. "Hopefully it won't end with us in hand-cuffs. Can you believe we're finally going to get Shit-For-Brains?"

Jo and Luce marched to the Driftwood Room, leading the team in their all-or-nothing assault. Jo felt her heart beating with a warrior's joy, victory within her grasp, singing *Go big or go home, baby.*

Jo turned to Luce. "Can you think of anything we forgot?"

Luce shrugged. "Parking validation? Last rites?"

Jo's eye caught the sweet no-nonsense lady sipping from a china tea cup and waved to Grandma. "Let's get our secret weapon."

Luce followed Jo's gaze and grinned. "Manny is toast."

Jo chuckled. "We said GuardShark was the Make-A-Wish product that needed a miracle, and we had our miracle all along." The geek Amazons, one short, one tall, resumed their march to ground zero.

50

Moment of Truth 101

To: rookie-pup
From: Lord&Master

This is it. It's show time. It's our time. This is the critical moment when everything about you, your character, courage, and skill are put to an extreme test. This is our *momento de la verdad*, our moment of truth.

We have covered all our bases by giving the underlings a false goal and finding a way to blame them for their failure to achieve it. The beauty of this particular win is they will never know how we achieved our goal at their expense. We are moments away from pulling off your first kill. Be proud of your part in it.

You are ready for the final scene of our performance. It comes down to this moment of winning it all, and it is worth whatever we had to do to achieve it. You have learned to do whatever it takes to win, and you have changed who you are for one simple reason.

When you play the power game, the power doesn't change; power changes you.

~Sent from my iPad

51

Showtime

GRANDMA PLACED THE bone china tea cup in its matching saucer and looked up at Jo. "Can you tell me what to do?"

Jo squeezed Grandma's shoulder. "Don't worry, I will be right there. I'm glad you're with us." She offered Grandma her arm and held the beautifully upholstered chair as Grandma got up. "Here we go."

They walked a few steps to the little band of engineers, who parted to let them stand next to the Driftwood Room sign. The double doors were cracked open a couple of inches. Jo squinted to get a line of sight into the room. The friendly chatter of people seated around a table enjoying their coffee felt familiar to her.

Manny strode to the head of the table. He was attired in an elegantly tailored charcoal suit and a black silk tie with geometric gridding. *His Hugo Boss is wearing him*, Jo thought. Manny cleared his throat as the screen behind him displayed the PowerPoint title page announcing 'McWare, Inc., Q3 Board Meeting, Manfred Wimple, CEO.' "We will begin today's Board meeting with a report from our Chief Financial Officer, Mackintosh Rielle." He nodded and sat near the head of the table as Mackerel's reed-thin pinstripe strode crisply into Jo's view.

A woman's authoritative voice chuckled, "Give us the good news, Mack. Is it payday or poof day?"

Mackerel was concise. "McWare has reached a critical point. Since the last Board meeting in May, McWare has released the moderately successful Rhombus product and focused on developing the GuardShark software security product. The market is hungry for GuardShark now, but we will miss our revenue targets unless GuardShark is completed by tomorrow."

An annoyed male voice broke in, "C'mon, Mack, did the engineering talent we bought you pull it off or didn't they?"

Mackintosh Rielle did not react to the taunt. "Unfortunately, the completion of the GuardShark product has been delayed indefinitely due to gross negligence by the two lead project engineers. Given the binding agreement between the Board of Directors and the investors, McWare has no alternative but to declare bankruptcy under articles of Chapter 7, sell off the company assets, and distribute the proceeds of the sale."

Board members and investors erupted in a cacophony of questions. Mackerel's frame remained as taut as the set of his expression, his eyes alone registering the dead-on high beams of disdain. "This completes my report. Manny and Mr. Wimple, Chairman of the Board, will field all questions." Mackerel moved out of Jo's view as Manny returned to the podium.

An older gentleman sitting next to the podium demanded, "What evidence can you show us that the two lead project engineers are to blame for this? What are their names?" Jo noticed he wore the exact same ensemble as Manny, but that was where the resemblance ended. His command of the situation was apparent. *That's Glaston Wimple, in the flesh and matching Hugo Boss.*

Manny displayed the slide with the names of the accused. "Their names are Josephina Galvan and Luciana Savodsky." At that moment, Steve pushed open the double doors to reveal Jo, Luce, and the engineering team.

Steve's voice dominated the room of startled Board members. "I would like to present McWare's lead project engineers, Jo Galvan and Luce Savodsky. They brought their engineering team to show us the GuardShark software security product."

Manny froze, staring open-mouthed at the advancing group of engineers. Glaston Wimple stood, pointing angrily at Jo and Luce as he bellowed, "What are they doing here? This is a closed meeting. Get them out of here."

A tall, lean man in jeans took charge, looking around the table at each person. "Don't you want to see our new product?"

Glaston Wimple's face flamed with fury. "Shut up, Big Bill. As Chairman of the Board, I demand those criminals leave immediately." He pointed to Liz, Manny's assistant. "Call the police."

Liz reached for her iPhone, but hesitated for a long minute. She looked at Jo and Luce, and back to Jo, their eyes locked on each other. Glaston's bark startled Liz. "What are you waiting for? We're firing them, and we can always add you to the list. Call the police, *now!*"

Liz looked straight at him, inhaled, and said in a voice that resembled a steel cord, "No, and don't yell at me like that. I'm not your servant. Jo and Luce do their jobs brilliantly despite Manny's idiocy and incompetence, *and so do I.* Even if it costs me my job, I'm not calling the police because I don't believe they would do anything dishonest." She locked eyes with Glaston Wimple as she placed her iPhone on the table in front of her with a resolute smack.

Glaston's face was red as he banged his fist on the table. "We have reports proving that GuardShark does not work. The engineers failed. They have no right to be here."

Big Bill waved to the engineers to come forward. "Glaston, quit grandstanding and get off the stage. We all need to see the GuardShark product we paid for."

Manny stood helplessly at the head of the table. Jo stared, imagining her bobblehead version of him. *He's just never ready for prime time.*

Glaston jumped up, seething, "I have no intention of letting these thugs waste my time." He was across the room in a few commanding strides. He stormed past the startled engineers, just missing Grandma by a hair as he exited the Driftwood Room. At the head of the table, Manny stood frozen in place, staring at the retreating sight of broad shoulders in an obscenely expensive Italian silk blend.

Big Bill turned to Jo. "You're on. Set up your computer so everyone can see your demo displayed on the screen."

Manny cowered. "What about the Board meeting?"

Big Bill moved with the energetic confidence of a lifetime of conquering mountains in nature and in business. Ignoring Manny's whining, Bill unplugged the video display cable from Manny's computer, pushed the mobile podium off to the right, and moved a chair to the head of the table before stepping aside. Jo set up her Mac, attaching the video display cable.

As the GuardShark Getting Started window displayed in its multi-faceted glory on the screen behind her, Jo beckoned to Grandma, "Come, sit down." She pulled out the chair for Grandma.

Steve joined Jo and Luce, turning to the group. "Jo Galvan and Luce Savodsky lead the engineering team that developed the GuardShark product. I will let them introduce their team."

Jo felt the adrenalin rush as she glanced over the table of the rich and powerful, surrounded by the engineers arrayed like a troop ready for their last battle. She looked down at Grandma and smiled. *We're ready.* Jo willed her petite frame to stand ramrod straight and took a deep breath before addressing the powerful group. "Thank you, Steve. Good afternoon, and thank you for this opportunity to demonstrate the GuardShark product. Our team wanted to let you see how a first-time user would experience the product, and give you a chance to try out GuardShark yourselves."

Luce added, "GuardShark's rich set of security features will sell the product, but we believe the ease of use will make it a winner."

Jo put a hand on Grandma's shoulder. "This is Mrs. Illyena Galvan, my grandmother." Grandma's smile twinkled. "What you see on the big screen is what Mrs. Galvan is doing on her computer as she uses the GuardShark product for the first time." She turned to Grandma, bending a little closer, her voice still audible to the group. "There are three choices on the Home screen—Menu, Help, and Exit. Click on the one you want. You can always return to Home from any GuardShark window."

Grandma focused on the screen in the familiar posture of The Fixer researching a repair problem. A smile played on Jo's face as Grandma clicked on Menu, selected an option and followed the simple instructions for reviewing the security levels, encryption options, and other available settings. Jo watched Grandma click on the Help button and read the information.

Grandma looked up at Jo. "This is good information. It has simple explanations and examples. You need to add a way to make the text larger. Oh, I see, just click the plus sign next to the Text symbol. That's good. I'm going back to the Menu to see what else I can do."

Luce pulled out her iPhone to take notes. "That's great feedback, Mrs. Galvan."

As Grandma continued to click on selections from the Menu, Jo stood up and asked the group, "Are you all ready to try using GuardShark?" She waved her hand to indicate the geeks. "Each member of our engineering team has GuardShark running on their computers."

Jo nodded to Jim. "Jim McGraw is our lead software architect; he designed the features." Jim waved as he moved between two people dressed in business suits, offering them his Mac. A power-suited woman readily accepted his offer.

"Sherm Chrisman is our lead software engineer." Sherm nodded, placing his Mac on the table between an older gentleman in a business casual jacket and a younger man in a Polo shirt and Dockers, both of whom reached for the Mac before the younger man relinquished it.

"Wayne Oakley is a senior software engineer." Wayne grinned, giving a little nod as he placed his Mac in front of Manny, who sat stone-faced, not moving a muscle. A mature, elegantly dressed woman seated to his left casually pulled the Mac in front of her as Manny looked anxiously around the room. He pushed back his chair, stood and retreated to the wall with a bewildered expression.

"Steve Scott has been the engineering and quality manager at McWare since the company began." Steve nodded and offered his Mac to Big Bill Schuster, who stood near the head of the table. He rubbed his large hands together before tackling the mousepad with gusto. Jo felt oddly safer as she watched the tall, confident man.

"Vijay Patel is our newest engineer." Vijay grinned shyly as people sitting close to the head of the table waved eagerly to him.

Jo looked around the room at pairs, trios, and quartets of people clicking away, while Grandma was off on her own adventure that displayed on the projector screen. She sighed, relieved, feeling the positive atmosphere in the room. Luce nudged her. "Pretty cool, huh?" Jo's eyes lit on Manny standing alone next to an elegant Tiffany light fixture, barely a fixture himself.

Jo grinned. "Sure is. Let's get set up for the demo in a few minutes." She nodded to Luce, who began moving around the room whispering instructions to each of the engineers. Jo put a hand on Grandma's shoulder. "OK if I use the system for a few minutes?"

Grandma nodded and started to get up but Jo shook her head. "No, you stay there. I'm just going to move the computer to the podium." Big Bill quickly moved the podium a few feet behind Grandma's chair. When Jo had the system in place, she nodded to Luce.

Luce joined Jo at the podium, and began, "I hope you've all had a chance to try out some of GuardShark's many computer security features. Now we want to show you some of the things that can happen to your computer account when it doesn't have the kind of protection that GuardShark offers."

Jo continued, "We've been running GuardShark on McWare's network for the past two weeks. Everyone on our engineering team has GuardShark running on our systems, so our computers and email are protected."

Jo clicked the button on the screen for Suspicious Email. "Last week, GuardShark reported there was suspicious email coming into our network, so we used the features that analyze the sender's address and the content of the message to link all the messages from the same suspicious sender. Here is one of the messages from two days ago."

She scrolled to the beginning of the first smoking gun email, glancing around to check the display on the projector screen.

>>>
From: Lord&Master
To: rookie-pup

… Cinda is the designated scapegoat. We need her to keep in touch with CJ. As long as she is the go-between, our part in this can never be traced. She must handle all the payments and passing all the hacked files back and forth. You must stay on top of things with Cinda.

Make sure CJ has destroyed all the evidence from every computer system. I won't involve you in this because you are not yet ready to do what may be necessary.

>>>

Jo stole a glance at Manny, whose face had turned to stone, his eyes fixed on the projector screen.

A loud crash startled the busy little groups as Glaston Wimple angrily opened the door and strode into the room with a threatening gesture toward Jo and Luce. "What in the hell is going on? I just called the police to come and arrest these fired ex-employees."

He barked to the paralyzed mini-him quivering against the wall, "This is the annual Board meeting and we need to vote on putting McWare into bankruptcy. Manny, call the meeting to order."

The elegant woman with the power-suit chuckled as she read from the projector screen. "Lord and Master? It sounds like someone needs a designer mask to match the leather S&M outfit!" Glaston's eyes jerked to the screen, his face turning red as a ripple of snickers circled the table.

Jo stifled a grin as she clicked to display the next message. "The next email was sent yesterday."

> >>>
> From: Lord&Master
> To: rookie-pup
>
> … We have to stop those girls. CJ emailed that the business with the blonde has been handled. CJ is shark material, wastes no time on ethics or legalities.
>
> I have one job for you. Every night, get in touch with CJ at 10:30 PM to confirm everything has gone according to plan.
> >>>

Jo continued to scroll slowly as Big Bill said to Glaston Wimple, "You really never saw what GuardShark could do for McWare. You were playing us all along, planning to sell McWare to cash in. That's fraud in my book."

Glaston gave a dismissive wave in Jo's direction. "You can't prove those messages came from me."

Grandma piped up, "Oh yes they can, dear. The system knows your fingerprint, so all your messages are automatically tied to your account, and your son's too."

Glaston Wimple's mouth dropped open a split second before he barked at Manny, "Why didn't you warn me my identity wouldn't be hidden from the system?"

Manny shrugged his shoulders, his voice quivering as he said, "We needed fingerprint ID to be competitive in the market."

Glaston snarled in a barely audible growl, "Idiot," before turning to glare at Jo. "It doesn't matter if I sent those messages. You're taking them out of context."

Jo smiled triumphantly. "We thought you might say that. Here is the first email we found where you were schooling Manny in your strategy, almost four years ago."

>>>>

A start-up company provides the perfect situation for perpetrating The Big Lie. There is no information about the company that is publicly available, so none of the underlings has access to the company's financial status. Each quarter the investors and the Board receive a simplified, sanitized version of the numbers, but the Board members really only care about hobnobbing with each other while they are wined and dined before cashing their fat stipend. They are part of the cost of making us look legitimate.

Start-ups are incorporated as for-profit companies with a four-year plan to achieve profitability. At least that's what the government and the investors expect.

But remember, we have a different goal. We want McWare to report a loss to offset our financial gains in other investments. Creative accounting can report an annual loss. After four years, we can declare bankruptcy and easily convince the Board to sell McWare's assets at an additional loss. The investors pose a problem, and that problem is the reason you need to orchestrate The Big Lie I devised.

We don't have time to waste on a business based on ethics and a long-term commitment to innovative technology developed with top-notch technical expertise. Leave that to the Intel's of the world.

>>>>

Mackintosh Rielle lasered Glaston with angry eyes as he said, "You planned this treachery from when we incorporated McWare. I do not work for criminals." He turned to Big Bill. "We need to elect a new CEO and Chairman of the Board."

Big Bill turned to Glaston. "The engineers caught you and Manny red-handed. Your email ordered Manny to tell CJ to hack into the engineers' files, create errors in GuardShark's reports, and sabotage the brakes on Luce's car. The police caught him in the act of vandalizing Jo's car."

Luce nodded at Jo, who quickly pressed the button on the device on her belt. The vibration a few seconds later gave her a welcome sense of relief coupled with an electric thrill.

Glaston Wimple erupted, "This is a charade. We have test results that prove nothing in GuardShark works."

Grandma smiled at Glaston Wimple. "No, dear, I can show you. When I bring up the system monitor that comes with the computer, it shows that everything I selected is running, and I can see the backups it's doing for me to the Cloud." Her smiling face welcomed him with the same warmth she bestowed on every person she met.

Grandma's sweetness acted like poison on Glaston Wimple, who was shaking with rage. All eyes were focused on him when suddenly Officer Alvarez and a young male Boulder police officer marched into the room. Glaston's rage was replaced by a triumphant smile. "It's about time you got here, officers." He pointed at Jo and Luce. "Arrest those two women for fraud and theft of the company's intellectual property."

Officer Alvarez pulled out a pair of handcuffs. "Glaston Wimple, you are under arrest for suspicion of conspiracy to commit bodily harm to Jo Galvan and Luce Savodsky, and fraud."

Big Bill Schuster grinned. "They finally caught you, Glass. You've lost your touch, buddy."

Glaston Wimple looked down at Officer Alvarez as she cuffed him. "You're arresting me? Do you know who I am? Unlock these handcuffs or I will see you're fired."

Officer Alvarez looked at Glaston. "You have the right to remain silent, anything you say can be used in a court of law, you have the right to an attorney, and if you cannot afford an attorney, one will be provided to you." Her eyes roamed the room, found Jo, and a tight smile passed between them.

Glaston Wimple stood his ground as if handcuffs were a temporary annoyance. "You have no evidence on me. It's not my fault Manny decided to take short cuts that aren't legal. He's a grown man, and he's the one you should be arresting."

Manny looked stricken. "Dad, what are you saying? How can you blame me? You had all the ideas from the beginning, teaching me how to manipulate the underlings. I did what I thought you wanted. I thought we were partners."

Glaston was livid as he faced Manny. "Why in the name of every million I've ever made did I have to be stuck with such an idiot for a son?"

Big Bill gazed at Glaston. "You would finger your own son for the crimes you orchestrated? You can't possibly expect anyone to believe Manny could pull off a bubble gum wrapper, let alone a complex scheme to sell McWare down the river for your own gain."

Glaston yelled over his shoulder in Big Bill's direction, "Your son is an idiot too, but he's so lame that he'll never even try to play in the big leagues." Officer Alvarez forcibly turned Glaston around.

Big Bill sighed. "I'm not giving up on Lonnie. It's not too late for either of our sons." He turned to Manny. "I hope you learn from this and find a better mentor."

Glaston's growled, "You know where you can put your platitudes, Schuster."

Officer Alvarez turned to her partner. "You can handle this one while I make the other arrest. Manfred Wimple, I am arresting you for computer hacking, Internet piracy, and intent to libel and physically harm Jo Galvan and Luce Savodsky. You have the right to remain silent, anything you say can be used in a court of law, you have the right to an attorney, and if you cannot afford an attorney, one will be provided to you."

Manny's face registered the shock. "But I don't know how to do any of those things. I don't know anything about computers or software, except how to get a tee-time online."

Jo slowly scrolled through the email message on the screen. "Manny, we have evidence from an FBI investigation that you sent this wire transfer to an offshore account for the man you called CJ in payment for hacking the engineering team's confidential company files and sabotaging the brake system of Luce's and my cars. Luce has copies for everyone." She nodded at Luce, who passed out copies of the wire transfer confirmation.

Luce turned to look triumphantly at Manny. "CJ turned States' evidence against you."

Big Bill said quietly, "Manny, here's an opportunity for you to learn. You know, I'm going to miss having your father as a competitor."

Glaston glared at Big Bill. "I'm not done, Schuster. You know I'll come back to beat you again and again. I can already taste it." Officer Alvarez and her partner marched father and son out the doors of the Driftwood Room and through the mezzanine to the elevators.

Big Bill joined Jo at the podium. "What the engineers have shown us today convinces me the GuardShark product is poised to generate high revenue. There is no reason for McWare to go into either Chapter 11 or Chapter 7. Am I right, Mackerel?"

All eyes focused on Mackintosh Rielle for a tense moment before he responded, "The revenue projections we did a year ago for the GuardShark product forecast $1.7 million in U.S. sales in the first year, and we discussed partnering with distribution channels in Europe and Asia to extend our revenue base worldwide. If we declare bankruptcy, all assets would be frozen, prohibiting us from forming distribution agreements. Our best move is to continue operating as usual."

Big Bill grinned as he turned back to the money people. "Let's show our thanks to Jo and Luce and their outstanding team." Enthusiastic applause broke out as Board members and investors shook hands with nearby engineers, all grinning with pride. Big Bill smiled down at Grandma. "Mrs. Galvan, I think I speak for the Board and investors when I thank you for doing an excellent job of showing us the GuardShark product. We'll keep a spot open at McWare anytime you want to come and test products for us."

Grandma's smile blossomed like a rose in happy rays of sunshine. "Oh dear, no thank you. This is too stressful. I'll just stick with fixing things at home."

Big Bill turned to Jo and Luce, both still smiling down at Grandma. "That was a risky move, showing us GuardShark through the experience of a first-time user. It says a lot about your confidence in the product your team built. I think it would make a great marketing strategy."

As the room erupted in applause, Grandma gave him a mischievous look. "I would be happy to help you if Jo and Luce and their team can keep their jobs."

Big Bill grinned as he looked at Jo, Luce, and around the room at each of the geeks. "Mrs. Galvan, we have every intention of keeping this engineering team at McWare. We need them to help us build our business."

He turned to Jo and Luce. "You are the most talented group of engineers I've seen in a long time, and your commitment to delivering quality software products is outstanding. We need to rebuild this company, with you." Cheers filled the Driftwood Room as Jo, Luce, their team, and Grandma basked in a shared exhale of relief.

Mackintosh Rielle raised a hand. "Bill, we need to finish the Board meeting, elect a new Chairman of the Board, and formulate a plan to keep McWare solvent until the anticipated sales of the GuardShark product put the business back in the black. I nominate you for Chairman of the Board and CEO."

Shouts of "I second it" came from everywhere in the room, and Mackerel intoned, "All those in favor say Aye." Ayes were shouted, accompanied by wild applause. "It is unanimous. Congratulations, Bill."

Big Bill looked around the room. "I can't think of a group of people I'd rather work with. Thank you for your support."

Mackintosh Rielle's tone was infused with caution as he said, "Bill, the Board and investors need the results of an independent audit of McWare's books. That will take a week to put together and another week to give them time to study it before we can vote on a new business plan."

Big Bill nodded. "I couldn't agree more, Mackerel. The days of hype, threats, and empty promises by sleazy weasels are over. I want McWare to use only solid business practices that include the highest level of transparency. I believe in what we've got here, and I believe GuardShark will bring in the revenue we need to grow our business." He looked around the room. "Let's meet back here in two weeks to hammer out a business plan going forward."

Luce startled suddenly out of her silence and whispered to Jo, "Is this really happening? I think I'm having an out-of-body experience."

Jo nodded. "Yes, it's all true. We get to keep our jobs, we're putting Grandma in commercials, and we finally got to attend a corporate meeting that turned out to be a useful, positive experience. All our dreams have come true."

Luce feigned drooping. "I think I might faint."

Steve turned to Big Bill. "We can't have one of our top engineers losing consciousness at the Boulderado. I'm stealing Jo, Luce, and the team for a little celebration downstairs. I think the Board can manage without us for the rest of the day."

"Great idea, Steve. Expense it to McWare. Take the smartest people in the room and get out of here, with our thanks." Applause followed Jo, Luce, Grandma, and the team as they gathered up their laptops and backpacks, following Steve to the mezzanine.

As the engineers and Grandma assembled at the top of the grand staircase, Jo noticed Steve's strangely vapid expression, as if he had just learned the moon was really made of gruyere cheese. "Steve, is everything OK?"

Steve looked blankly at Jo and Luce. "I had no idea Big Bill Schuster knew my name. I'm pretty sure Glaston Wimple wouldn't have been able to pick me out of a crowd of two."

Wayne nodded at Steve. "Manny wouldn't know me from a can of paint."

Jo grinned. "I have a feeling McWare is going to feel like a different place from now on. And I mean that in the nicest way possible." Jo offered Grandma her arm, and the Galvan family led the team down the grand staircase to the Spruce Restaurant.

52

No Free Lunch

Jo PUSHED BACK from the large table in the Spruce Restaurant's porch, enjoying her second club soda. She surveyed the happy group of geeks encircling the table, ending with Luce sitting next to her. "You know, this is the same table where Shit-For-Brains and Red Nails dumped the GuardShark mess in our laps. Thank goodness I'm not superstitious."

Luce clinked her iced tea glass with Jo. "And now we're back here celebrating our GuardShark victory."

Jo raised her glass as a variety of beverages were held aloft. "Here's to the greatest team ever. Eat up! Drink up! Big Bill Schuster and the Board of Directors are buying." She clinked with Grandma's tea cup. "Did all that crazy stuff happen?"

Jim waved his beer bottle. "Did you see Manny's face when that cop put handcuffs on him? He looked like a scared rabbit."

Sherm rapped his fork rat-a-tat on the table. "What about Glaston Wimple pushing all the blame on Manny? What a jerk, trying to make his own son take the fall."

Wayne took a long swig of his beer. "Manny's got a rough piece of road ahead."

Steve grinned. "No golf, no Porsche, no caviar." Jo and Luce laughed out loud.

Jim put down his beer. "This feels great to be celebrating, but I'm a little afraid of our next project. Jo, do you and Luce know anything about that? I'm just not up for another nightmare."

Sherm hoisted his Fat Tire beer. "Big Bill and the Board said great things about us, but I'm afraid all CEOs have a natural habit of expecting the big miracle no matter how many we've pulled off in the past."

Steve tabled his beer. "Nothing has been decided yet, but it makes sense for us to set up the customer support mechanism for the GuardShark product, getting feedback from the first customers for ways to improve the product and fixing any bugs that are reported."

Jo swirled the ice in her club soda. "Let's brainstorm on Monday what we want to propose to Big Bill later next week, and see how he responds to our ideas."

Luce nodded. "We need intelligent work, but no deadlines or overtime."

Steve looked around the table. "If that type of work doesn't sound like your particular brand of java, let us know where you think you would be more productive."

Vijay grinned at Steve. "Does the Honolulu Cricket Club count? I need to spend quality time improving my game and learning to surf. That qualifies as cross-training, right?"

Sherm elbowed Vijay. "You finally took my fitness advice. That's an excellent example of setting the right priorities."

Vijay elbowed Sherm back. "No, the *right* priorities would be you finally checking out the Cricket For Dummies website. I'll text you the link, again." Sherm feigned ducking his head in shame as Vijay pantomimed texting his cell phone.

Wayne leaned on the table, looking at Jo and Luce. "Where's our buddy Seth? He should be celebrating with us."

Jo gazed toward the main entrance of the restaurant. "I texted him to meet us here, but he texted back that he's busy with something. We're trying to figure out a way to convince Big Bill to hire Seth without saying anything that might sound negative about Lonnie, Big Bill's son."

Wayne shrugged. "Now that's a pickle, ma'am. We can understand how you wouldn't want to be the one to tell Big Bill that his son is so useless, if he had a third hand he'd need an extra pocket to stick it in."

The entire table erupted in laughter, and eventually Luce found her voice. "I can't tell if Lonnie is dumb or lazy."

Grandma sipped her tea. "Parents always hope their children will turn out well. I was very lucky with my children, and with my granddaughter." Jo squeezed Grandma's hand as they shared a smile.

Jo suddenly turned to Grandma in a wave of concern. "I just remembered that you got out of the hospital this morning. We should get you home so you can rest."

Grandma laughed softly. "Honey, I haven't had this much fun in a long time. I feel fine."

Luce winked at Grandma. "You just charmed the pants off Big Bill and the Board."

Grandma grinned. "It was fun."

Sherm waved a french fry. "When are we doing the cartoon contest? I've been working on my entry for 101 Things To Do With A Dead CEO."

Vijay sighed. "Could we do it tomorrow? I'm not going back to work today."

Jim nodded. "Same for me. I'm going home to my wife."

Jo grinned. "I have to admit that I'm not thinking about anything right now but getting Grandma and me home to pet the kitties before we crash. One more toast to our amazing accomplishment, and to Grandma's new career!" Glasses were raised aloft, but halted as the group watched Jo's eyes move in the direction of the porch's wood-paneled entrance, where Liz was waving frantically at Jo.

"Liz looks upset. I hope she's not warning us Manny and his father were released from custody," Luce said.

Grandma grabbed Jo's arm. "What's the matter, honey?"

Jo stared as Liz quickly made her way through the Friday lunch tables, dodging servers and chairs. "Liz is, was, Manny's assistant. I wonder what we're in trouble for now."

Grandma frowned. "But everyone's so happy with your team." Everyone at the table glued their eyes on Liz as she approached the table.

Luce put down her fork. "Hi, Liz. What's up?"

Liz handed Jo a McWare envelope with Jo's name handwritten on it. "Mr. Schuster wanted me to deliver these before you left the restaurant. Luce and Steve." She handed each of them a similar envelope.

Jo frowned at the envelope. "This can't be from a lawyer. Recent experience tells me lawyers insist on using my Christian name. Jo is my heathen name. Is something wrong?"

Liz smiled and winked. "I doubt it's bad news. Bill Schuster is a nice man."

Jo did a double-take. "Liz, that's the first time I've seen you smile when mentioning a CEO's name. Are you working for Big Bill now?" A grin spread over Liz's face as she nodded vigorously.

Luce deadpanned at Liz, "I hope it's not too hard to get over the loss of Manny. Jo could give you another drawing of him, you know, in case you miss him."

Liz laughed. "Fat chance of that. You all have fun. I'm going to celebrate all weekend." She waved as she hurried out of the restaurant.

Luce looked around the table. "I wonder why the rest of you didn't get envelopes."

Wayne pointed at her envelope with his beer bottle. "Open them. We're here for you if it's trouble."

Jo, Luce, and Steve opened their envelopes, each unfolding the single handwritten sheet, eyes quickly scanning the short note. Steve sighed. "If an invitation to breakfast tomorrow morning with a rich guy is trouble, then I'm a goner. I'm not sure where that address would be."

Luce read over his shoulder. "That looks like an address you couldn't afford, up on the second ridge of Boulder Heights."

Jo frowned at Luce. "Breakfast with Big Bill Schuster and probably Lonnie. I'm having mixed emotions."

Steve pointed to his invitation. "Look at the bottom of the invitation. A driver will arrive at my home at 8:00 AM."

Jo mugged, "I will definitely need fashion advice for what to wear to breakfast at an estate, let alone the ride in the limo. My little black dress is at the cleaners."

Luce looked horrified. "No LBD for morning events. Definitely go with a power suit and heels, or a nice fall dress with a hemline below the knee, paired with a suit jacket in a complementary hue and calf-length boots."

Jo folded the invitation and put it back in the envelope. "A clean tee-shirt with my annual pair of jeans it is." Her iPhone announced an incoming email from work.

Steve grinned. "You'll fit right in. Big Bill appears to dress for comfort." His iPhone chimed the announcement of a new email.

Luce looked down at her beeping phone as several other engineers received email on their phones. "It's from Seth. He forwarded a notice for an all-hands meeting and all-hands lunch at the Boulderado conference center at 11:00 AM tomorrow."

Vijay looked at Steve. "What is an all-hands lunch? Does that mean we have to keep our elbows off the table?"

Steve grinned. "So did everyone get the same lunch meeting announcement?" Quizzical faces around the table nodded.

Luce frowned. "I wonder if we have to call ahead to get the limo to come back and take us to the lunch thing?"

Steve drained his beer. "I'm sure we'll all just carpool with Big Bill."

Snickers circled the table, and as it died down, Luce turned to Jo. "What do you think this is all about?"

Jo shook her head. "I have no idea, but I think that's because I just ran out of energy. Grandma, it's time for us to hit the road."

53

Breakfast of Champions

Big Bill minimized his long-legged stride to match Jo's shorter one as they crossed the wide flagstone terrace to the wooden railing where Steve and Luce were staring at the stately mountains. The Second Range of the Rocky Mountains loomed tall in the distance.

Bill leaned on the railing. "I never take this for granted. I grew up on a farm out on the plains in Southeastern Colorado. When I first saw the Rocky Mountains up close, I knew this was where I wanted to live. I bought this land with a downpayment from the money I saved working two jobs during college. I've been even happier here than I imagined I would be."

Jo couldn't take her eyes off the texture of the rock faces as the morning sun glanced off their surface. "Where did you go to college?"

Big Bill turned to Jo. "School of Mines. I double majored in electrical and mechanical engineering so I could understand how things worked and how to design things to work better. I loved being an engineer."

Steve gazed at the shimmering peaks. "That's a good engineering school. Do you still do any hands-on engineering?"

Big Bill laughed quietly. "I like to tinker with old machines, find old parts so I can fix them or restore them. Every time I get into some project in my shop out back, I decide I'm going to retire. But the next morning, ten more things need a decision or a crisis management plan. Someday."

Jo grinned. "My grandmother is like that. She sold the repair shop after my grandfather died, but she still fixes things for all her friends, especially older things that people want to try to keep using instead of replacing."

Big Bill's eyes smiled down at Jo. "Your grandparents owned Galvan's? Your grandfather fixed my Dad's old push lawn mower. I'm sorry your grandfather died, but your grandmother seems to be quite a lady."

Jo laughed. "One of the officers who arrested the Wimples yesterday is the daughter of good friends of my grandparents. I'm beginning to think the whole town knew them."

Big Bill nodded. "They were the kind of people you have to look harder to find these days, especially in Boulder. The L towns around Boulder still have small shops owned by people like that."

Steve recited the list. "Longmont, Lyons, Louisville, Lafayette, Loveland. I guess Leyden and Littleton don't count."

Jo smiled. "Grandma thinks of Boulder as if it's still the way it used to be. So many people know her and would do anything for her."

Big Bill gazed at the mountains. "My parents were like that, always helping people." He looked at Jo. "Were you around your grandparents when they had their repair shop?"

Jo gazed at the stunning peaks. "Yes, I came to live with my grandparents when I was six, after my parents died in a car accident up in the mountains. They showed me anything I wanted to learn about whatever they were fixing."

Big Bill paused for a moment, looking away, then back at Jo. "That must have been sad and confusing for you, but you got to be around such great people in your grandparents. From such beginnings come great engineers."

Jo grinned but was suddenly aware of Bill waving a greeting to someone behind him. She turned around to see Seth walking barefoot across the flagstone terrace. He was wearing comfortably worn cut-off jeans and a well-washed Norton motorcycle tee-shirt. *When did Seth get here? Who rides a motorcycle barefoot?*

Seth sauntered to the railing, looking at Big Bill. "Sorry I'm late. I was working on a problem and lost track of time."

Big Bill grinned at Seth. "If I know you, halfway through breakfast you'll have a breakthrough blockbuster thought and off you'll go."

Seth shook his head, grinning. "I will be more social once I have this figured out." He looked at Jo, Luce, and Steve in turn. "Hey, good to hear everything went great yesterday, good work. Your ploy paid off."

Jo stared at Seth with the distinct feeling that something was out of place, not making sense. "Hey, Seth. Do you two know each other? Did you ride up here on your Commando?"

Big Bill leaned comfortably against the railing. "Seth and I have a story to tell you, and we hope you will understand why we didn't tell you sooner."

Jo struggled with the sudden shift in her reality. "Why do I get that cloak-and-dagger feeling again?"

Seth looked at Jo. "It will make sense when we've explained, but let's do this with food and caffeine. I am in desperate need of Anya's banana muffins." Seth padded toward the outdoor sideboard, where a middle-aged woman with dark hair deftly completed the arrangement of a breakfast buffet, greeting her as he helped himself to coffee.

Jo shifted her gaze to Big Bill. "Seth has been here before? What is he working on?"

Big Bill grinned, nodding toward the buffet. "Better get it before it's gone. We'll explain after we're all seated."

Jo moved as if unpinned from gravity. She took an acacia wooden plate from the short stack at the near end of the sideboard, and selected fresh fruit, scrambled eggs, and a perfectly golden-tinged banana muffin from the array of beautifully enticing foods. She placed her plate at one of the table settings before filling a large mug with the enticingly dark rich brew from the polished silver urn. Seth placed his own plate at the setting to Jo's left as he pulled out her chair.

They sat next to each other in silence for a few clock ticks as Jo focused harder than necessary on her coffee, her mind whirling around too many questions to grasp an opening topic of conversation. Seth's voice held easy warmth as he extended a hand in Jo's direction, holding his coffee mug. "Here's to finishing GuardShark in fine style," he toasted.

Jo raised her mug to his and let her eyes focus on the two mugs clinking, unable and unwilling to make eye contact that would betray her overwhelming curiosity and the creepy tinge of dread.

Bill looked around the table. "Dig in while Seth and I lay our cards on the table."

Seth got up and sauntered to the sideboard. "Wait a sec, I almost forgot the most important thing." He retrieved a bottle of Tabasco and another bottle with the proud label, Dave's Hurtin' Habanero Hot Sauce. He set them next to Jo. "Give these a shot. They probably last longer in our house. I like that Hurtin' one on my eggs." He sat down and reached for his coffee mug.

"Our house?" Jo re-capped the Hurtin' Habanero bottle before handing it to Seth. "Do you mean you live here?"

Seth nodded while enjoying a forkful of eggs with habanero sauce. "I have an apartment on West Arapahoe, but Comcast Internet isn't working right and I couldn't afford to lose a day re-reading back issues of *Easy Rider* while I waited around for their tech to show up. I've been working upstairs in my old room until everything's solid with GuardShark."

Jo stared at Seth, her image of him turned upside down.

Bill grinned. "I'm used to him rattling around in his cage all hours, day and night."

Seth stretched his neck and back. "Hey, it's usually worth it. I found a security hole while I was doing some last-minute testing of GuardShark. I worked pretty late last night trying several variations of a fix."

Jo looked at Seth, looked at Bill, and turned back to Seth, choosing her words carefully from the rush of questions zinging through her mind. "You live and work here? We thought you might be living off the grid, with friends."

Big Bill sipped his coffee. "I met this guy when my son Lonnie was in high school at Alexander Dawson Academy. You've had to deal with Lonnie, so you can understand why I hired a very bright math and engineering sophomore at CU/Boulder as a tutor."

Seth stabbed habanero-soaked home-fried new potatoes absently with a fork. "One afternoon I came back from a bathroom break to find Lonnie gone. He left a note saying that he wasn't into studying. He'd taken off without his math book and wasn't answering his cell."

Big Bill shook his head. "I could kick myself for not paying attention to what was going on with my son."

Seth sipped coffee. "Kids don't always make the best choices. I called Bill at his office and agreed to meet him here to deliver the book and talk about Lonnie's progress. That's when I met Celia." He looked at Bill for a long moment. "It never gets easier, does it?"

Big Bill set down his coffee. "Everyone loved my daughter, I loved her like the dickens, and she fell in love with this guy. They got married and left for Seth's graduate program at Harvard. Celia got a job with the EPA in Massachusetts, working with nuclear waste clean-up."

Seth said quietly, his gaze locked on Bill, "I started working at Mitre while going to Harvard. We had four of the happiest years. We didn't find out until it was too late that one of Celia's clean-up sites had radioactive waste that had been improperly stored. She died of cancer from the contamination, surrounded by her family and the

Boulder mountains she loved so much. I fell apart after the memorial, just couldn't function. Bill was amazing, moved me in here. I don't even want to think where I would be if it hadn't been for him."

Bill looked at Seth. "We were there for each other. I lost my wife to breast cancer ten years ago and couldn't handle the bottom falling out of my life again."

Luce looked at Bill and Seth. "I'm so sorry."

Jo felt a lump in her throat. "I'm sorry, too. I'm glad you have each other. It helps so much when you have someone in your life who understands what you lost, who you lost."

Seth nodded. "Mitre and some old friends kept me busy with contracting work that I could do telecommuting from here. I couldn't face the company politics and stress of a full-time job."

Big Bill took a bite of bacon. "Boulder is a small town and the entrepreneurs all know each other. Glaston Wimple founded McWare and made Manny CEO to train him to follow in his footsteps. Manny and Lonnie were in the same frat at CU. Glaston conned me into being on the Board and becoming an investor by offering Lonnie a job."

Seth buttered a banana muffin. "Lonnie got me an open-ended contract with McWare, so I thought I was just doing work to fill in the gaps. But Lonnie got lazy and forwarded your instructions for SharkNet to me. That's when I realized I had been doing his work all along."

Big Bill continued, "Having Seth work with Lonnie gave me a way to protect my investment. I made the mistake of believing Lonnie would eventually shape up."

Seth continued, "I worked here, telecommuting to McWare under Lonnie's computer account until you figured out I was doing Lonnie's work. It was a miracle when I could work directly with your great team."

Jo grinned. "I'm glad they use their talents for good, not evil. So do we get to hire you officially?"

Big Bill looked at Jo. "First we wanted you three to know the whole story, and let your team work through any concerns you have about Seth's relationship to your new CEO."

Seth nodded. "It would be great working with all of you, but only if we can all trust each other to be honest and open. Ask us anything."

Steve rearranged his scrambled eggs before asking, "Where does Lonnie fit into the picture?"

Big Bill grinned as he shook his head. "Lonnie no longer works at McWare. The good news and the bad news is his grandparents' trust fund will kick into high gear on January 1st and he will never need to work again. He's at the Arnold Palmer Golf Academy in Orlando, and said something about going to Pebble Beach or a Club Med golf resort with his fraternity buddies."

Jo sipped her coffee. "Having Seth full-time will be great. My only concern is about our team. They worked so hard getting GuardShark done, and we're all ready for a break. We need time off before starting the next big project."

Big Bill's eyes twinkled. "I'm way ahead of you, which I doubt will happen often. I worked with Mackerel to allocate the funds for a two-week, all expense paid trip to Hawaii for everyone on your team, including Seth. Hey, buddy, don't shake your head. This is a part of teamwork too."

Seth smiled. "OK, I'm willing to take one for the team. But I have to fix that security hole first."

Jo said, "I just hope Grandma's OK being home alone. She has several things lined up that need fixing, but she was in the hospital for a couple of days for her sodium and blood pressure."

Big Bill laughed. "Your grandmother *is* a part of the team. She's getting a ticket too."

Jo grinned. "Wow, she won't believe it. Of course, she unofficially adopts pretty much everyone she meets, so Hawaii better watch out. You and Seth are probably next."

Seth laughed. "Sounds good to me. We can always use more family."

Steve looked at Bill. "Back on the topic of Seth coming to work at McWare, how would you feel about all of us sitting down together with the team, laying it out and letting them ask questions and get comfortable with everything?"

Seth winked at Bill. "Bill, try not to intimidate the engineers."

Jo deadpanned, "We're all pretty quiet, never make waves, never share opinions."

Luce nudged Jo. "Jo is our role model." They all erupted in laughter as Jo feigned ducking under the table before Luce continued, "But we've had to work around one of the worst examples of management, and people just don't switch gears that fast. No matter how cool you are, you're still the CEO."

Steve nodded. "Give us time to get to know you, Bill, and the trust will happen on its own."

Seth looked at Jo. "They have to trust me too if we're going to work together every day."

Jo nodded. "That's true. You know what we went through with Manny and Cinda, so they will grill you. We were suspicious of you until you proved yourself. This is a lot of change to absorb. Twenty-four hours ago we were all sure we were going to lose our jobs, so we're still getting used to the luxury of staying employed."

Seth said, "I'm OK with proving myself to the team. Do you have any concerns of your own about my relationship with Bill?"

Jo tried to project a serious tone. "I'm concerned about your ability to go toe-to-toe in the cartoon contest."

Bill's face brightened. "What do you call 101 dead CEOs? Not even a good start." He grinned at Jo and Luce's shocked faces. "I've gone over there a few times with Seth late at night. He showed me the Tomb of the Unknown Meeting and the cartoons."

Seth laughed. "He's your biggest fan, trust me."

Jo looked at Luce and Steve. "Is my head spinning? I can't believe everything that has happened in the last couple of weeks. We're actually still employed, by people we want to work for."

They talked more easily for a while, lingering over cups of rich dark coffee, until Big Bill stood up. "I need to get us to the all-hands meeting. I can take all of you in my SUV if Seth takes his rocket bike."

Seth nudged Jo as they stood up. "I've seen you eyeing my Commando. I think it's time you got a new taste of mountain air. You up for riding with me?"

Jo felt something zing inside her, kicking her heart rate into overdrive as her words stumbled over each other. "That sounds … great. Uh, I didn't bring a jacket …" She glanced at Luce, whose face held a playful grin.

Seth turned toward the staircase. "I'll find you one of my sweatshirts. I have to get into my jeans and leathers. I'll be right back."

Jo watched his lithe, athletic body take the stairs two at a time, a warm flush creeping up her neck as she made an effort to keep her voice even. "That'll work," she said.

54

Career Path 102

To: rookie-pup
From: Lord&Master

Quit whining and listen. My attorney told me to stop communicating with you, so this is my last chance to teach you for a while. Anyone can be bought, and I know people in this town. But prison wouldn't be that different from the corporate business world. There are people there with access to power and money who naturally control the underlings. We could do well there.

I was disappointed to learn that CJ will be tried separately and will likely be sentenced to a different facility for all his past crimes. You did well manipulating Cinda, but your dealings with him were dismal.

You made several key mistakes. You learn slower and have less affinity for focusing on a goal than I anticipated. You couldn't remember our priorities. We had one goal—to bring down McWare and sell it for a lot of money, not making GuardShark competitive. I made it as simple as possible for you, but you still couldn't get it right.

You're angry now, but you have no reason to mistrust me. My ploy of foisting all the blame on you was the best move for us in that moment. We must be equally committed to doing whatever it takes to achieve our ultimate strategy of achieving the most money and power. Stop pouting and learn from my skillful handling of the situation. Using you as a sacrifice in that crucial moment was the optimal strategic ploy for us.

Don't squander this opportunity by getting a bad attitude about this turn of events. You must knuckle down and learn from this failure so you are better prepared next time. This is just one dip in a long road filled with power and money. You're no CJ, but you have potential.

You kids just don't take pride in your work. You expect everything to be handed to you. When you show me that you are willing to do whatever it takes, we can resume your training.

~Sent from my iPad

55

That Great Rewards Thing Again

J O WALKED ACROSS the familiar hallway of the Boulderado Hotel's conference center toward the meeting room for Friday's all-hands meeting. She was engulfed in Seth's hoodie and still felt the exhilaration of flying down the winding mountain road, leaning against his strong back as she held tight around his lean waist. The rock and roll dance of their bodies in sync with the animal power of the motorcycle as it matched the curves of the road's descent was intoxicating. She didn't realize she had closed her eyes, giving herself over to the sweet freedom of it all in sheer bliss until Seth suddenly slowed the bike at the stoplight on Broadway.

As she unzipped the extra-large sweatshirt, a surprising thought made her heart skip a beat. *This is what he was wearing the first night I saw him in the Tomb with Lonnie.* She carefully folded the jacket over her left arm, absently smoothing the fabric with her right hand. She looked around, realizing where she was, and continued walking toward the double doors.

Inside the meeting room, she spotted Luce standing next to Steve. She took a deep breath to shake off the glowing feeling, and teased, "Did you really just carpool down the mountain with our new CEO after letting him feed us breakfast?"

Luce struck a Vogue pose with one hand on her hip. "I have to admit I was feeling pretty special being chauffeured by our new CEO in his 8-speed Jeep Grand Cherokee until he dumped us at the curb. How was the ride?"

Jo willed her voice to an even tone as she replied, "Seatbeltless." Jo felt the hoodie's fabric on her arm, reminding herself to return it to Seth. *Why didn't I remember to give it back to him in the parking lot?*

She surveyed the odd arrangement of furniture until her eyes landed on the lavish lunch buffet, grateful for an opportunity to avoid discussing her ride with Seth. "That's a lot of food." She draped the hoodie across the back of a chair.

Luce snickered, "That should last about ten minutes around software engineers."

Steve looked puzzled. "Why aren't the chairs set up for the meeting?" Dozens of chairs were arranged haphazardly in small groups around the room.

Jo took in the scene. "Red Nails quit. Chairs were one of her strong suits. Or maybe it's intentional so people can talk to each other."

Luce said, "How inclusive. Imagine the honchos as part of a small group instead of on their thrones on stage."

Jo smirked. "Shit-For-Brains and Red Nails would be as comfortable here as they would have been in the Tomb."

Wayne joined them, his eyes twinkling. "It looks like we got ourselves a mighty fine spread here." Jim, Sherm, and Vijay wandered over.

Jo greeted them, "Hey, geek squad, what's new in your lives?"

Jim grinned. "The likelihood of having permanent jobs. I could get used to these new work hours."

Wayne nodded at the abundantly laden tables. "Let's get this feed on." He made a beeline for the buffet table.

Sherm tailed close behind him. "Pace yourself, not that I plan to follow my own advice."

Vijay grinned. "Free is my favorite food group now, thanks to you delinquents." Jim followed him, grabbing a plate from the stack.

The Boulderado catering staff replenished the buffet as the twin lines of McWare employees made their way along the deliciously colorful variety of mouthwatering selections, each with a discreet sign indicating the ingredients and warnings for foods associated with allergies.

Jo moved in line behind Jim. "I don't think I've conked out that fast in a long time. My kitties could have danced on the desk and fought on my bed all night long without waking me up."

Luce yawned from the line across the buffet table. "I'm pretty sure I was sleepwalking when I took my dogs for a walk last night before I crashed."

Jo's salad defied gravity. "I was so nervous at breakfast I didn't eat much. I've got to get some of that habanero hot sauce."

Luce piled a vegetarian color palette on her plate. "I thought you were a little subdued this morning. Were you nervous before the limo picked you up?"

Jo whispered, "I got in the shower and realized I had my bra on."

"That's a good indicator of social discomfort." Luce looked around the room. "OK, where to sit?" Luce, Jo, Steve, and the rest of the team nudged chairs here and there to form a haphazard grouping, akin to the variety of personalities represented.

Jo looked around at the team happily munching away. "This reminds me of my kitties bonding over food."

Vijay paused mid-muffin. "We're more like a tiger team, making a meal of our latest kill."

Wayne speared a forkful of potatoes. "A few more snarky lines like that and even the marketing people won't think of you as an intern anymore."

"How will I know when I've achieved that status?"

Steve waved a french fry. "They move to the other side of the room when they see you coming."

Jo dipped a carrot in Tabasco sauce. "Did you notice how Red Nails seemed to rearrange herself when we were joking around?"

Luce munched a tortilla chip. "Ah, you miss your Red nemesis."

Jo smeared her slider with hot mustard. "I miss her as much as the flu. Look, our CEO has arrived, tardy. Grandma?" She stopped eating at the unexpected entrance of the odd couple. Grandma's eyes twinkled as she entered the room on the arm of Big Bill, who carefully matched the much smaller lady's pace.

Jo stood up, put her plate on her seat, and joined them. "I didn't realize you were going to be here, Grandma. I haven't seen you in that dress in a long time." Her fingers traced the lovely old black Spanish lace of Grandma's heirloom shawl, lightly embracing the elegant simplicity of a rich Italian silk wool blend dress in deep blue hues that were accented subtly with tiny gold and silver threads.

Grandma smiled. "Mr. Schuster asked me yesterday after the Board meeting, while you were gathering your things, and we decided to surprise you. I was so excited I was afraid I would give it away before you left this morning."

Big Bill looked down at Grandma with the same familiar fondness Jo noticed on everyone who met Grandma, except the Wimple men. "It's Bill, Mrs. Galvan, always Bill. You're a big part of our success."

Grandma glowed with the compliment. "You come over anytime you want, Bill." Her eyes twinkled again. "You can be my assistant."

Big Bill grinned. "It's a deal. I need a back-up plan in case this engineering thing doesn't work out. Let's get some lunch from the spread over there." He winked at Jo. "Didn't you hitch a ride here with Seth?"

Jo blushed. "He's still in the parking lot taking notes on his iPhone about a fix for the security problem he found. He's an interesting combination of geek and pit bull. He fits right in." Bill nodded to Jo as he escorted Grandma to the buffet table.

"That would make an interesting cartoon." Seth's warm voice turned Jo around. "Hey, brainiac, how's the habanero situation here?" He tossed his leather jacket on an empty chair next to Luce and Steve, who waved forks in his direction.

Jo shook her head. "Zero hot sauce, but I have fond memories of that Hurtin' Habanero heaven. Get some food and come hang with us."

"You bet. All that work on the secure password generator gave me a righteous appetite." He joined Big Bill and Grandma in line at the buffet.

Jo retrieved her still-laden plate and caught Luce's happy expression. "Let the feeding frenzy continue."

Twenty minutes later, Big Bill, Grandma, and Steve sat in a little grouping next to Jo, chatting easily as they enjoyed their lunch. Jo felt a rush of gratitude that Bill had magically found a little table he set up for Grandma. Bill casually visited with each little group, greeting people by name.

As plates emptied, Steve stood in the middle of the gathering of employees. "Good afternoon, everyone. I think most of you know me. I'm Steve Scott. You received an email this morning announcing a few changes our Board of Directors made at their annual meeting yesterday. I have the happy job of introducing our new Chairman of the Board and CEO, Bill Schuster."

A polite round of applause accompanied Steve's return to his seat, leaving Big Bill the focal point of the roomful of eyes. His faded jeans and flannel shirt matched his easy smile.

Big Bill spoke casually. "Thank you. I'm glad I had a chance to meet most of you. We hope the changes in McWare's management will be more supportive of your talents in building our company. This time is primarily for your questions and comments. Anything is fair game, so who's got a question?"

One of the Ken dolls from the marketing team raised his hand. "Where is Manny?"

Big Bill glanced briefly at Jo, Luce, and Steve. "Manny's term as CEO was for four years, which ended yesterday. Glaston Wimple, his father, also ended his term as Chairman of the Board. The Board elected me to replace them as CEO and Chairman of the Board, but my performance will be reviewed every year just like yours are. Transparency is key to an organization to build the trust it takes for everyone to feel valued as a part of the team." He turned to Steve. "I'm proud to announce that Steve is our new director of engineering. Steve, can you share the news from your organization?"

Bill sat down as Steve rose. "Thanks, Bill. I am very happy to announce that our new security product, GuardShark, will be launched to the market as soon as it has received official security certification. I will oversee marketing for our software products, and we have plans for creating a new customer support organization that will involve our customers in defining our new product ideas. Any questions?"

The other Ken doll raised his hand. "Manny always came up with ideas for software products." Jo winked at Luce, pantomiming writing on her paper napkin.

Luce mumbled, "The marketing guys look terrified they might be expected to do real work."

Steve nodded at the two men in designer ties. "The Board members, Bill, and the investors have pooled their extensive networks of contacts in business and industry to form an incubator of industry leaders who will work with our existing customers to generate new product ideas."

Bill rose and stood next to Steve. "We anticipate sales of GuardShark for this year alone will be over one million dollars. That will enable us to launch our European, Asian, and South American roll-out next year."

Steve waved toward Jo, Luce, and the engineering team. "Today is about celebrating the outstanding team of engineers who built the GuardShark product in record time and with the highest standards of quality and performance. It is my pleasure to introduce Jo Galvan and Luce Savodsky, the software leads for the GuardShark project. Can the rest of the team stand? Please join me in showing our appreciation." Applause broke out in the room.

As the engineers stood up, Steve introduced them. "Jim McGraw, the lead architect." Jim gave a parade wave. "Sherm Chrisman is the lead software engineer." More applause as quiet Sherm couldn't keep the proud smile off his face. "Wayne Oakley is the lead for test and validation." Applause and whoops from the engineers accompanied Wayne's grin. "Vijay Patel was our engineering intern, but as of this morning he is one of our newest full-time software engineers, with time off for good behavior to attend his last classes at CU/Boulder for his final semester." Applause accompanied the cheers from the engineers as Vijay's face became one huge smile.

Big Bill nodded to Steve before he continued, "In appreciation for the team's outstanding work and commitment to quality, the Board approved some decisions for the GuardShark engineering team. The first is to send the whole team on an employee retreat to Hawaii to enjoy some much-needed time off." Liz handed him a stack of thick envelopes and Bill handed a packet to each engineer, including Steve, as he shook their hands. The engineers floated back down to their chairs, speechless for once.

Big Bill continued, "The Board approved a new employment package for each engineer, and also approved hiring two more new members of our engineering team." He extended a hand to Grandma. "Illyena Galvan will continue the outstanding work she did for us in product testing. Mrs. Galvan is Jo's grandmother. She is going to Hawaii too." Grandma's face lit with her trademark twinkling eyes. Warm applause surrounded her as Bill handed her an envelope.

"Our other new engineer is also family. Seth Ackley is my son-in-law, and served as an engineering consultant to help us get the GuardShark product built and tested. Since I won't participate in annual performance reviews for the engineers, the Board also approved hiring him. So let's welcome Seth." The engineers applauded loudest and whooped in approval of the former Mystery Geek's permanent home with them as Bill handed Seth an envelope.

Big Bill looked around the room. "Enjoy yourselves here as long as you like. McWare will be getting new office furniture over the next month that was selected in response to suggestions from many of you. The furniture company needs to take measurements this weekend, so we'd like you to pack anything on your desks right after lunch, take your company laptops home over the weekend, and take the rest of the day off. Any questions?"

Liz, Big Bill's administrative assistant, waved her hand. "What about our ergonomic chairs and the dropdown keyboard trays? It was a nightmare getting those approved." Several people nodded in agreement.

Big Bill reassured the group, "Thanks for reminding me, Liz. All the existing chairs, and anything else you currently use in your offices, will be placed in your new office cubicle with a new type of chair that you can try out for comparison. If there are no other questions, thank you all for your hard work. Enjoy yourselves."

Applause broke out as Bill turned to Grandma, taking her arm. "Let me drive you home, Mrs. Galvan. What did you think of your first company meeting?"

Grandma patted his arm. "You have very nice employees. But my favorites are still the engineers."

Big Bill turned to Jo, Luce, and Steve. "Are you OK sharing the back seat of the Jeep? I'm heading to the office after I take Mrs. Galvan home. I'm probably the only one who doesn't have to pack up this afternoon."

Jo looked at Steve and Luce. "Luce and I can ride home with Grandma, and we'll go to Toyota to pick up Luce's car on the way to the contest."

Jim said, "Steve, I don't have a limo, but you can ride with me. I'll take you home after the contest."

Steve grinned. "I'll make do."

Vijay's face lit up. "We're doing the contest today?" He turned to Wayne and high fived.

Jo grinned. "1:47 PM sharp, in the Tomb." Jo turned to Seth. "You have to come to McWare to pick your new cubicle, so you're staying for the contest."

Seth waved his motorcycle helmet. "OK, but I'm limited to software and cartoon captions."

Jo winked. "Just bring your opinionated self and your sense of humor."

"Deal."

56

We Think We're Funny

A s the engineering team noisily descended on the Tomb, Jo's mental movie screen was suddenly flooded with clips from the harrowing rollercoaster of the past two weeks. The team sat around the table. Wayne nodded to them. In unison, the engineers, including Steve and Seth, gave a thumbs-up with their left hands, each with a bright red nail.

Jo doubled over laughing. "You are too much, painting your nails red just to help me celebrate."

Luce gasped, "That's our team, still subtle as a Mack truck."

Jim waved his thumb closer to Jo. "Not quite that committed. Take a closer look."

Jo burst out laughing. When she finally got her voice under control, she grinned. "Red tape, even more appropriate. She never really appreciated all of you. Thanks for sharing the joy of her good riddance."

Luce smirked. "Operation Red Aloha, accomplished!"

Seth grinned. "Somewhere in Boulder there's a group of engineers at risk."

Jo sighed. "Thankfully, Red Nails' career will be on hold for a while. Before the contest, I've got good news and bad news. Which do you want to hear first?"

Sherm grabbed a chair. "I've gotten used to living with a parade of good news over the past twenty-four hours. What's up in the happy department?"

Jo opened her arms wide. "Big Bill said the Tomb won't be part of the company makeover. All of our notes, art work, and food spills will remain intact."

Luce joined Jo standing next to the table. "Shall we tell them the bad news?"

Jo put on a solemn face that took every ounce of control to maintain. "Can you do it?"

Luce couldn't control her big grin. "It looks like Manny and his father will be indicted, and if they are convicted they could be sentenced to a minimum security prison for fraud and criminal intent to injure Jo and me by getting that CJ character to tamper with our brake systems."

Seth looked puzzled. "Where's the bad news in that?"

Jo mugged as the team stared at her like she had two heads. "It won't be maximum security, hard labor, or Devil's Island. Since it's their first offense, with no loss of life or limb, Officer Alvarez warned us they might get a reduced sentence. But CJ will likely be looking at a much stiffer sentence due to his list of warrants and indictments."

Luce nudged Jo. "Tell them the rest of the bad news about CJ. Poor guy, so sad."

Vijay frowned as he sat down. "Why would you feel sorry for someone who tried to hurt you two, and almost cost us all our jobs?"

Jo pulled out an empty chair and sat. "Cormac Janx is Red Nails' brother." Groans and moans swirled around the table. "He hacked into Manny's computer to find a way to set Red Nails up with Manny at a conference, hacked into the conference to create a bogus registration for her, and infiltrated the executive matchmaking services

Manny used to get his confidential questionnaire. Red Nails prob-ably used that information to tailor her, uh, behavior with him."

Luce sat down next to Jo. "Her strong suit is the willingness to do whatever it takes to manipulate key people to pull off a con."

Jim looked at Jo. "That's twisted. What happened to Red Nails? Didn't she get a job at another company?"

Jo looked at Luce and shrugged. "She landed a job with MailMeister, a junk mail company both Jo and I rejected before coming to McWare because they are sleazebags." The team cheered.

Steve said over the laughter, "But the FBI's investigation of CJ's long criminal career found that he and Cinda had conned their way through several small start-up high-tech companies. CJ accused her of masterminding the plan, but she turned on him and handed over copies of all her documents and email for every one of their crimes."

Steve continued, "She isn't capable of orchestrating crime, but she will likely do some time in a minimum security prison for being an accomplice."

Luce smirked. "Can you picture her in an orange jumpsuit?"

Wayne settled back comfortably in his chair. "Not like the Wimples. Those two smelled bad to me, worse than a cattle feedlot. There's somethin' honest about cow shit the Wimples seem to be missing." The team snickered as heads shook in amazement around the table.

Jo curled up in the chair. "The Wimples were pretty weird. It's creepy that Manny's father referred to himself as Lord&Master."

Vijay stared, wide-eyed. "I didn't know people like that owned software companies."

Steve looked around the table. "The smell of big money in high-tech is like blood in the water to sharks."

Luce nudged Jo. "OK, that's the news of the soon-to-be-incar-cerated. I believe we have a contest to conduct." Whoops, cheers, and table-pounding erupted. "Jo, how are we doing this?"

Jo rubbed her forehead. "I'll admit I'm winging it here, but feel free to make up your own rules as we go along. This is, after all, a sport that relies on ridicule, sarcasm, and the ability to undermine your opponent." She turned to Seth. "Can you be the judge for the cartoon contest? You already have experience judging my cartoons."

Seth crossed his arms, adopting a serious tone. "Are bribes involved? Winter is coming and my Commando needs a tune-up."

Jim reached in his pocket and tossed Seth a quarter. "Let the bribing begin. Enjoy your next video game on me."

Steve threw in two quarters. "I'll see your quarter and raise you one. I'm terrified of the competition in this room."

Vijay waved his hands. "Hey, no fair throwing big money around. I'm still a student. I can't compete with half the cost of drying a load of laundry. But I have a jar of sambal oelek from Indonesia that I can attest will be the hottest chilies Jo has ever tasted."

Seth looked puzzled. "How does Jo's decidedly heathen worship of gastronomic fire figure as a bribe for me?"

Vijay grinned. "Someday you will have a disagreement with Jo. Bribing her works, and you are going to want that jar."

Seth nodded. "Bribe accepted, and may I congratulate you on your meteoric rise as one of the weirdos." The team whooped and applauded as Vijay gave a mock bow.

Sherm raised a hand. "I've got an unopened bag of pretzel M&M's. That's salty, crunchy, and sweet, so covers all the geek food groups."

Jim shook his head at Sherm. "You forgot free and frozen."

Seth held up his hand. "Enough with the bribes. This has to be the craziest contest I've ever heard of. We haven't seen one cartoon yet and I already know enough about you people to scare me silly."

Wayne grinned. "What's really scary is how quickly you've become one of us. A few short weeks ago you were doing secret software for a certified idiot by day and jotting secret cartoon captions at night. Life made sense. Now you're selling your soul for a jar of chili paste, a handful of coins, and a bag of salted candy."

Seth couldn't control his wide grin. "Which proves I'm no better than the rest of you, but no worse. I'm good with that. Let the contest begin."

Jo gestured toward a wide blank spot on the whiteboard. "So, who has a cartoon?"

Jim, Sherm, and Steve all raised their hands. Sherm jumped up and went to the whiteboard. "Me first." He drew a caricature of Vixen with a rendition of a corpse-like Manny at the wheel as it careened into a wall while a group of people in lab coats with stop watches and clipboards observed. The caption read 'Crash Test Dummy.' Sherm waved the marker at his cartoon. "Ta da. The winning entry if I ever saw one." He walked back to his seat with a grin.

Jo shivered. "It's painful to imagine Vixen at the hands of that idiot, dead or alive, but definitely a valiant entry. I still can't believe he ran this company."

The team cheered as Jim stood up and sauntered to the board. Stalks of corn populated a field under ugly-faced crows circling in a cloud-dotted sky. A goofy-faced rendition of Manny appeared on the board, wearing a ragged business suit, with one outstretched hand propped lifelessly around a pitchfork. "Scarecrow," he said triumphantly. The team cheered.

Luce nodded at Jim. "What's scary is that job fits his abilities to a T."

Steve moved to the board. "It's an honor just to be nominated. Here goes." He drew a long empty highway with the black marker, and several renditions of Manny near the center line in the right lane. Using the orange marker, he drew a triangular covering around each Manny-kin, the narrow end near the neck and the wide base near the feet. "Highway construction cone." The team cheered and applauded.

Seth laughed. "It's unfortunate that you have career ideas that actually match his skill set. He could have avoided prison if he had let you people mentor him."

Luce shook her head. "He's probably blaming Daddy, and with good reason. It should be a crime for an evil mutant like Glaston Wimple to be a father."

Jo grinned. "Vijay and Wayne, you're up. I feel for you being up against this competition, but you've got the power of collaboration. Show us your stuff."

Wayne moved his chair next to Vijay, who popped his Mac open and clicked the mouse a few times. "Pick a number for the seed," Vijay said.

Wayne said, "42."

Jo rolled her chair next to Wayne. "An electronic entry. That's a gutsy move. This could be trouble for the competition."

The team gathered around Vijay's Mac. 'What do you do with a dead CEO?' flashed on a simple drawing of a paper flip chart. The number 42 appeared on an 8-ball game icon that spun for a second before spewing a blob of ink that formed the answer, 'Garden gnome.' Vijay double-clicked on the text to pop up a photo of a garish ceramic statue. The team roared.

Wayne grinned. "That's one of the numbers we've linked to a graphic image."

Jim stared at the screen. "You're using a numeric matching scheme? OK, try 47." Vijay clicked to highlight the 8-ball, typed 47, pressed Enter, and the spewing ink blob landed on the flip chart as 'CEO-In-The-Snow Paperweight.' More laughter erupted as the team members threw out numbers and applauded each new answer. 5 became HOV lane seat filler. 86 flashed Coral Reef Reinforcement. 99 popped Shark Bait. 55 flashed Speed Bump. 13 displayed Casino Cooler.

Jo stood grinning as the numbers revealed more comedy turns. "You really did the whole 101 Things To Do With A Dead CEO. That's so cool."

Jim shook his head. "I'll concede. I nominate Wayne and Vijay as the winners." The room filled with wild applause, whoop whoops, stomping feet, table pounding, and more laughter as Vijay and Wayne stood in unison and took their bows.

Seth was shaking with laughter. "I know when to give in to peer pressure. OK, I declare Vijay and Wayne the winners and return all bribes as completely unnecessary. This is the best first day on the job I've ever had."

Jo cocked her head at Seth. "Hey, we do what we can to make newbies feel welcome. I say we call it a day and let the weekend begin."

Luce shut her Mac, grabbing her backpack. "Just one bit of home-work. Be thinking about when you want to take your trips to Hawaii. We don't have to go together as a group, but if we do it's only fair that we warn the locals to take cover."

Jim turned to the contest winners. "Can we get copies of your cartoon program? How many entries do you have?"

Wayne grinned. "101, but we thought of more, just wanted to stick to the spirit of the contest."

Sherm turned to Vijay. "Is there a way to add our own new ones?"

Vijay nodded as he closed down his Mac. "Yes, it runs off a text file named deadceos.txt. All you have to do for a new entry is add the next number, comma, and a string of quoted text, with an optional comma and a hyperlink. There is also a random number generator option that works on any length of file that has at least six entries, in case players just want to roll the virtual dice."

Steve grinned. "That's really inventive."

Wayne stood up. "We had fun. We got on a roll one night and couldn't type fast enough."

Jim sat back, exhaling. "This is weird, not working against a killer deadline."

Sherm nodded. "It's good weird."

Jim's cell phone rang, and a minute later he yelled, "Jenna's water broke. I'm outta here!" His thick body sprinted down the hallway to the back door.

Shouts of "Go Dad," whoops, and cheers followed Jim out the door.

Luce shouldered her backpack, smiling at the engineers. "See you Monday. Have a great weekend, everyone."

Wayne, Vijay, and Sherm headed down the hall, with Jo, Luce, Steve, and Seth exchanging grins at their happy chatter. "We work with weirdos, thank goodness," Jo said.

Steve held the Tomb door open for her. "I couldn't agree more." Jo clicked off the light and winked at him as she pranced under his outstretched arm.

Luce sighed. "I used up all my energy laughing."

Jo emitted a matching sigh. "You and me both. But once we've had the weekend to rest up, I'm sure we'll be back in our usual good form."

Seth sauntered through the Tomb's door. "Steve, I can take you home. You can borrow the sweatshirt Jo used. Then I can get back to work on that security hole." He turned to Jo and Luce. "I'll see you two at work on Monday. That's something I didn't expect to be saying."

Steve followed Seth. "I can't believe I'm really going to be home with my wife weekends and evenings, and in Hawaii. *If* I survive Seth's motorcycle. What a ride, literally."

Jo called after the two tall men, "Be prepared for speed. Seth drives it like he stole it." She was rewarded with Seth's warm grin and a wink before he and Steve walked down the back hallway.

Jo sighed as she walked down the hall with her best friend. "I'm having a little trouble shifting gears. Is this all too good to be true?"

Luce shrugged. "It feels like dating someone new. You never notice their flaws on the first date."

"We could start looking for the first signs of trouble now," Jo said.

Luce said dreamily, "Or we could just enjoy it while it lasts."

Jo waved her arms to one side and the other as she did little side steps. "I think I'll learn how to hula in Hawaii. I need a break from worrying. We can always deal with trouble later."

Luce mimicked Jo's dance steps. "Hawaii sounds like a great place to take a break, and if not, what could it hurt?"

Jo grinned at Luce. "We'll be better at the next crisis with a tan. Are you emotionally ready to see your baby Prius?" Luce nodded as they walked through the back door, unhurried, unscheduled.

In the parking lot, Jo sighed as she unlocked Vixen. "The end."

Luce smiled at her best friend from the passenger side of the Mustang. "Maybe not. How will the two Wonder Geeks make sure they never have to work with scum again?"

Jo gazed into the beauty of the high blue Boulder sky, her face bathed in the golden fall sunlight. "Faith healers, miracle workers, we never sleep."

57

Once Upon A Virtual Time

J O TURNED OFF Vixen's engine, removed the key from the ignition, but sat still, enjoying the quiet embrace of the magically
looming half-moon gracing the late afternoon sky. Her heart, hands,
and head were calm, here, now. She breathed in, sighed out, and
opened the car door to begin her last short journey of the day.

The lunar hemisphere rocked on its side, winking through the
branches of the tall old cottonwoods. A wisp of gauzy cloud fingered
its way across the faintly glowing orb floating in the milky blue sky.
It all felt so right, quietly eternal, at peace in the constancy of nature.
Jo closed her eyes, breathed in slowly, deeply, before sighing as she
let her breath go, go until the end. *Home.*

She opened her eyes to gaze at the wide front porch of Grandma's
house. Her thoughts replayed scenes from the whole GuardShark
adventure and the faces of Seth and Big Bill. She willed herself to
forget CJ, Red Nails, Manny, and Glaston Wimple.

*Did all that really happen in the past two weeks? Manny and Red
Nails forcing us to finish GuardShark, but all the time working with CJ
to sabotage it and us. Grandma was in the hospital, Luce's car brakes were
zapped, and mine came too close. Seth the Mystery Geek pulled off miracles*

and now he works with us. Our team is amazing. They should tackle world peace next.

Jo caught the momentary flicker of light through the window. *I'll bet she's fixing something.* She took a few deep breaths and made her way to the porch, anticipating the warmth and love that always gave her such happy relief.

Jo stopped to look through the lace curtains to the workroom. She smiled at the long old oak table covered in an assortment of tools and greasy parts. Grandma moved into the frame, the little grey head and small but strong body happily working on her next project. Grandma sat in her work chair, picking up a small tool from her organized layout of parts, her focus fixed on a repair manual. The lamplight caught her frame in her favorite pose.

Jo unlocked the front door and walked into the house. Grandma turned around to meet her granddaughter's eyes with a delighted smile. *Grandma the Fixer.* Jo smiled and let go, breathing a sigh of welcome relief and a newfound joy in the assurance of working only with good people. *I'm the Fixer's Granddaughter. How lucky am I?*

"Hi, Grandma, did you start packing for Hawaii yet? I don't think you'll be able to take the socket wrench set through airport security. Better put it in your checked bag."

Acknowledgements

Nothing of value that I've ever done, except petting my kitties, has been accomplished without the support and collaboration of a village of the gutsiest, most generous, and coolest people. The friends and writers who were with me on this journey are the best examples of those attributes, and the fact that they are brilliant, wildly creative, and hands-down some of the funniest weirdos only added to my delight in sharing this experience with them.

Writing a first book is akin to getting a graduate degree. My development editor, Max Regan, jumped on the joyride of my crazy ideas for story, villains, banter, and shenanigans, guiding me in shaping the book. As teacher and mentor at his annual Writers' Retreat and in a gazillion private sessions, Max is as astute in teaching the craft of writing as he is fierce in his collaborative support throughout the adventure of bringing a book to completion. In a word, Max is brilliant, and that daredevil says he's up for doing it again.

Thanks to Lisa Birman for timely discussions on structural aspects of an early version, advice on the art of manipulating red herrings to enhance villainy, and proofreading par excellence.

Jack Pollock did a bang-up job as cartoon editor, greeting each ink-stained draft with fresh eyes and his indefatigable sense of comedic timing.

My peer reviewers were so generous with their time and detailed notes on the first full version of the manuscript. Deirdre Garvey, Meg Grant, Carol Lackman-Smith, Ann Loar-Brooks, Beverly

Major, Jean McCormack, and Dorothy van Soest, you are all geeks in my book. When you stop quaking over that, you will understand that it's a compliment.

I am indebted to my fellow students at Max's annual Boulder Writers' Retreat, who encouraged my early attempts with writing comedy and stayed with me through three years of crafting this book. Now you see what happens when you laugh at my jokes and pester me about what my characters are going to get away with doing and saying next.

Thanks, Mom, for teaching me to read before I was old enough to go to school, and taking me to the library each week to borrow books beyond my age that intrigued and ignited my imagination. I love that at ninety-five, you're still going to the library every week for those thousand-page books you devour.

Thanks to my brother Bucky, the funniest person I've ever known. He was my first buddy in banter who could find the humor in anything and anyone, and I miss him every day. I would love to know if this one made him laugh.

About the Author

BONNIE AONA HAS published several technical papers on optimization of applications and computer games, but *101 Things To Do With A Dead CEO* is her first foray into fiction.

She received a Master's degree in electrical and computer engineering from UC/Davis, and a degree in comparative literature from Warner Pacific College. She lives in Longmont, Colorado.

www.bonnieaona.com